"In the Underearth,

at the borders of Azhrarn's kingdom, winds a river with waters heavy as iron and the color of iron, and white flax grows on the banks. The river of sleep that river is, and on the shores of it sometimes stray the souls of slumbering men. There the demon princes hunt those souls with hounds.

"If you dare it, I can mix you a drink that will send you fast down into the pit of sleep and wash up your soul on those shores. It is a place of snares, but if you can escape its dangers and the running hounds of the Vazdru, and cross the plains, you will reach the City of the Demons and confront, if you will, Azhrarn. Then ask him for your girl created from a flower.

"If Azhrarn grants your request—and he may for who can guess his mood on that day—he himself will speed you and her safely back to the world of men. But if he is merciless and cruel at the hour when you find him, then you are lost, and the gods know what torment or what pain he will send you to."

NIGHT'S MASTER

Tanith Lee

Illustrated by
George Barr

DAW BOOKS, INC.
DONALD A. WOLLHEIM, PUBLISHER

1633 Broadway, New York, NY 10019

Dedication

To Hylda Lee, my mother, in thanks for the first
fading horse.

First Printing, November 1978

3   4   5   6   7   8   9

PRINTED IN U.S.A.

Table of Contents

BOOK ONE
Light Underground

PART ONE:

1) A Mortal in Underearth   9
2) Sunshine   16
3) The Night Mare   25

PART TWO:

4) Seven Tears   37
5) A Collar of Silver   46
6) Kazir and Ferazhin   60

BOOK TWO
Tricksters

PART ONE:

1) The Chair of Uncertainty   79
2) King Zorashad's Daughter   86
3) The Starry Pavilion   100

PART TWO:

    4) Diamonds   111
    5) A Love Story   119
    6) Love in a Glass   127

BOOK THREE
The World's Lure

PART ONE:

    1) Honey-Sweet   145
    2) Shezael and Drezaem   157
    3) Night's Sorcery   174

PART TWO:

    4) The Anger of the Magicians   183
    5) A Ship with Wings   196
    6) The Sun and the Wind   205

BOOK ONE:
Light Underground

PART ONE

1   A Mortal in Underearth

One night, Azhrarn Prince of Demons, one of the Lords of Darkness, took on him, for amusement, the shape of a great black eagle. East and west he flew, beating with his vast wings, north and south, to the four edges of the world, for in those days the earth was flat and floated on the ocean of chaos. He watched the lighted processions of men crawling by below with lamps as small as sparks, and the breakers of the sea bursting into white blossoms on the rocky shores. He crossed, with a contemptuous and ironic glance, over the high stone towers and pylons of cities, and perched for a moment on the sail of some imperial galley, where a king and queen sat feasting on honeycomb and quails while the rowers strained at the oars; and once he folded his inky wings on the roof of a temple and laughed aloud at men's notions of the gods.

As he was returning to the world's center an hour before the sun should rise, Azhrarn the Prince of Demons heard a woman's voice weeping as lonely and as bitter as the winter wind. Filled with curiosity, he dropped to earth on a hillside as bare as a bone, beside the door of a wretched little hut. There he listened, and presently took on his man's shape— for, being what he was, he could assume any form he wished— and went in.

A woman lay before the exhausted flames of her dying fire, and he could see at once that she, as was the habit of mortals, was dying too. But in her arms she held a new-born child, covered by a shawl.

"Why do you weep?" Azhrarn inquired in fascination as he leant at the door, marvelously handsome, with hair that shone like blue-black fire, and clothed in all the magnificence of night.

"I weep because my life has been so cruel, and because now I must die," said the woman.

"If your life has been cruel, you should be glad to leave it, therefore dry your tears, which will, in any case, avail you nothing."

The woman's eyes grew dry indeed, and flashed with anger almost as vividly as the coal-black eyes of the stranger.

"You vileness! The gods curse you that you come mocking me in my last moments. All my days have been struggle and torment and pain, but I should perish without a word if it were not for this boy that I have brought into the world only a few hours since. What is to become of my child when I am dead?"

"That will die, too, no doubt," said the Prince, "for which you should rejoice, seeing he will be spared all the agony you tell me of."

At this the mother shut her eyes and her mouth and expired at once, as if she could no longer bear to linger in his company. But as she fell back, her hands left the shawl, and the shawl unfolded from the baby like the petals of a flower.

A pang of indescribable profundity shot through the Prince of Demons then, for the child was of an extraordinary and perfect beauty. His skin was white as alabaster, his fine hair the color of amber, his limbs and features formed as carefully and wonderfully as if some sculptor had made him. And as Azhrarn stood gazing at him, the child opened his eyes, and they were of darkest blue, like indigo. The Prince of Demons no longer hesitated. He stepped forward and took up the child and wrapped it in the folds of his black cloak.

"Be consoled, O daughter of misery and wailing," said he. "You have done well by your son, after all."

And he sped up into the sky in the shape of a storm cloud, the child still nestled to him like a star.

* * *

Azhrarn carried the child to that place at the earth's center where mountains of fire stood up like thin ragged and enormous spears against a sky of perpetual thunder and dark. Over everything lay the crimson smoke of the mountains' burning, for almost every crag held a craterous pit of flame. This was the entrance to the demons' country, and a spot of awful beauty where men seldom if ever came. Yet, as Azhrarn sped over in his shape of cloud, he heard the child chuckle in his arms, unafraid. Presently the cloud was sucked into the mouth of one of the tallest mountains, where no flame burned but there was only a deeper darkness.

Down fled the shaft, through the mountain and beneath the earth, and with it flew the Prince of Demons, Master of the Vazdru, the Eshva and the Drin.

First, there was a gate of agate which burst open at his coming and clanged shut behind him, and after the gate of agate, a gate of blue steel, and last a terrible gate all of black fire; however, every gate obeyed Azhrarn. Finally he reached Underearth and came striding into Druhim Vanashta, the city of the demons, and, taking out a silver pipe shaped like the thighbone of a hare, he blew on it, and at once a demon horse came galloping and Azhrarn leaped on its back and rode faster than any wind of the world to his palace. There he gave the child into the care of his Eshva handmaidens, and warned them that if any harm befell the boy their days in Underearth would be no longer pleasant for them.

And so it was in the city of demons, in Azhrarn's palace, that the mortal child grew up, and from the earliest all the things that he knew and which, therefore, became to him familiar and natural, were the fantastic, brooding and sorcerous things of Druhim Vanashta.

All around was beauty, but beauty of a bizarre and amazing sort, though it was all the beauty the child saw.

The palace itself, black iron without, black marble within, was lit by the changeless light of the Underearth, a radiance as colorless and cool as earthly starlight, though many times more brilliant, and this light streamed into the halls of Azhrarn through huge casements of black sapphire or somber emerald or the darkest ruby. Outside lay a garden of many terraces where grew immense cedars with silver trunks and jet-black leaves, and flowers of colorless crystal. Here and there was a pool like a mirror in which swam bronze birds, while lovely fish with wings perched in the trees and sang, for the laws of nature were immensely different beneath the ground. At the center of Azhrarn's garden a fountain played; it was composed not of water but of fire, a scarlet fire that gave neither light nor heat.

Beyond the palace walls lay the vast and marvellous city, its towers of opal and steel and brass and jade rising up into the glow of the never-altering sky. No sun ever rose in Druhim Vanashta. The city of demons was a city of darkness, a thing of the night.

So the child grew. He played about the marble halls and plucked the crystal flowers and slept in a bed of shadows. For company he had the curious phantom creatures of the Underearth, the bird-fish, and the fish-birds, also his demon nurses with their pale and dreamy faces, their misty hands and voices, their ebony hair in which serpents twined sleepily. Sometimes he would run to the fountain of cold red fire and stare at it, and then he would say to his nurses: "Tell me stories of other places." For he was a demanding though an endearing child. Nevertheless, the Eshva women of Druhim Vanashta could only stir softly at this plea, and weave between their fingers pictures of the deeds of their own kind, for the world of men was to them like a burning dream, of no consequence except to make delightful enchantment in, and wickedness, which to them was not wickedness at all, merely the correct order of things.

One other being came and went in the life of the child, and he was not so easily accounted for as the fair nonsensical women with their tender snakes. This was the handsome, tall and slender man who would come in suddenly with a sweeping of his cloak like the wings of an eagle, and his blue-black hair and his magical eyes, who would stay only for a second, glance smiling down at him, and then be gone. No opportunity to ask this wonderful person for stories, though the child felt sure that he would know every story there might be, no space in fact to do more than mutely offer his look of worship and love, before the eagle-wing cloak had borne its wearer away.

The time of demons did not at all resemble human time. By comparison, a mortal life flashed by like the span of a dragonfly. Therefore while the Prince of Demons went about his own midnight business in the world of men and out of it, the child, glancing up, seemed to see the man in the inky cloak only once or twice a year, while Azhrarn had perhaps gone to the nursery, as it were, twice a day. Nevertheless, the child did not feel neglected. Worshipping, he claimed no right to ask for any favor—indeed, did not even think of such a thing. As for Azhrarn, the frequency of his visits indicated his great interest in the mortal boy, or, in any event, his great interest in what he had guessed the boy would become.

So the child grew up to be a youth of sixteen years.

The Vazdru, the aristrocracy of Druhim Vanashta, sometimes watched him walking on the high terraces of their lord's palace, and one might observe: "That mortal is indeed most beautiful; he shines like a star." And some other would answer, "No, more like the moon." And then some royal demoness would laugh softly and say, "More like another light of the earth sky, and our wondrous Prince had best he careful."

Beautiful the young man was, just as Azhrarn had foreseen. Straight and slim as a sword, white of skin, and with his hair like shining red amber and his evening eyes, it is certain there were few so exceptional in Underearth, and fewer still in the world above.

One day, as he walked in the garden under the cedars, he heard the Eshve handmaidens sigh and bow from the waist like a grove of poplars in the breeze, which was their form of homage to their Prince. And turning eagerly, the young man beheld Azhrarn standing on the path. It seemed to the mortal that this special visitor had been absent far longer than before; perhaps some more than usually complex venture had kept him on earth, the twisting of some gentle mind or the downfall of some noble kingdom, so that possibly four or five years of the young man's life had gone by without his seeing him. Now his dark glory burned there so tremendously that the mortal had an impulse to shield his eyes from it, as from a great light.

"Well," said Azhrarn, Prince of Demons, "it appears I chose excellently that night on the hill." And coming closer, he put his hand on the young man's shoulder and smiled at him. And that touch was like a spear thrust of pain and joy, and the smile like the oldest enchantment of time, so that the mortal could say nothing, only tremble. "Now you will listen to me," said Azhrarn, "for this is the only harsh lesson I shall teach you. I am the ruler of this place, this city and this land, and also I am the master of many sorceries and a Lord of Darkness, so that the things of the night obey me, whether on earth or under it. Nevertheless, I will give you many gifts not generally bestowed on men. You shall be to me my son, my brother and my beloved. And I will love you; for such as I am, I do not give my love lightly, but once given it is sure. Only remember this, if ever you make an enemy of me, your life shall be as dust or sand in the wind. For what a demon loves and loses he will destroy, and my power is the mightiest you are ever likely to know."

But the young man, staring into the eyes of Azhrarn, said: "If I should anger you, my lord, then all I would wish would be to die."

Then Azhrarn leaned and kissed him.

The head of the mortal swam and he closed his eyes.

Azhrarn led him to a pavilion of silver, where the carpets were thick as fern, and scented like night-time woods, and dark shining draperies hung down like clouds across the moon.

In this strange place, part real, part mysterious, Azhrarn pondered the adult virgin beauty of his guest once more, caressing the ivory body, and combing with his fingers the amber hair he had cherished. The youth lay dumbfounded by ecstasy beneath the Demon's touch. He seemed lapped by the heatless burning of the garden fountain of fire. He was an instrument designed expressly for one master musician. Now the master tuned his body and woke the nervous strings of his flesh to an exquisite and suspenseful agony. In the embrace of Azhrarn was nothing brutish or even merely urgent. Eternal time was on the side of his lovemaking, pleasures that thrilled and spilled over upon each other, measureless and prolonged. Melted and remolded in the limitless furnace, the youth became at last only one throbbing sounding-board for this mounting theme. Then a note of awful and marvelous dimension was sounded within him, filling the waiting vessel he had become to its brim. The phallus of the Demon, (neither icy nor burning), entered him as a king enters a kingdom conquered, adoring, this by right of surrender. The phallus was a tower which pierced the gate, the vitals of the citadel of his inner world. The dark colors of the pavilion merged with the darkness of those imminent and unclosing eyes that watched him with a terrible, cruel, unsparing tenderness. The body of the mortal leaped and flamed and shattered in a million shudderings of unbelievable delight, the last chords of music, the cupola of the tower which smashed the roof of the brain's sky. He sank back in delirium with the taste of night, Azhrarn's mouth, upon his own.

2   Sunshine

Azhrarn gave the youth a name. It was Sivesh, which in the demon tongue meant the Fair, or perhaps the Blessed. He made Sivesh his companion and lavished on him many incredible gifts, as he had promised. He made him able to shoot with an arrow farther and more cleverly than any other, man or demon, and to fight with a sword as if he had had ten sword arms inside this one. Touching his forehead with a ring of jade he made him able to read and speak each of the seven languages of Underearth, and with a ring of pearl each of the seventy languages of men. And, with a spell more ancient than the world itself he made him proof against any weapon, steel or stone, wood or iron, snake venom, plant poison or fire. Only water he could not protect him from, for the seas were of another kingdom than the earth and had their own rulers. However, Azhrarn planned one day to take the youth to the cold blue lands of Upperearth, and trick the Guardians of the Sacred Well into giving Sivesh a draught of immortality.

Meanwhile, there was much for the young man to see and do, for now not only did he roam Druhim Vanashta with the Prince, and share in all its miraculous delights, but he rode beside him through the wild wastes of Underearth. Azhrarn had given him, along with all the other gifts, a demon horse to ride, a mare with a mane and tail like blue smoke and the remarkable quality that she could run over water. Azhrarn and Sivesh would gallop together across the lakes of the Underearth, beneath trees made of silver wire or bone, or go

16

hunting with blood-red hounds on the shores of the great river of Sleep, where white flax grew like rushes. Azhrarn did not hunt deer or hare or even lion on those shores, for the little cruelties of man were as nothing compared to the huge cruelty of demon-kind. The Vazdru hunted the souls of men asleep, which ran shrieking before the hounds; though it was only the souls of the insane or those near death which the dogs were able to catch and rend, and even these always escaped in the end—it was merely a sport to the demons. And Sivesh, who had no memory of what he was, and knew no other laws than the laws of Darkness, hunted merrily and thoughtlessly with his lord.

Eventually Azhrarn began to hanker after the earth above. Then he took Sivesh with him also. They journeyed, of course, by night, for no demon loved the world's day. Azhrarn rose from the volcanic shaft like an eagle, but he had changed Sivesh to a feather on his breast. Up into the sky they flew, and the feather trembled against him. There below blazed the craters of the fire mountains, there above blazed the face of the moon, framed by her mantle of sky, the stars flung like diamonds across it. *I have never seen such radiance as this*, Sivesh thought. *The fountain in the garden gives neither light nor heat*. He was, though he had forgotten, a child of earth. His mortal soul reached out for her blindly.

So, seeing that Sivesh enjoyed the world, Azhrarn came to spend much time in it.

Sometimes, in the garb of travellers, they would visit the nighttime cities of men, and enter by stealth the treasure houses of kings, and all the gems and metals they found there Azhrarn would transform to heaps of dust or drifts of withered leaves, for such was his pleasure. And often they might lead astray some caravan in the desert or some ship to founder on the teeth of an unfriendly coast. Yet all these things were childish games to Azhrarn; his wickedness was of a far larger and far more subtle order. Nevertheless, it pleased him to see how Sivesh obeyed him gladly and unthinkingly in everything, and how adept the youth was. Azhrarn humored him like a beloved child.

Then one night, as they came from the hills of some

earthly kingdom, where they had left fire and murder behind them, riding on the demon horses of Underearth with their smoking manes, they came on an old shriveled witch woman by the roadside. The moment she set eyes on the riders and their strange mounts she called out: "Blessed be the name of the Dark Lord, and let him do me no harm."

To which Azhrarn, smiling, replied: "Time has harmed you enough with his claws."

"So indeed he has," cried the witch, her eyes glittering greedily. "May the Dark Lord grant me my youth again?"

At that Azhrarn laughed coldly: "I do not often grant favors, hag. But though I will not give you your youth, I will see to it you grow no older," and a lightning slipped from his hand and struck the witch down. It was never wise to ask a boon from a demon.

Yet the witch did not die at once, and as she lay there she stared up at Sivesh. Marking the handsome face, and guessing him to be mortal, she said: "Scorn me while you are able. You, too, are a fool, earthborn, to trust in demon-kind and to ride on a mare of smoke and night. What demons love they slay in the end, and the gifts of demons are snares. Go nowhere on a horse that fades, for your dreams will betray you." Then she lay back and said no more.

It was by now near dawn, and Azhrarn was impatient to return to the center of the earth. But Sivesh, who was oddly troubled by the witch's words, dismounted and bent over her body. As he was kneeling there a curious pallor in the sky made him look up once more, and on the rim of the hills he saw a glow like a burning rose.

"What light is that?" he asked Azhrarn, wondering and in awe.

"That is the light of dawn, which I abhor," the Prince replied. "Come, mount your horse and let us ride swiftly, for I would not see the sun."

But Sivesh kneeled on the ground as if in a trance.

"Either come now, or I must leave you here," Azhrarn told him.

"Am I then born of earth, as the woman said?"

"You are. The sun to you, perhaps, looks fair, but to the Lords of Darkness it is a thing of ghastly ugliness."

"My lord," Sivesh cried, "let me remain here for one day. Let me see the sun. I cannot rest until I have done so. And yet," he added, "if you command me to return with you, I must, for you are dearer to me than anything."

This softened Azhrarn's mood. He did not wish to let the young man remain, but he foresaw unease if a sight of daytime earth were denied him.

"Stay then," said Azhrarn, "for one day." Then, throwing him a little piece of silver shaped like the head of a serpent, he said: "Sound that at dusk, and it will draw me to you wherever you are. For now, farewell." Then he dug spurs into his beast, and galloped away faster than thought, and even Sivesh's mare, which had been stamping and whinnying nervously at the lightening sky, fled too.

Sivesh felt a sudden fear at being left in the world of men, alone on the hills beside the witch's body, with the terrible glare of dawn filling the east. But then there began in him a swelling happiness, that grew like a melody in his heart. So he had felt when first Azhrarn had spoken to him at Druhim Vanashta, but this time he could find no cause, except for the light over the hills.

First came jade, next ruby, then a disc of gold which shot out rays like arrows of flame, and set the whole world ablaze. Then such color filled the land as the mortal, who had lived in the Underearth, had never seen, such greens, such saffrons, such reds—his whole body seemed to catch alight with them as the world seemed to catch fire from the sun. Never in Azhrarn's midnight halls or the shadowy bright streets of the demon city had he seen a comparable splendor. He stood and wept at it like a lost child which suddenly finds its home.

All day long Sivesh wandered about the valleys and the slopes, and what he did there no one knows. Perhaps he charmed the wild foxes to follow him or the birds of the air to his hands; perhaps he stopped at some shepherd's hut and found there a pretty girl who brought him a drink of milk in an earthenware bowl, and a deeper drink, perhaps, from that other bowl the gods had entrusted to women. Whatever he did, when the sun sank like a fiery tide into the sea, he lay exhausted on the hill and fell asleep, and did not remember to sound the pipe Azhrarn had given him.

Presently Azhrarn came, passing like an inky wind across the land, and searching. Sivesh had not strayed far; the Prince found him easily. Azhrarn was angry, yet seeing him asleep, his beautiful eyes fast shut with weariness, he let his anger rest, and woke the youth with a gentle touch. Sivesh sat up and looked about, and soon made out Azhrarn in the wind.

"You neglected to call me," said Azhrarn, "so I must come looking like your slave or your dog." Nevertheless he spoke quietly and with some amusement.

"My lord, forgive me, but I have seen so much—"

"Tell me nothing of it," Azhrarn said sharply. "I hate the things of day. Now get up and I will take you to Druhim Vanashta."

So they returned, the youth with his talk locked in his mouth and sadness in his face, for he wished to share with Azhrarn, since he loved him, all the joy he had felt at the world.

And how cold the city seemed, and how dismal, all its jewels and its glamor faded by the brightness of the sun. While the eternal cool light of Underearth was like a breath of ice upon his soul.

Azhrarn saw all this in the eyes of Sivesh, but he set aside his anger, as before. He sought to divert the young man's mind.

Azhrarn summoned the Drin, the canny dwarfish smiths of the Underearth, and had them construct for him, in a single night, a vast palace on a high place in Druhim Vanashta. It was built of gold, a metal not generally favored by demons, lit by a thousand many-colored lamps, and girded by a moat of volcanic magma. Such a house had no rival, even among the diverse glories of the city. Sivesh marveled at it, but he could not hide his thoughts from Azhrarn, for the gold was not like the gold of the sun and the magma in the moat did not warm him.

Next Azhrarn gathered his people to a feast, and guiding Sivesh lightly by the arm, he walked with him among the glittering guests. "It is time you sampled women, my dear. You must take a bride," he said. "See, here among the Vazdru and the Eshva are the most magical beauties of my kingdom. Choose, and any one of them shall be yours." Sivesh looked about him, but the lovely faces of the demon women were like masks of paper, their black hair sullen, their eyes like stagnant pools, the movement of their limbs like snakes. He grew paler still with anguish and could not answer. Azhrarn merely stroked his hair, and smiled.

He went alone by night to the hill where he had found Sivesh asleep, and there, adopting the shape of a black wolf, he dug in the earth with his claws. After a while he found a little seed which was sprouting. Quickly he grasped the seed, and in his swiftest form, that of a lightning flash, he sped back to the Underearth. There in the dark garden, beside the fountain of fire, he planted the seed in the ground and spoke over it certain words and sprinkled on it certain dusts. . . . Soon he sent for Sivesh.

Sivesh stood beside the Prince of Demons, and at first he saw nothing, only the bed of freshly turned soil. Then from the center of the bed there spread a crack like a wriggling worm, and after the first, six more. Shortly, there came an opening, and out of it the tip of some growing thing thrust like the snout of a mole.

"Oh, my lord, what is this?" Sivesh asked, halfway between horror and fascination.

"I have grown a rare flower for you," Azhrarn replied, and slipping his arm about the young man's shoulders, bade him wait and see.

The shoot of the mysterious plant now came springing up. As soon as it had shaken itself free of soil it began to put forth leaves and buds, though mostly they withered as quickly as they formed. One bud, however, swelled like a bubble on the stem, swelled until it was of unusual size and then split open. Inside stood a full-grown flower, shaped rather like the closed cup of a magnolia, the palest violet in color, but veined with rose.

This was wonderful enough; the young man caught his breath. But what came after was more wonderful still.

The tight-shut petals of the flower stole open one by one, each revealing behind itself another of a deeper and more ravishing blue, until at last the entire blossom was spread wide like a fan. And at the heart of the flower lay a sleeping maiden, naked among the flames of her own hair.

"Since the women of my country were not fair enough to please you," remarked Azhrarn, "I have grown you a woman from a flower of earth. See. Her hair is the yellow of wheat, her breasts white pomegranates, her loins honeydew." Leading Sivesh to the flower, he leaned forward and lifted the maiden out, and as her white feet left the flower's heart there came a little snapping sound like the breaking of the stalk of a plant. At once the maiden opened her eyes; they were as blue as the world's sky.

Azhrarn the Prince of Demons gave her hand into the hand of Sivesh with a secret smile, and as if to echo him, the maiden smiled also, looking into Sivesh's bemused face. And so sweet was that smile and that loveliness that Sivesh forgot the sun.

Her name was Ferazhin, Flower-Born. Sivesh lived with her in harmony in his palace at Druhim Vanashta for one mortal year.

Azhrarn had taught him many of the ways of love. Demons did not adhere only to a single road, a solitary room in the vast treasure store. The delightful door of one chamber led into another. Ferazhin, with the honeycomb of her loins, her apple sweetness, her wheat-field hair able to couch both her lover and herself upon a resilient carpet of fragrant gold, was as ripe for the pleasure of Sivesh as was the earth.

Certain it is that for that time he loved her, and maybe that she loved him. She was not of demon-kind, though made by demons. Neither was she human. She was a creature grown of earth-seed in supernatural soil. She bore the stamp of both.

So for a year, Sivesh lived much as before, hunting the wilds of Underearth, feasting in the subterranean city, going sometimes by night with Azhrarn over the earth, and at last returning to his flower-wife across the magma moat. And if he adored her, still he worshipped the Prince of Demons before everything, all the more because of this last gift which he had given him. Maybe there was too some spell cast over him when he took her hand, for otherwise it is strange that he forgot so long and so completely the daytime world that he could visit it contentedly by night, and could even hunt the souls of men on the margins of Sleep River.

But the Prince of Demons could not foresee everything, and it was Ferazhin herself who caused the breaking of the spell. She had come from the world, though demons made her, and her heart was still the kernel of the seed that obeys the natural laws, and yearns for air and light.

Suddenly, on the last day of the year, rising from their bed, she murmured to her husband Sivesh: "I dreamed a curious dream when I slept. I dreamed I lay in a cavern and I heard a bronze horn sound in the sky and I knew it called me. So I rose, and I went up the steep stairs of the cavern towards it. The way was very hard, but at last I reached a door, and thrusting it open, I came out on to a lawn, and above was an enchanted bowl, all blue, with set in it one little disk of gold, and though it was so little, the disk gave off a light that filled the land from end to end."

When Sivesh heard her, his heart seemed to leap and catch fire inside him, and he recalled at once the dawn when he had seen the sun. It was as if a shadow had fallen all around him, except in his breast and brain, which flamed. He looked at beautiful Ferazhin, and she was like a figure of mist. The palace about them both was dull as yellow lead. He ran out into the city; its splendor had grown cold, it was a tomb. Then, as he walked dazedly into the streets of the tomb, he met Azhrarn.

"I see you have remembered the world of clay," said the Prince of Demons in a voice of iron. "What now?"

"Oh, my lord, my lord, what can I do?" cried Sivesh, weeping. "The flesh of my mother calls me from its grave in the earth above. I must go back to the land of men, for I can remain in the Underearth no longer."

"So you deny you owe me any love," said Azhrarn in a voice of steel.

"My lord, I love you more than my soul. If I leave you, it

will be to me as if I left half of myself behind in your kingdom. But I am in torment here. I cannot stay. The city is a shadow and I am like a blind worm crawling in it. Therefore pity me, and let me go.''

''This is the third time you have angered me,'' said Azhrarn in a voice of winter. ''Consider well whether you wish to leave me, for I shall not any more set my anger aside.''

''I have no choice,'' said Sivesh, ''none, my lord of all lords.''

''Then go,'' said Azhrarn in a voice of death. ''And remember after, what you have cast away and why, and who it is that tells you this.''

Then Sivesh went with leaden steps to the outskirts of Druhim Vanashta, and all the way the demons shrank back from him. The great gates opened. A whirlwind snatched him up and tossed him through the maw of the volcano and out upon the earth for which he ached.

In this way Sivesh returned to the world of men, and walked with sorrow under the sun.

3   The Night Mare

This was the tragedy of Sivesh: while he could no longer endure to live in the city below, he knew no other life, and while he yearned for the sun of the world, having left him, he yearned as much for the dark sun of Druhim Vanashta—Azhrarn.

He had been a prince in a palace, with horses and hounds and a fair wife. Now he worked for the herdsmen on the hills and in the valleys, driving the rough goats all day in the heat, sleeping in a tent of hide or a little wayside house of stones at night. His pay was a slice of coarse bread, a handful of figs; he drank from streams as the goats did. All this was nothing to him. The sun was his motive. He watched for its rising, he watched it go by like a fiery bird, he watched it fall beyond the world and the ravens of darkness gather. The sun was his joy, his happiness. The herdsmen, as they drove their flocks across the land, wondered at the strange and handsome youth who spent so much of his time staring upward. He made no friends among them, though he was gentle and modest. They thought he might be some rich man's son who had fallen on hard times. He said no word of his past, though sometimes in his sleep they heard him call out a name which some of them knew, and it struck their spirits with fear. For in sleep, the soul of Sivesh, wandering by Sleep River, stared across the wild lands of its dreams, looking for the Dark Lord and his hunting dogs.

He discounted all Azhrarn had told him. Sivesh did not

believe the Prince could ever bring him to harm. He loved wholly and with his open mortal heart, bearing the pain of his loss like a heavy burden he never wished to set down. Azhrarn, who had loved him also, would bear his loss similarly, and as Sivesh could never hurt what he loved, therefore neither could Azhrarn. For all his years in the Underearth, Sivesh's generous melancholy nature had learned little of the demon-kind.

One day the herders reached a city, where they planned to sell their goats in the market place. It was a city of earth and, to Sivesh, very ugly and terrible. There had been no poverty or diseases, hovels or beggars in Druhim Vanashta, only rare gardens and slim minarets of metal, while the demon-race were very good to look on. After a time, Sivesh grew sick. He left the herders to their bargaining, and walked out of the gates and away to the seashore. Here he sat upon a rock in the profoundest grief, and presently the sun swam beneath the water and the night came blowing down from the land.

For a long time he had avoided the night, covering his head with goat skins and falling swiftly asleep. It was pain to him to recall how he and Azhrarn had ridden over the earth by night and played their devil-tricks on humanity. Partly too, he had come to understand the evil they had done in the world under the cold moon. Confusion and a sense of awful loss beset him. Yet now he remained on the shore, for it seemed that tonight his heart would crack in any case. He was almost glad of it.

So there he sat. And the stars grinned like naked daggers. Perhaps Sleep, the fisher, came to him once or twice then drifted away again, trailing her filmy net, cheated.

At midnight a wind whispered in his ear. It spoke of a strange music.

Sivesh listened, and roused himself. He heard a curious halting melody, sad and dreaming; it matched his mood. He looked out toward the sea. He saw a wonder. The moon had fallen from the sky, and floated there. But then he shut his eyes, and looked again, and through the pale radiance that surrounded it he saw an incredible ship. It was formed like a great flower of beaten silver, but at its center there rose a slender silver tower pointing up into the night, its roof shaped to resemble a diadem. And in the tower, just beneath the diadem, there burned a single ruby window. The ship had neither oar nor sail. There was a movement before it, a glistening of starlight on wet ancient skin, a creaming of foam: huge beasts were drawing the vessel through the waves as a team of horses would draw a chariot. What they were— enormous whales, dragons even—Sivesh could not tell. He stood staring, and as he did so, the ship turned and came nearer to the land.

All around him the lovely sorrowful music seemed to play. The vast beasts toiled, the ship went gliding after. Sivesh walked into the sea some distance, until the breakers burst against his knees. As he watched, the window in the tower opened wide. Out looked a face.

The weakness of Sivesh was his love for beauty. As others loved riches or pleasure or power, so he loved this. And so he worshipped Azhrarn, and for a while Ferazhin the Flower-Born, and so he worshipped the light of fire and at last the lord of all fires, the sun. Thus he looked up at the face of the maiden leaning from the tower, and she became the sum of everything.

Having told of so much beauty, how is it possible to tell of her? There are no words left on the earth in any tongue that will do. Such words vanished from the world when it shook itself free from the ocean of chaos, in a cataclysm that reshaped it like one of the balls small children throw in the air at play.

Yet there was something of Ferazhin in her, and something of Azhrarn also, and she shone from her window like the sun, and presently, like the sun, slowly unveiled herself of her draperies, and let her silver nakedness dazzle inch by inch on Sivesh, till he trembled and fire filled his loins.

Then the great ship turned once more, and began to move away over the sea, leaving behind it on the water a reflection like a path. Sivesh called aloud after the vessel—he gazed at the path and struggled out through the waves. But the heavy sea thrust him mercilessly back, and its cold brought him to his senses.

He stood on the shore like a man in a trance all through the hours of darkness, his eyes fixed on the far horizon where the ship had vanished like a setting star. When at last the sun rose, he had no eyes for it. He lay in the rock's shadow and fell into blind slumber.

He woke at sunset and watched all night. The ship passed, far out, two hours before dawn. He called to her, but she did not turn for land.

The next day too he slept. The herders were looking for him on the beach at noon, but he did not stir and they did not find him. They had made a profit in the city and had money to spend. Besides, the youth was strange, perhaps half-witted. Shortly they went away. When night fell, Sivesh stood on the shore and waited with wild and hungry eyes. This time he did not see the ship, though she passed, for he heard the music. He trembled for joy at the sound, and waded out into the sea until again it pushed him angrily off. Then he wept with anger at the angry sea. He was quite mad with longing.

He was also bewitched. He, who had seen such spells worked out on others, had no judgment left to free himself from the enchantment when it fell on him. And he, who had lived in the City of Demons for seventeen years, still had no guard against their sorceries.

It was Azhrarn's doing. Who but Azhrarn?

The Prince of Demons had spoken truly from the first. What a demon desired and lost, he would destroy. It was as natural to him as it was to a mortal to burn the sheets of the sick man after fever, or to bury the dead.

At first, he had been perplexed, this Lord of Darkness, as to how it should be done. In the days of their companionship he had made the young man proof against all the weapons and perils of earth. Then Azhrarn remembered the one thing he had not been able to do.

Presently, the youth went to the shore, and Azhrarn fashioned from smokes and dreams the magic flower-tower ship. It was a ghost-thing, but like the mirage men glimpse in the desert which seems as real as the sand all around. Azhrarn was very pleased with the toy. For a long while he admired his handiwork, and he looked longest at the phantom woman he had created to ride in it and capture Sivesh's heart and mind. Even he, the Prince, felt a half amused wonder at the beauty he had made. He sent her out upon the sea. He himself, in the appearance of a black gull, circled high above the shore, and watched the spell take hold of Sivesh.

Three nights and three days he let the youth suffer his despair and yearning. On the fourth night, about an hour after the sinking of the sun, Azhrarn modelled for himself the form of a fisherman, and leaning over Sivesh, who lay asleep, he sang softly in his ear, in the way of demons.

Sivesh started up. It seemed a coaxing melodious voice had woken him—he thought the silver ship had come. But getting to his feet he neither saw nor heard the ship; only an old grizzled fisherman sat mending his net on the shore.

"Did you call me?" asked Sivesh, for there was something about the fisherman which strangely attracted him and urged him to speak.

"Not I," answered the man, "there would be no profit in that."

But his voice was odd, did not seem to belong to him. It had a unique quality, like the brilliant and marvelously intelligent eyes with which he now regarded Sivesh. The young man felt comforted by this presence, he did not know why. He had an impulse to unburden his trouble to the fisherman. Yet he was shy too; he had never grown used to human men and women.

"A good catch today?" he therefore murmured.

"No, a bad," said the man. "The fish are anxious and will not rise. I will tell you a wonder, if you will listen. There is a great silver ship which haunts the sea by night. I have seen her pass with my own eyes. A maiden sits in a tower at the center of the ship. She waits for a lover she heard of in a prophecy, and her foot may not touch land until he claims her. The prophecy says that his hair will be red as amber and that he will know certain magics of the Underearth, taught him by a Lord of Darkness."

The young man turned very pale, and stared at the empty waves.

"Tell me then," he whispered, "if you know the prophecy, how will this lover reach the maiden in the ship?"

"Why," said the fisherman, "the story goes that he will have a demon mare which can run across water, and will therefore ride to her over the sea."

Sivesh covered his face with his hands. The fisherman, rising, put an arm about his shoulders and inquired kindly what ailed him. And at the old man's touch, which seemed as amazingly thrilling as the voice and eyes had done, Sivesh felt once more the irresistible impulse to confide his misery.

"I am the one the prophecy spoke of," he stammered, "destined to love the maiden on the ship. Already I have seen her, and love her more than my life. I have, too, lived in the Underearth and there learned some magic, and owned such a horse as you mention, which can run on water. But I renounced that world to live on the earth, and now can ask nothing of my Lord Azhrarn."

"Do not speak that fearful name aloud," implored the fisherman in apparent fright, making a sign against evil, his eyes glinting as eyes only glint with extreme terror, or laughter. "But I will ask you this. Did the Demon ever give you anything by which you might summon him? For there are mystic tokens that will call such creatures whether they wish to come or not."

At once Sivesh gave a cry and fumbled in his coat. Presently he drew out the little pipe shaped like a serpent's head which Azhrarn had thrown to him when first he stayed on earth to see the sun rise.

"This he gave me," said Sivesh, "and said that it would draw him to me wherever I might be."

"Well and good then," said the fisherman. "But do you not tremble at the thought of his anger? Or do you think he may be gentle with you after all?"

"I do not fear him. I can think only of the maiden."

At this the fisherman's face seemed to melt for a moment, to reveal behind it another face, all iron. But Sivesh did not see; indeed, he could see nothing but his dreams. He set the pipe to his lips.

"Wait!" shouted the fisherman, in evident horror, "let me be gone before you sound. I have no wish to stand here when he comes."

So Sivesh waited, and the fisherman ran down the shore.

Perhaps, after all, it had been a sort of test which Azhrarn had set for Sivesh. If Sivesh had been able to resist the enchantment of the magic ship, and recalled for a moment his love of Azhrarn, and also the power which Azhrarn possessed which made him so fearful in men's eyes (since the demons were vain of their beauty and their power) is it possible that the Prince might have turned from his vengeance? But the sorcery Azhrarn himself had made had proved too great. Sivesh remembered only his longing for the maiden and for those moments set the Prince of Demons at nought. He could, after that, expect no mercy.

Once the old man was out of sight—and did he not run fast for one so old?—Sivesh again put the pipe to his lips, and blew.

There was no sound, at least no sound that could be heard on the earth. Then suddenly the air was full of a noise like beating wings, and on the shore there whirled up a pillar of smoke. There was no form to the smoke. Azhrarn would never more deign to appear to Sivesh in the fair mortal shape which demons generally put on and which caused them to be adored and magnified by humans.

From the smoke came a voice which asked coolly:

"Why have you called me here? Have you forgotten we are parted?"

"My lord, forgive me, I ask one thing only and then I will ask nothing further."

"Be sure of that. You shall not dare sound that pipe a second time. What then do you require?"

"Loan me, for one night merely, the horse of Underearth which once you gave me. The mare with the mane like blue steam, who can run across water."

"Never say I am not generous," said the voice of Azhrarn

out of the smoke. "For this one night you shall ride her. See, here she comes."

And abruptly some of the dunes of the beach burst open, and out flashed the demon mare, shaking the sand and soil from her back. Sivesh called to her joyfully, and recognizing his voice, she trotted to him and let him mount. When he looked back the pillar of smoke had blown away into the night and the shore was empty. Sivesh felt then a pang of guilt and sorrow; he had not even given Azhrarn his thanks. But soon he forgot, and sat patiently at the edge of the sea, the mare, eager to run over the waves, fretting under him, while the moon rose and sank and the stars glittered like drawn steel.

It was late when the ship came. She stood far out near the line of the horizon and, having appeared, she did not move.

Sivesh heard the music in the wind. He thought: *My beloved stays the ship, she waits for me to ride to her.* So he set spurs to the mare which were hardly needed for she was glad to be off.

Her hooves darted like cymbals through the foam, over the silver path that was reflected shorewards from the flower-tower ship.

Sivesh called to the mare, to the night, to the maiden in the tower. He was alight with the sort of extraordinary unreasoning happiness that only the victim of a spell could know. A happiness like the flame of a candle, burning down even as it glows, at its brightest in the instant before it gutters out.

When he was about a quarter of a mile from it, the ship began to move leisurely away from him. This did not seem ominous or even curious to him. It was like a kind of delightful playfulness, a game devised by the girl in the tower just to see if he would follow. Besides, the ship moved only very slowly, though somehow just fast enough that he could not quite catch up with it, no matter how he might try.

Then, through the moan of the sea, the enchanted music, the jingle of the harness, through everything, there came to Sivesh as he rode a voice made of the wind itself. He did not know what brought it, he did not remember to whom it had

G. Barr

belonged, but the words it spoke repeated themselves over and over in his ears: "You, too, are a fool, Earthborn, to trust in demon-kind and to ride on a mare of smoke and night. What demons love they slay in the end, and the gifts of demons are snares." All at once, he saw himself as if he had been a gull circling round in the sky above—a man on a horse riding impudently across the sea, over the path of light cast by a ship which forever ran away from him. A cold serpent twisted in Sivesh's vitals. He drew rein and looked behind him. How far the shore was, only a line like lavender chalk dividing water and air. He saw too, in looking back, another thing, a thing which until now had always filled his heart with gladness. The east was paling, soft as the breast of a dove. Soon the sun of day would rise.

The wind, fresh with dawn, blew more strongly.

"Your dreams will betray you," sang the voice of the wind. "Go nowhere on a horse that fades."

Sivesh gave a groan of horror and of anguish. He turned the demon mare about, leaving the fleeing ship behind him. The moment she faced the lightening east, however, the horse whinnied and reared with terror.

Sivesh held her firm. He cajoled her with endearments, or cursed her. He forced her to make toward the distant shore, over the rolling sea which now was turning luminous as nacre. She ran finally like the whirlwind; her mane lashed his face. She snorted and stared with fear.

Sivesh glanced back. The silver ship had grown transparent in the brightening sky, it flickered like shadow before light, now it was gone. And now the sun rose.

It rose like the phoenix, the whole of the east opened like a flower. The rays of its vast light struck out across the sea, so that now a path of gold, not silver, lay emblazoned there, and as the arrows of fire struck the demon mare she gave a scream more dreadful than any legitimate sound of the earth; the burning shafts seemed to pass right through her.

Immediately Sivesh felt the reins dissolve in his hands, the stirrups run like wax. Next, the firm body of the horse collapsed and crumpled like a thing of paper. Sivesh stared down at her. She was only a wisp of night fog beneath him, fading in the sun.

He fell. The sea received him, opening its jaws greedily. He was not proof against the sea. Even the Prince of Demons had not been able to protect him against it, for it was not of the kingdom of earth, and had its own rulers. In the second before the waters drank him down, Sivesh cried one name aloud. It was the name of Azhrarn, and in that name was all the pain and loneliness and despair and accusation that any mortal throat could utter. Then the waves swallowed and the morning was filled with silence.

If Azhrarn heard that last cry, who knows. Perhaps he was watching in some magic glass for the end of the youth, and saw him drown; perhaps for a moment some of that awful pain hurt in his own throat, and in his mouth, which spoke so wondrously and with such charm, perhaps there came, for the moment of a moment, a taste of green salt water.

It is said that a great fire was made in Druhim Vanashta, and that in the fire was burned the palace which Azhrarn had built for Sivesh. When its roof of jewels fell in, a huge glare thrust up, and seared the eyes of all who watched, a light too fierce to be welcome in the Underearth, for it resembled the sun.

PART TWO

4 Seven Tears

Far down in the Underearth, yet outside the phosphorescent walls and shimmering steeples of Druhim Vanashta, lay a wide dark mirror-lake between shores of black rock. Here, all through the unchanging day-nights, the Drin worked at their anvils, the red forges smoked and the hammers rang.

The Drin had none of the beauty of the higher echelons of the demons, the Vazdru—who were princes—or the Eshva, their stewards and handmaidens. The Drin were little and grotesque and full of small grotesque jokes. They loved to make mischief, like their lords, but seldom had ideas of their own as to how it might be done. Therefore they served the Vazdru, ran the errands of the Eshva, and when powerful mortal sorcerers set about their brews and conjurations, the Drin would rush up on the earth to aid them, and where possible wreck more woe than the sorcerers had bargained for.

And one other thing the Drin could do; they could be metal-smiths. If they were not beautiful themselves, yet they could fashion beautiful things. They hammered out earrings for demonesses, rings for demom princes, cups and keys, clockwork silver birds to fly round the towers of the palace of Azhrarn, lord of all demon-kind. And once they had built a mansion of gold for a mortal youth Azhrarn favored, though now nothing remained of it but golden ash.

There was a Drin called Vayi: he was given to ambitious thoughts, and sometimes roamed by the lake looking for the

37

precious stones or translucent pebbles that in places littered the gloomy shores, thinking: *Presently I shall make the most magnificent ring in Underearth, and Azhrarn will wear it and praise me,* or, *Soon I will invent a magic animal of metal that will stop all tongues with wonder.* For Vayi wanted above everything to do better than all the other Drin who carelessly strove and hammered, he wanted to be unique and known. Sometimes he dreamed of living in Azhrarn's palace, the pet of the Prince of Demons. Nothing would be too good for Vayi then. At other times he thought he might go above ground and thrive at the courts of famous kings, renowned and honoured by all, with a special velvet-lined day-box in which to hide from the unpleasant sun.

As he was walking and dreaming and muttering, Vayi suddenly saw a figure moving along by the lake's edge just ahead of him. He knew at once that it was no Drin, being too tall, slender and, even when seen from the back, somehow too fair. Possibly here was some gorgeous Vazdru or Eshva lady come to ask for a wonderful jewel, and perhaps willing to offer payment in a particular fashion very pleasing to the Drin. Vayi pattered stealthily after her, and soon she seated herself on a rock before the lake. Her veil fell back then, and Vayi knew her at once. Long yellow hair drenched her shoulders and her face was the face of a flower. There was no other like her in all Underearth, and probably none like her on the earth above. For this was Ferazhin Flower-Born, the maiden Azhrarn had grown from a flower to please the mortal, Sivesh, who now lay under the sea.

Ferazhin sat by the lake. She held out her white hands to the cold black water and to the unchanging sky. She bowed her head and wept.

Vayi was fascinated. Did she weep for Sivesh? Or did she weep, as Sivesh had wept, for the cruel blazing sun of earth? Then Vayi saw how the tears of Ferazhin fell down on the rock and gleamed and glittered there. *What gems those tears could make,* thought Vayi all at once, *bright as diamonds, yet softer; more like pearls, yet clearer than pearls, spangled; rather like opals, yet purer than opals; more like pale sap-*

*phires, though not spoiled with color. But how, how shall I
capture them and harden them?*

Vayi fumbled in his belt, and drew out a little box and spat
in it and sprinkled a spell into it from his woody hands. Then
he capered out and took up a tear on the tip of his little finger
and dropped it, unbroken, into the magic box. Six more tears
he took after it and added to his collection before Ferazhin
looked up from her weeping and noticed him. She gave him
only one glance of fear and hurt and, gathering her veil round
her, rose and went slowly back toward the gates of Druhim
Vanashta. Hunt as he would, Vayi could find no further tears
shining among the rocks, so he scampered after her, crying:
"Pretty Ferazhin, come back and weep some more, and I will
give you bangles and brooches, and earrings." But Ferazhin
paid him no heed, and soon he hurried away toward the lake,
clutching the precious box, muttering: "Seven is enough.
More would be vulgar. Seven is rare."

Into his own cave Vayi ran, blew up the fire and poked
about among his untidy hoard of metals, pebbles, and stones.
Shortly he went to a cage where three round spiders were
sleeping, and rattled on the bars.

"Wake, wake, daughters of sloth," cried he. "Wake and
spin, and I will bring you cake soaked in wine and the Prince
of Demons will stroke you with his wondrous fingers."

"Oh, lord of liars," said the spiders, but nevertheless they
obeyed him, and soon the twilight cave was festooned with
their filigree webs.

Hour after hour Vayi worked in his forge. The fire leaped
and smoked, and other fires—magic fires—also glamorized
the air. He was inspired, and called to his use every one of
the small strange sorceries the Drin had access to. Sometimes
other Drin would come to the cave entrance and peer in,
curiously. But the cave was full of smoulders, and they could
not catch the words of Vayi's spells, for all the Drin were
somewhat deaf from their constant hammering. How long
Vayi worked altogether it is not easy to reckon. It was
thought a long time in the Underearth, and certainly on earth
itself many seasons had given way to each other, and many

human years elapsed between the beginning and the ending of his labor.

At last there was silence in the forge.

The other Drin stole up, but now Vayi had magnified one of his spiders to enormous size and stuffed the poor thing in the opening, so nobody could pass either in or out.

"Ho, there, Vayi!" cried the Drin. "Show us what you have been fashioning that has taken you so many ages."

"Go drown in mud!" shouted back Vayi rudely from within. "Nothing here is for your eyes."

The Drin went off a little way and mumbled together by the lake. One of them, Bakvi, was very jealous and unsettled in himself, for he remembered Vayi's ambitions, and how he had hoped to win Azhrarn's especial favor by making something finer than all the rest for him. All the Drin adored and feared Azhrarn, and Bakvi began to think to himself. *Suppose I were to be able to steal Vayi's trinket, and give it to my lord myself. Then I should be the favored one.*

So, when the other Drin had gone off grumbling and chiding, Bakvi hid behind a rock and waited.

After a long while, Vayi thrust the spider out of the way, stuck his long nose round the cave wall and looked nervously about. Assuming himself alone, he emerged from hiding, and running onto the shore performed a wild dance by the lake, squealing to himself joyfully.

Bakvi meanwhile sidled up to the spider.

"Fair lady," said he, "how you are grown! Your size is matched only by your excellence."

"Flattery is no use to me," said the spider. "Be off, or I shall bite you, for I am hungry."

"Easily remedied," said Bakvi. And he produced from his pocket a large honey cake baked only that morning. The spider licked her lips. "Luscious madam," said Bakvi, "pray eat this cake before you swoon from lack of nourishment. Who could expect you to be loyal to such a master as this Vayi, who stuffs you in cave entrances so disrespectfully, and brings you no food." With this the spider agreed, so Bakvi gave her the cake, and tried to sidle within the cave, but no sooner was the spider done eating than she got in his way again. "Dear me," said Bakvi, "I wished only to peep at what your wicked unkind master has made. Surely you can be persuaded? Is there not some other service I can render you?" At which he commenced tickling the spider in a certain part of her anatomy. Presently she became excited, and suggested a bargain. Bakvi accordingly mounted her and began to work vigorously on her behalf. She sighed and squealed, but she was a difficult lady to please. Bakvi bucked and heaved away with a will, and fancied himself near ruined if she should not seen be satisfied. Eventually, with a violent hiss, the spider tossed him from her back and declared he might now leave off and enter Vayi's workroom instead.

Nursing his bruises and rather short of breath, Bakvi hobbled into the cave.

And there on Vayi's bench lay a collar of white silver, fiery pale as the moon and hung with chains of silver spiderweb made metal, as fine as the finest thread. And in this mesh were caught, like star-birds in a snare, seven wonderful flashing gems, bright as lightning yet soft as milk.

"O most marvelous Vayi," said Bakvi, much recovered. And snatching the collar, he hid it in his jacket, and ran as fast as he could out of the cave, along the shore, and over the dark slopes toward Druhim Vanashta.

Soon enough Vayi came hopping back. The spider was exquisitely grooming herself with her eight furry limbs, a picture of utter content, but this Vayi did not notice. Straight into his cave he bounded and straight up to his bench, and then what a wailing and screeching was heard, and what a turning over of tables and chairs, and upheaving of braziers and throwing of bellows and gnashing of teeth and thrashing of spiders. Then came silence, and then came Vayi hurtling out of his cave and along the shore and over the slopes toward Druhim Vanashta, screaming for justice and vengeance, and this was how he arrived at the palace of Azhrarn, Prince of Demons, one of the Lords of Darkness.

Azhrarn was walking in his garden of velure trees, a Vazdru princess at his right hand playing a seven-stringed harp more delicately than an evening breeze playing in a

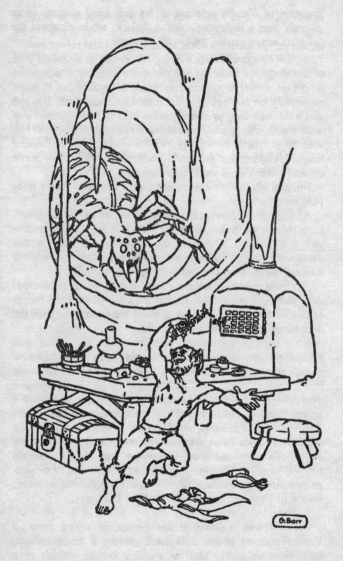

fountain, a Vazdru princess at his left hand singing more sweetly than a nightingale and a skylark, while all about the jeweled wasps visited the crystal flowers.

Into this dark harmony came an Eshva woman who bowed low, and next a little gamboling Drin.

"Well, little one," said Azhrarn, passing over Bakvi a pair of mesmerizing thoughtful eyes, "what is it you seek?"

Bakvi flushed and stammered, but drawing his courage together at last, he cried: "Oh, Incredible Majesty, I, Bakvi, least of your subjects, bring you a gift. For unknown eras I have toiled in secret, while others have made a great fuss and show of their work. All my skill and all my love have I poured into this unworthy token of my worship. Pray deign to glance at it, O Prince of Night."

And, producing the silver collar, he held it out to Azhrarn.

Both the Vazdru princesses gave a cry and clapped their hands. Even the jeweled wasps swooped closer. As for the Eshva woman, she shut her eyes in sheer delight.

Azhrarn smiled, and that smile filled Bakvi up like a cup with pride, but before another word could be spoken, into the garden erupted Vayi. At the sight of Bakvi and the collar, Vayi turned the color of blue gas, and let out a most dreadful howl of rage.

"Cursed be all thieves, and cursed be all the furry daughters of gluttony and lust, my eight-legged handmaidens, and cursed be all the Drin but me!"

The Vazdru and the Eshva shrank aside, terrified at Azhrarn's anger which would surely blast the Drin to ashes. But Azhrarn did nothing, merely stood where he was, and soon Vayi became aware of him, like a tall shadow thrown upward on the air. Slowly then, Vayi's eyes traveled up until they met those coals that were the Prince's.

"Mercy, Peerless One," whimpered Vayi, "I forgot myself in my fury. But this son of a deaf bat and a blind owl has stolen my work. That collar is mine, mine!"

"And did you also intend," said Azhrarn, smooth as honey and hemlock, "to give the collar to me."

At this Vayi beat his fists on his head and his feet on the ground.

"What else, O Wondrous One? Is it not fair? Is it not without equal? Who else should possess it but the Lord without equal?"

"Well, well," said Azhrarn. "And how am I to judge who made this gift for me? Shall I put you both to the test?"

Bakvi and Vayi both cast themselves down on the black lawn and squealed for pity, but presently Vayi gave over chewing the grass and stuck up his head again.

"There is only one way to test us, Prince. If he made the collar, ask him where he came by such rare and lucent jewels."

Azhrarn smiled once more, a smile unlike the first. He looked musingly at Bakvi, and he said:

"That seems reasonable enough, little hammerer. The jewels are strange and beautiful. Tell me, where did you mine them?"

Bakvi sat up and looked about wildly:

"In a deep cave," he began, "I found a curious cleft," but at this Vayi let out a gale of laughter. Bakvi checked and began again. "Strolling by the lake I found a lizard with a brazen skin, and, holding it up by its tail, shook out its eyes."

"Did it then have seven eyes?" barked Vayi.

"Yes, yes, it did," gabbled Bakvi, "two on either side of its nose, one in the top of its head—ah—one in its chin, and—um—"

"Pah!" exclaimed Vayi exultantly. "See how the wretch lies. I will tell you, oh Fabulous Lord, where I got my seven jewels." And coming close, he whispered it.

"That is easily verified," said Azhrarn, and he took from one of the Vazdru princesses a magic glass, and summoned up in it the image of Ferazhin Flower-Born, and bade her, in his low melodious voice, to weep. So irresistible was his command that all wept who heard him; even the flowers put out dew. Ferazhin's tears fell like rain, and each resembled one of the seven jewels.

"Cease weeping," murmured Azhrarn, darkening the glass, and the Vazdru brushed the drops from their damask cheeks though the Eshva woman wore her tears like opals, and the two Drin continued to snivel from fear. "Now," said Azhrarn, "I know that Vayi made the collar and Bakvi stole it. How shall I punish him?"

Bakvi gibbered, and Vayi cried:

"Boil him in the venom of the snake who is his mistress, boil him for ten human centuries. And then boil him in lava for another ten. And then give him to me."

"Be still, little greedy one," said Azhrarn, and Vayi paled. "I alone mete out justice in Druhim Vanashta. I see that, though one is a thief, the other is ambitious, boastful, impetuous and loud. Bad little Drin. Bakvi must crawl on his belly and be a worm and turn the soil of my garden until I remember him, for thieves cannot be tempted when there is nothing to steal," and next minute Bakvi had shrunk and thinned and fallen down and slipped away a little black worm into the ground. "As for Vayi; I decline his gift, since its value has been lost in wrangling. Bad little Drin, you are too proud of your cleverness. I will send your collar to the world of men and there great mischief will come of it, which will please you, and who will doubt that a Drin made it, but they will never learn your name and you shall get no credit for your work, no kings will keep you in state, or make you velvet boxes in which to hide by day."

Then Vayi bowed his head, seeing Azhrarn read all his dreams.

"I am punished," he said, "and rewarded too. You are just, as ever, Master of the city. Only let me kiss the grass where the sole of your foot has most recently rested, and I will go."

And this he did, and trotted away, and lay in his cave by the lake, thinking of Azhrarn the beautiful, and of Bakvi the worm tunneling in the garden, and of the silver collar with the seven tears in it lost in the wide world of men.

5   A Collar of Silver

The secret in the collar was quite simple: being magic, a thing of the Underearth, it was attractive to men and to mortal things in a way no earthly adornment could ever be. More than its beauty, it was a lure. Whoever saw it coveted it, and besides, it was wonderfully made—even Azhrarn had received it with pleasure, at the first. Lastly, the seven gems set in the mesh of the collar were tears, and cast on it their own pale sorcery. A collar constructed in ambition and pride and jeweled with sorrow could only stir up greed and smiling fury, and bring weeping after.

One of the Eshva brought the collar to earth. In the form of a slim dark young man, he wandered dreamily from place to place through the night, glancing in at lighted windows, calling the night things, the badgers and panthers, to play on the forest lawns, and staring through moonwashed pools at his own reflection.In the lavender twilight before dawn, the Eshva crossed the market place of a vast city and found a beggar asleep on the steps of a fountain. The Eshva laughed softly with his eyes, and fastened Vayi's collar about the beggar's neck. Then, leaping in the air, fled away toward earth's center like a dark star.

After a time the sun rose and the market stirred. Pigeons flew to the fountain to drink and women came with their water jars to gossip. The beggar got up and stretched himself in his rags, picked up his begging bowl and set off for his day's work, but he had not gone far before a voice bawled out to ask him what it was he wore about his neck. The beggar paused, and felt the collar. No sooner had his hand encountered the smooth hardness of silver and his eye the cool brightness of jewels, however, than a huge crowd came pressing around him clamoring.

"Good sirs," cried the beggar, "I am surprised you are so interested in this cheap bauble—it is only a talisman I bought from an old witch to keep me safe from the plague. But, alas," he added, "I fear it has done me no good," and he exhibited a few spots and sores he had previously painted on himself for begging purposes. The crowd uncertainly drew off a little and the beggar ducked through and rushed down a side street, but in a moment the mob were after him, yelling. Into a jeweler's shop he flew, and flung himself down before the jeweler. "Succour! Aid me, sweet sir!" screamed the beggar. "Only rescue me, and I will shower on you the riches of the world."

"You?" inquired the jeweler scornfully, but he wanted no trouble, and hearing the crowd coming, he thrust the beggar into a chest, slammed down the lid, and went and stood in the doorway as if waiting casually for business. Presently the crowd came cramming into the street, and implored him to tell if he had seen a beggar run that way.

"*I?*" asked the jeweler loftily. "I have better things to look out for."

The crowd debated noisily and then began to break up in confusion, some running on down the street, others back up it, and shortly the way was empty.

"Now," said the jeweler, throwing open the chest, "be off as fast as you can."

"A thousand thanks," said the beggar, stepping out, "but before I leave you, regard this necklet, and tell me how much you would give me for it."

Immediately the jeweler's face altered. His eyes and mouth narrowed and his nose twitched. Be sure he wanted the collar more than anything, but it seemed to him quite silly to pay a beggar for it. *Such creatures are not used to coins,* he thought. If I pay him what the collar is worth he will only get into trouble with the money. So he said cautiously: "Just give me the trinket and let me examine it a moment."

The beggar did as he was asked, but no sooner did the jeweler have the collar in his hand than he shouted: "Ah! I hear the mob coming back. Quick, into the chest again. Make no sound whatever happens, and I will try to save you."

The beggar in fright jumped straight back in: the jeweler banged down the lid, and this time secured the clasps. Then, hiding the collar in his robe, he went out into the street and called over two porters who were idling near the wineshop.

"Here is a gold coin each," said he, "if you will only take this wretched old chest off my hands. It has been cluttering up my place of business for days, and no one will help me get rid of it, since it is so heavy. But you two strong fellows should make light work of such a job. Just carry it down the street and tip it off the bridge into the river."

This the two porters gladly did. The unfortunate beggar kept quiet all the while as the jeweler had instructed him, and indeed, was never heard much of again.

No doubt the jeweler had intended to make his fortune with the collar of silver, selling it to some rich lord or lady, perhaps even to the king of the city. But as he lovingly examined it, the thought of parting with the collar at all became horrible to him. Presently he found an ivory box lined with velvet, laid the collar inside, shut the box and locked it. Next he went stealthily up to the top of the house and put the ivory box inside a box of cedarwood, and this cedarwood box inside a larger box of iron, and finally all three boxes into a great old chest, very like the one in which he had imprisoned the ill-starred beggar. Last of all he lugged the chest into a tiny room where the odds and ends of the household were kept, hurried out and locked the door. Then he took the key of the door and hid it up the chimney. Such was his condition since acquiring the collar of Vayi.

As he sat mopping his brow after his exertion, the jeweler's wife came in and stared at him.

"Why, husband, how hot you are. Do you know, I just saw two men tipping a chest, remarkably like our own below in the shop, into the river, and when I stopped and asked what they were at, they laughed and said some old idiot had given them a gold coin apiece to do it.''

"Be silent!'' roared the jeweler, starting up. "Say no more about it or I will turn you out of doors.''

The jeweler's wife was greatly puzzled, for her husband had always been a very moderate man until now. Accordingly, she began to keep a careful watch on him. Imagine her surprise and alarm therefore, when, in the dead of night, the man, quite obsessed with his treasure and thinking her sound asleep—which she had pretended to be—stole out of bed and went creeping about. She was quick to follow, however, so she saw exactly how he behaved, first taking a key from the chimney, then using it on the room above, going in the room and securely locking the door again from the inside. Not amazingly, the jeweler's wife kneeled down and applied her eye to the keyhole; but she could see very little, only a great many boxes being opened, and her husband crouching over something and crooning, and when a mouse ran across the floor, he hissed at it frenziedly: "Ssh! Ssh!''

The jeweler's wife got up and went quietly back to bed, but her husband did not return for three or four hours.

Whatever can he have up there? wondered his wife, remembering certain street criers' tales of invisible sprites and certain titillating arts they would practice in return for human blood or souls.

The next night it was the same, and the next, and the lady became quite beside herself with anxiety and interest.

"Well, well,'' said she to her husband on the fourth day, "I think I will turn out that room at the top of the house.''

"No!'' shouted the jeweler, "I forbid you to go near the room. Dare lay one finger on it and I will have you whipped through the streets.''

"Please yourself,'' said the wife. But she determined to see whatever it was that made the man so foolish.

That very day, as it happened, the jeweler had to go out on business.

"Shut the door, and let no one in till I get back,'' he said, "and mind you stay down here and do your work and refrain from snooping."

"Of course, O best of husbands," murmured the jeweler's wife. But as soon as he was off, so was she; first to the chimney, then up the stairs, into the room, into the chest, into the boxes, and—

"Ah!" cried the jeweler's wife.

Before long the jeweler's wife fell to thinking as she held the collar in her hands: *A man or a woman could equally well wear this necklet, and it will therefore look very nice on me. But if my husband returns and finds what I have done, he will never let me wear it; he will whip me or worse.* So, and it seemed quite natural to her, she ran down to the river wharves where there was a little dark hovel, and here she purchased a certain medicine and ran back home again with it.

When the jeweler came in at the door, there was his loving wife waiting for him with a brimming goblet.

"How I have missed you!" she cried. "And see, I have mixed you a cup of spiced wine."

The jeweler drank and promptly fell dead, for his lady had added the medicine to the liquor.

What lamentation there was then, and the neighbors ran to comfort the poor widow, never suspecting anything. But no sooner was the jeweler in the ground than his wife sold up his shop and all his wares, and moved to a fine house where she kept peacocks to walk on the lawns, wore black velvet, and the magical collar always glittering on her breast.

The king of the city also had a few wives, and one of these was his queen. She wore a veil of golden threads sewn with emeralds, and each day she would ride through the city in her chariot drawn by leopards. Her slaves would walk behind, beside and before the chariot, crying: "Bow down to the king's first wife, queen of the city," and everyone would bow down at once, or if they did not, the slaves would seize them and cut off their hands or their feet, whichever most took the queen's fancy that day.

One afternoon as the queen went riding, she saw something shining up on a balcony.

"Go, fourth slave on my right," said she, "and fetch me whatever it is that glitters there."

The selected slave hurried away, and quickly returned dragging a terrified woman, who was no other than the jeweler's wife with the silver collar round her neck.

"O Imperial Mistress, this jewelry is what your beauteousness saw gleaming, but the woman refuses to give it up, and see, she has bitten and scratched me when I tried to take it."

"Strike off her head then," said the queen, "for I will not abide meanness in my husband's city."

This was at once done, the collar washed free of blood in scented water (which was always carried for just this purpose, the hands and feet the queen ordered subtracted frequently having ornaments on them), dried on a silken cloth, and handed up to her. With sparkling eyes, the queen placed the collar round her own throat.

Soon the sun sank, and the queen came into the banquet that every night the king her husband gave in his hall. All there marveled at the collar, and many gazed at it with hungry eyes, forgetting the food on their plates. The king himself reached out to toy with the seven jewels.

"What a necklet, my dove. Where did you come by it? It looks very fair on your whiteness, but think how magnificent it would seem about the neck of a man, for surely it is too heavy for your delicate throat and you mean to give it to me?"

"Not at all," said the queen.

"But you will loan it me?" wheedled the king. "Loan it me, and I will give you a certain turquoise I have, larger than the palm of my hand."

"Nonsense," said the queen. "I have seen the turquoise in question, and it is no bigger than your thumb."

"Well then, I will give you five sapphires bluer than sadness. Or a casket of rare wood filled with pearls, each from a different shore."

"No," said she, "I am content with what I have."

So the king chafed in his skin, and grew very angry, but he did not show it. When the feast was done, he went out secretly into the night and up to a high place in the palace gardens. Here, by starlight, he turned east, north, south and west and uttered certain incantations which he had learned from a magician in his youth. At first all was still, but presently there came a noise like a winter wind beating over the sky, the crests of the garden trees combed the moon, and a wide shadow was cast like a net across the ground. The king trembled but stood firm. A fearsome dark bird had settled on the turf, greater than three eagles, with a cruel curved beak, talons like hooks of bronze, and ruby eyes as hot as fire.

"Speak," said this terrible Bird, "for you have brought me, with your little spell, from a feast high in the crags of my home."

The king shuddered, but he said: "My first wife has a necklet she will not give me, though I am her husband and have a right to it. Seize her and fly up with her into the sky. When she screams for clemency, make her render you the necklet, and then bring it here to me."

"And she?" said the Bird.

"I care nothing for her," said the king, "and care nothing for what you do, so long as I have that necklet, and am clear of blame."

"Then, because you have called me by the spell, I must act as you say."

It was not a demon, the Bird, but an earth thing, one of the monstrous creations left over like fragments from the first garment of time. It really belonged nowhere, neither on the world nor under it, a bit of chaos that had taken on a shape and roamed at large, sulky and evil, for men to call, if they dared, but mostly for men to dislike and avoid.

It spread its huge wings like vast fans of palm leaves, and soared up to the saffron window where the queen sat before her glass, caressing the collar.

"Beloved," the Bird called softly, "beloved, beloved, second moon of the night, come out and show your beauty to the shadows."

And the queen came to the window, wondering and haughty, and the Bird grasped her suddenly in its awful talons, and bore her shrieking into the vault of the night.

The Bird flew high and far. Near to the gardens of the stars it flew and brushed their silver roots with the breath of its wings. Below, the land lay like a smoky map, here and there on fire with the lamps of cities, while at its edge crept the violet deserts of the sea.

The queen wailed for terror.

"Give me your necklet, and I will let you go," said the Bird to her.

All else was lost in fright. The queen tore off the prize she had bought with blood, the Bird snatched it in its beak. And then, true to its word, let her go indeed, and down she fell towards the world. Some say she perished so, some say a wandering elemental of the Upperearth took pity on her cries and turned her into a bird herself, a little spiteful falcon, which forever after fluttered about the sky screeching.

The great Bird, glad to be rid of her, shook the collar in its beak.

It did not mean to give it to the king of the city after all, but to keep the ornament for itself. But as it beat homeward for its crags, a storm was born with the sun over the mountains, and came running across the heaven, clashing together its cymbals. A lightning struck the Bird, only a glancing blow, but it cried out and the collar of Vayi dropped from its mouth and was lost. Three times the Bird wheeled, searching for its spoils and then, finding nothing, flew on furiously into the west after the trailing rags of night.

The collar plunged like a meteor. Misty hills, tinged by the sun, opened and fell away, a river flashed, a forest lay like a green-furred beast. There was a valley, walled in by tall towers of rock, carpeted with flowers at its bottom. Here, by a narrow waterfall, a small white temple stood in a grove of trees.

The seven jewels rang together as the collar fell, like bells. It caught suddenly among branches, and its descent was checked.

Who knows what god was worshipped in that place? Three priestesses tended his shrine and lit for him a flame on his altar. They had no other company than each other and one little snake, which was said to be the god's oracle. At festivals the people of the valley and the surrounding hills would come to the temple, and the priestesses would take up the little snake—which was dear to them and which, at all other times, they treated quite as a pet—and place it in a marble tray of sand. Then they would put to it certain questions concerning harvest, birth, death and fortune, and when the snake wriggled, they would read the marks left in the sand, and this would be the interpretation of the oracle, the god's answer. Also they would milk the little snake of its venom which they used to make a special incense. They did this quite safely for, although poisonous, it never bit them since it liked them too well. They fed it honey cakes and cream.

Every morning one of the three priestesses would go to the narrow waterfall with a ewer, and today the youngest set out. All the birds in the valley were singing and so was the youngest priestess. Yet, as she drew near the water, she saw something sparkling in the grove of trees.

"A star must have fallen from the sky in the night," said she, but when she went closer, she saw well enough what it was. The ewer dropped out of her hands, which she clasped before her, and her eyes burned very bright. All she wanted in the world was to take the collar and put it round her neck and let the jewels shine on her breast, but she could not reach the bough where the prize was hanging. While she stood there like this, the second priestess came looking for her.

"Why, sister, what are you gazing at?"

"At nothing. There is nothing here!" cried the youngest. Of course, the second priestess looked up at once and saw at once. "It's mine!" cried the youngest. "I found it first. You shall not have it."

"Not so," said the second. "I am older than you and I *will* have it." And, snatching up the ewer from the ground, she struck the youngest such a blow with it that she fell down dead.

Just then the oldest priestess, hearing these violent noises, rushed out to the grove.

"Here comes another of the pests," muttered the second priestess, and taking up the ewer again, she hid behind a tree, and it was not long before the oldest priestess suffered the same fate as the first. Then, regardless of her grim work spread around her on the flowery grass, the second priestess seated herself before the tree and gazed up at the collar.

"Soon," she murmured, "I shall think of a way to bring you down and wear you about my throat, but until then I am content merely to watch over you."

The sun rose high, and still she sat beneath the tree. The rocky towers turned gold then crimson as the day beat on its wings toward the west. Then all the blush was gone from the land and the sky, and green twilight filled the valley. And still the last priestess sat beneath the tree, seeing nothing but the collar among the branches.

Presently, the little snake came winding from the temple, lonely and hungry and out of sorts, for no one had petted it or fed it. When it saw the last priestess in the grove, it moved to her gladly and coiled about her ankle. But she took no notice. At this, the snake looked up and saw what was in the tree.

It was as if a spark kindled in its brain. Such was the collar of Vayi that all earth things, human or otherwise, coveted it. As if it bled from a mortal wound, every drop of the snake's gentleness drained away. *Mine*, it thought, as had thought all the others, and it nipped the priestess in her heel with its venomed fangs, so that soon she also lay unbreathing on the ground.

The snake felt one moment of awful desolation and loss, then a sensation of anger and power. Its desperate loneliness was changed to boiling pride. It stretched itself to encircle the broad trunk of the tree, and it began to grow. It bloated with hatred and arrogance, it swelled and lengthened. Three times three its sinuous body wound round the trunk, and it rested its flat cruel head on the bough where the collar hung.

Night came and blackened the face of the world, and the snake blackened also to the color of its furious spite, and its eyes turned to silver slits from gazing at seven bright jewels.

Years passed, mortal years. The roof of the temple fell in, the pillars crumbled; it was a ruin. The waterfall dried up at its source and the flowers died, the trees withered and died too. Only the great tree, the tree with the collar in its branches, continued to live and to grow, though, like the snake, it had become dark and unlovely. The snake lived too. While its anger and jealous pride persisted, it could not die. It never slept, roped about the tree, and when men approached with torches, songs or knives, it spat from its clashing mouth a poison rich with its hate, that destroyed everything it touched. The grass was shriveled and full of new flowers, white flowers: bones.

There was a blight on the valley. People abandoned it, it was deserted. The legend grew of a treasure in a tree and a serpent which enviously guarded it. Then the heroes came.

Some came with armies, some alone; some came on horses, in armour, protected by spells, with swords of blue metal; some on foot with native cunning and wild hearts. All perished. Their bone flowers were added to the others which lay in the rank grass, and their names passed away into myth, or were forgotten. After five centuries, or ten, the heroes ceased to come.

And after the time of heroes, there was a time of emptiness.

The snake lay stretched all its black length along and about the tree, its jaws dripping ready venom, thinking merely: "The treasure is mine, only mine. You shall not have it."

But behind its thought, an ache began, an ache in its serpent soul. An ache for what? It did not know, as it lay wide-eyed through the centuries. Sometimes, when the dry wind stirred the grass, it would dart up and spit death at the wind, hungry for another hero. But then it grew weary, and only lay with its flat head on the bough, dazzled and unseeing, thinking: "Mine, only mine. No one shall take my treasure from me."

Though it had forgotten by then what its treasure was.

One day, when the sky was like a dome of sapphire glass over the barren valley, the snake heard a human footfall some way off, in the porch of the ruined temple. It raised itself, and its eyes cleared a little. It saw a shadow—it saw only in shadows now—a shadow like a man. The snake hissed, and poison sizzled on the ground beneath the tree.

The shadow stopped where it was, not as if timorous, rather as if listening.

The snake had learned the speech of man centuries before, for hatred and jealousy must find a tongue; only the creatures which never feel those things have no need to talk. Therefore the snake spoke.

"Come closer, man born of woman, that I, the serpent of the valley, may kill you."

But, instead of running away, or drawing nearer—as the adventurers with their swords had foolishly done—the shadowy figure seated itself on one of the broken columns of the temple.

"Why should you wish to kill me?" asked the man, and his voice was strange and new in the valley, not brazen and shouting, or wheedling or pleading like the voices of the heroes, neither harsh like the wind nor monotonous like the rain, but musical and very pleasing. It was a voice which seemed to have a color like that of a topaz.

The snake held very still at the voice, for it seemed to make the ache in its soul far worse, yet at the same time, oddly, soothed it.

"I kill all those who trespass here," the snake said, nevertheless, "for all who come, come to steal my treasure."

"What treasure is that?"

"Look up into the boughs of the tree," the snake declared with bitter pleasure, "and you will see it."

At this the voice laughed, very gently, almost kindly, and the laugh was like water to the parched earth.

"Alas, I cannot see your treasure, for I am blind."

The words cut through the snake, sharp as any hero's sword. That a man who spoke in such a voice should be blind somehow hurt the snake, perhaps since it too had grown almost sightless.

"Were you born without eyes?" it asked.

"No, I have eyes, though they see nothing. But I come from a land with one ancient custom."

"Tell me," rustled the snake on the bough, because, for the first time in long, long years, pity had touched it, and interest.

"The land which birthed me," said the stranger, "lives in great terror of its gods. The people there believe that if an infant is born with unusual beauty, the gods will conceive an anger for it, and strike it down. Therefore, each child, either male or female, is examined by the priests on its third birthday, and if any are judged likely to incur the gods' punishment, they are made to look on white hot fire until the sight is burned from their eyes. In this fashion the gods' jealousy is averted. And for this reason, in my land, all who are fair are blind."

"Are you then fair?" the serpent asked.

"It seems they found me so," replied the stranger, yet there was no rancor or sorrow in his tone.

"Come near," whispered the snake, "and let me look at you, for I too am almost blind from staring at a silver fire. I will not harm you, never fear me. You have been harmed enough."

The stranger rose. "Poor serpent," he said, and came close, quite unafraid, and feeling his way with his hands and with a slim staff he leaned on. Soon, gaining the tree, he reached up, not for the collar of silver, but to caress the body of the snake. The snake let down its head and gazed at him. The stranger was a young man, handsome indeed as a god might have been. His hair was pale as barley under white spring sun. His eyes showed no mark of their blinding; they were as green and as clear as the finest jade. His body was slender and strong.

The snake, feeling a great weariness, rested its long head on the shoulder of the blind man.

"Tell me who took your sight, tell me your name and theirs, that I may wish evil on them for your sake."

But the stranger stroked the head of the snake, and said:

"My name is Kazir, as for the others, they are troubled enough. They took my eyes, but my other senses have grown sharp. When I touch a thing, I know it. Walking through this valley, I have learned all its history, merely from the brush of long grass on my wrist or a warm stone picked up from the track. And touching you, I grasp your sadness and your burden far better then if I had seen you and been afraid."

"Ah, you understand me," sighed the serpent, its face against his neck. "Once I was happy and innocent. Once I was loved and loving. I have yearned so long and never known my hope. Oh, give me peace, blind Kazir, give me rest."

"Rest then," said the young man, and he sang to the serpent a quiet golden song. It had to do with ships made of cloud, and the drowsy country where sleep rose like a mist to comfort the grief of the world. Hearing it, the serpent slept, the first sweet sleep of centuries, and in its sleep its envy and its fury died, and presently it also died, as softly and as gratefully as it had slept.

Kazir felt the life of the serpent leave it, and, since he could do no more, he kissed its cold head and turned away. Suddenly a branch snapped sharply behind him, and there came the sound of bells falling through the air. Kazir put out his hand before he reasoned and into it splashed the collar of Vayi.

He held it only for a moment.

This thing is cursed, he thought, *demon work. It has done much ill and will do more unless I hide it in the ground.* Then, his fingers going over it, he touched the seven magic jewels.

Others, seeing them, had hungered for them. But Kazir saw only through his finger-ends, and this with his own curious power. For an instant he held his breath, and then he said:

"Seven tears shed in despair beneath the earth, seven tears shed by a flower who is a woman."

In that second he knew everything—not only the bloody story of the collar, but what had gone before, the little Drin hammering in his forge, Bakvi the worm in Azhrarn's garden. But more than all this, he knew Ferazhin Flower-Born who wept beside the lake in Underearth, for Sivesh and for the sun.

6   Kazir and Ferazhin

For many months Kazir wandered over the earth, Kazir the blind poet, Kazir the singer of gold. He was searching for a way to the Underearth, a way to Ferazhin. A spell had been laid on him, not of avarice but of compassion, and of love. But who could tell him what he must know? The name of Azhrarn was only filtered in shadows and in whispers; besides, he had so many names: Lord of Darkness, Master of Night, Bringer of Anguish, Eagle-Winged, the Beautiful, the Unspeakable. The entrance to his kingdom was the core of a mountain at the earth's center, but who could find the place, what map showed it? And who would dare to go, dare to guide a blind man to such a spot where funnels of rock erupted flame and the sky was all vermilion smoke?

Kazir did not despair, though his heart was heavy. He earned his bread by making songs, and sometimes his songs would heal the sick or cure the mad, for such was his magic. Although he was blind, almost any house was glad to shelter him, and, although he was blind, almost any woman who saw him would have been glad to spend her days at his side. But Kazir passed by as a season passes, seeking only the way to Ferazhin.

He carried the collar hidden in his shirt, understanding the evil it would bring to men, but when he was alone, he would reach in and touch the seven jewels, and into his mind would steal the presence of Ferazhin. He did not see her, not even with an inner eye, for he had been blinded too young to remember much of images, colors or visual forms. Rather he knew her as others might know a rose by smelling its perfume in a darkened garden, or a fountain by feeling its refreshment play over their hands.

One twilight, high on an open tableland, he came upon a stone house. An old woman lived there who had once practiced the arts of sorcery, and although she had wisely put away her books at last, a scent of spells still clung around the spot.

Kazir knocked. The old woman came out. She had kept one sorcerous ring: when the wicked stood near her the ring burned, when the good were close at hand the stone turned green. Now it shone like an emerald, and the old woman bade her visitor enter. She saw that he was beautiful, and blind, and she was clever from her years of witching. She set food before her guest, and presently she said:

"You are Kazir, the foolish one who seeks the way to Underearth. I have heard you slew a terrible serpent in a desert valley, and came away with a fabled treasure."

"Wise lady," said Kazir, "the serpent died of age and sorrow. The treasure is steeped in the blood of men and worth nothing. I came away only with an agony in my heart for another, a damsel weeping in the Underearth for light and love."

"A fair damsel," said the witch woman, "a damsel made from a flower. Perhaps I know a way to her. Are you brave enough to take it, blind Kazir? Brave enough to search without eyes along the margins of death?"

"Only tell me," said Kazir, "and I will go. I cannot rest till she has rest, that fair one underground."

"My price is seven songs," said the witch. "A song for each of Ferazhin's tears."

"I will pay you gladly," said Kazir.

So Kazir sang, and the witch listened. His music loosened the stiffness in her joints, undid the knots in her hands, and a little of her youth stole back to her like a bird flying in at the window. When the songs were done she said:

"In the Underearth, at the borders of Azhrarn's kingdom, winds a river with waters heavy as iron and the color of iron, and white flax grows on the banks. The river of sleep that river is, and on the shores of it sometimes stray the souls of slumbering men. There the demon princes hunt those souls with hounds. If you dare it, I can mix you a drink that will send you fast down into the pit of sleep and wash up your soul on those shores. It is a place of snares, but if you can escape its dangers and the running hounds of the Vazdru, and cross the plains, you will reach the City of the Demons and confront, if you will, Azhrarn. Then ask him for your girl created from a flower. If Azhrarn grants your request—and he may, for who can guess his mood on that day—he himself will speed you and her safely back to the world of men. But if he is merciless and cruel at the hour when you find him, then you are lost, and the gods know what torment or what pain he will send you to.''

Kazir only reached for the witch's hand, and holding it in a steady grip he said:

''The child may fear to be born and the mother to give birth, yet neither can choose otherwise when the time is come. Neither have I a choice. This is my only path. Therefore, mix your drink, kind sorceress, and let me go down my road tonight.''

Kazir passed through the house of sleep as all pass there, unknowing, and woke by the shores of the great river.

Sometimes, sleeping, the blind might see, if they had seen much in life before their blindness, and who could doubt all souls can see when once forever free of the body. But the body of Kazir still lived and had seen little before his sight was taken. Therefore his soul also, stirring on that cold bleak shore, was blind as was his earthly shape. In fact, the soul resembled exactly the flesh of Kazir, had his clear eyes, wore his garments even, and held in its hand the ghost of his blind-man's staff.

So he stood on the banks of Sleep River where the white flax grew, and he smelled the icy smell of the water and heard the iron sound of it, and away from him stretched the black lands with their trees of ivory and gilded wire, though he did not see them.

Then Kazir kneeled up and placed his hand on a pebble lying on the bank.

"Which way lies the City of the Demons?" asked Kazir. And he felt the pebble warm very slightly on one side, and so he rose and went on in that direction, striking away from the river, and feeling before him with his staff.

He walked for a long stretch, yet sometimes he would reach out and touch the metallic bark of a tree, and know from that which path he must take and how far the City was. There was no sound all this while save the wind of Underearth. But suddenly he felt a presence, swirling like smoke, and a voice murmured:

"Mortal, you have come far in your dream. I am Forgetfulness, the slave of sleep. Do you seek me? Let me wind my arms about you and drink all your memories from your brain's cup, so that when you wake men will ask your name and you will not recall. Think what peace I offer you—no past crimes or shames to cloud your mind, free as the air of earth, casting off your old life like a garment."

But there were no crimes or shames in Kazir's past which he needed to forget.

"No, I do not seek you," Kazir said, "I seek Azhrarn, the Prince."

"Go then," said the smoky thing. "If you are to be his, you must not be mine."

So Kazir went on, but later there came another presence, sweeter and more persuasive than the first:

"Mortal, you have come farther than far in your dream. I am Fantasy, the child of sleep. Do you seek me? Let me wind my hair about you, and fill your brain cup with dancers and palaces, so that you beg me not to let you wake but walk forever in my many-colored balls. Think what delight I offer you, a second world more lovely than the first."

But Kazir understood fantasy, for he wove his songs from the stuff of it.

"No, I do not seek you," he said, "though I know you well. I seek Azhrarn, the Prince."

"Go then," said the sweetness. "If you are to be his, then you are mine already."

After this, Kazir found a road. Of marble it was, and lined with pillars, and the touch of it told him that it led to the gates of Druhim Vanashta, City of Demons.

But he had not been long on the marble road before he heard behind him a noise so horrible, so fearful, so like the baying of wolves—yet worse, much worse—that he knew the hounds of the Vazdru had picked up his scent.

Instead of fleeing on or seeking cover, Kazir stopped and faced about. He heard the snarling and baying draw nearer, the hoof-beats of the demon horses, the bells of their harness, the calling of the Vazdru. Then Kazir, lifting his own voice gently above the din, began to sing. And the soul of Kazir sang with all the beauty of his mortal voice, and maybe more. He sang, but what he sang of is lost. Whatever it was, the hounds ceased running and lay down upon the road, the horses dropped their heads, even the princes sat attentively, their pale handsome faces resting on their ringed hands, listening.

When the song was done a silence came, and into the silence another voice, a voice as marvelous as the voice of Kazir, but a voice that was like snow falling over the poet's singing flame, and in color not golden, but black as night.

"Dreamer," said the voice, "you are far out of your way."

At this voice, Kazir lifted his blind gaze, and his sightless eyes rested on the being who spoke, uselessly, yet with a sort of courtesy.

"No longer," said Kazir, "since I traveled here hoping to meet with you, Lord Azhrarn, Prince of Demons."

"What, are you blind?" asked Azhrarn. "Blind soul, you have been foolish, daring this place which even men with two wide eyes tremble at. What can you want from me?"

"To give you back, Lord of Darkness, something which your people made," said Kazir. And he took out the silver work of Vayi which he had carried with him to the Underearth, since the collar, being made of shadowy items and in shadowy lands, could return through the river of sleep as a mortal thing—flesh or metal—could not. Kazir extended the collar, then he let it fall on the road before the Vazdru. "Oh,

Prince," said Kazir, "take back this, your toy, for it has drunk enough blood that even you must be content."

"Be wary," said Azhrarn, soft as velvet, soft as a cat's paw with all the claws ready in it, "be wary, singer of songs, what you say to me."

"Lord Prince," said Kazir, "if you wished, you might read me like a book. Knowing I cannot hide my thoughts from you, I speak plainly. The virtues of demon-kind are different from the virtues of men. I only tell the truth of the matter: the collar has made much trouble and butchery in the world, which is only as you would wish. Therefore rejoice, illimitable prince, though I, being mortal, must grieve."

At this, Azhrarn smiled, and, though Kazir did not see it, he sensed the smile.

"You are brave, blind soul, and truthful, as you say. Do you also dare to enter my slender-towered city and sing there for me?"

"Gladly will I sing for you. But I shall ask a fee," said Kazir.

Azhrarn laughed. Was ever such a laughter heard by a man's soul in sleep?

"Bold, blind hero," said the Prince, "your fee may be too high. Ask it now, and I shall see."

"A woman weeps in your city. Her tears are in this collar of blood. She is a flower and craves the sun. My fee is her freedom to roam in the lands of men."

Azhrarn did not answer for a long while. Only the harness of the demon horses sounded. The blind poet stood still, leaning on his staff.

"I will make a bargain with you," said Azhrarn then, suddenly. "Come to my halls, and I will ask you one question, and you shall sing me your answer in one song, and if the song is true and the answer the right one, you shall have Ferazhin, and Ferazhin shall have the sun. But if you fail, I will chain your soul in the blackest deep of the Underearth and there my hounds shall tear you until your body is dust on the earth above, and longer than that. Now, either accept my bargain, or go. And I will let you go without pursuit, for you have entertained me."

"There is no road back for me alone, Dark Lord," Kazir returned. "Lead me into your city and ask me your question, and I will sing my answer as best I can."

So Kazir entered Druhim Vanashta, where mortals did not generally come.

Everywhere strange music played and strange incenses perfumed the air. They led him, the Vazdru, till he stood in the wide hall of Azhrarn.

Azhrarn was very courteous. He had laid before his visitor delicious foods and mysterious wines, and he pointed out to him how this goblet was made of malachite with rubies, how this plate was finest glass, how many candles in silver sconces burned around him, and the color of every drape and the subject of all the mosaics on the floor. He spoke too of the princely Vazdru, the worshipping Eshva, the handsome demon men, how they were beautiful and how they were subtle; he described the princesses and the hand maidens, the lovely shapes of their breasts, the fragrance of their hair and limbs.

Then he conducted Kazir through his palace, and, standing on high places, instructed him what towers glittered north or south, and what parks unrolled their carpets east and west. He told him, too, the numberless subjects of his city, the countless horses in his yards, the impossible extent of his power and his mage-craft and his knowledge. This took a great while, and when he was finished, Azhrarn said gently:

"All this I have, poet's soul. And more of the same I might have, if I wished it. Now I will ask my question and you shall answer with your song."

"I am ready," said Kazir, and he heard the rustling all about of the Vazdru and the Eshva as they waited.

"Do you suppose," said Azhrarn, "there is anything, which, having all this about me, still I cannot do without?"

The Vazdru applauded, the Eshva sighed. They saw no possible answer to the Prince's question. But Kazir bowed his head a moment, and then, lifting it, began to sing his answer as Azhrarn had said he must.

This was the substance of Kazir's reply: For all Azhrarn's supernatural riches, for all his eternal kingdom under the earth, one thing he needed. That thing was human-kind. "We are your plaything, your amusement,'' Kazir told him. "Always you return to us, to throw down our glories, to laugh your dark laughter when you have tricked us. Without man on the earth, the time of demons and the time of the Demon Lord would hang heavy indeed.''

When they heard this, the Vazdru cried out scornfully though Azhrarn kept silent. But Kazir's song was not ended.

He sang a cold dream to the demons.

He sang of how a plague came from the edges of the world and erased from it all mortal life. Not a man or a woman remained, not a child, not a baby. No crones creaked over their potions, no princes rode on heroic quests, no armies made war, no fair maidens looked out from their towers, and no infants cried in their cradles. Only the desolate wind moaned over the earth, only the grasses stirred. The sun rose and set on emptiness. And he sang of how the Prince of Demons flew by in the form of a night eagle, over the noiseless cities and the deserted lands. Not a light burned in a single window, not a single sail moved on the seas. And the Prince looked for men. But not one high heart was left to corrupt, not one rapacious jeweler to make mischief with. And on all the wide earth, not one tongue remained to whisper in reverence and terror the name of Azhrarn.

The demons had fallen very still. As the last of the poet's words shifted down among them, they seemed frozen in ice.

Kazir stood in the hall of the Prince through that long quiet. Then Azhrarn said: "I am answered.'' No more, no less, and maybe only the poet, with his sensitive ear, heard in that acknowledgment how the voice of Azhrarn was chilled and changed—as if with pain, or even fear.

But the bargin had been made, and shortly out from the palace sped one of the Eshva, and found Ferazhin walking in some shadowy garden.

She entered Azhrarn's hall meekly, dolefully, in her cloudy veil, her face hidden.

Azhrarn beckoned her near, and said:

"A mortal has bought your freedom with a tomb-cold song. His soul must go back through sleep river, but some bird of night shall carry you to the soil of earth from which you came.''

Ferazhin looked up.

"And shall I see the sun?'' she asked.

"Till you are sick of it,'' answered Azhrarn. "And he also, your rescuer, you shall see, for you are to be his.''

But although he spoke low, Kazir heard him, and he called out:

"No, Lord Prince. She has been too long the property of others. I do not claim her. I bargained with you only to set her free.''

"Yet you love her,'' said Azhrarn, "or else you would not have come.''

"Since I encountered her tears set in the collar of silver, I have loved Ferazhin,'' said Kazir calmly, "and now, sensing her near me, I love her more deeply. But she knows nothing of me.''

However, Ferazhin had turned to look at him, for his voice had the color of the sun. She gazed at his face, his form, his hair, his eyes, and going up to him, she saw that he was blind. He had risked flesh and spirit for her, and asked nothing in return. She loved him at once; how could she not?

"I will come to you gladly,'' she said, "and love you for as long as you will wish it.'' Then she went back to Azhrarn, and she said softly:

"You grew me from a flower, and I was immortal while I lived in your dark kingdom. When Kazir grows old. as all men do, let me also grow old beside him, for I do not want to be other than he is, and when he dies as all men do, let me also die, for I do not want to be parted from him.''

"When you leave my land and go to walk the earth, you will be subject to earth's laws,'' said Azhrarn. "You will grow old and you will die, and I wish you joy in so doing.''

"And after death, shall I be with Kazir?'' asked Ferazhin.

"Ask the gods,'' said Azhrarn. "All things of earth have souls, even the flowers that grow there, but you may lose each other in the mists of the threshold of death.''

"Then let me die in the moment that Kazir dies, so we may go hand in hand.''

Azhrarn's coals of eyes grew blackly bright, but Ferazhin, her own eyes dazzled by her dreams, did not see it.

"Then let that be my gift to you," said Azhrarn. "In the instant you know Kazir is dead, you shall die also."

Ferazhin thanked him. The hall filled with a beating of wings. One starry bird carried Ferazhin away, up through the bewitched gates, out of the mountain, to the hills and valleys of the world, while another bore Kazir back to the river of sleep through which he must return in order to regain his body.

Azhrarn meanwhile stood on a high tower, the collar of Vayi in his fingers. The Prince of Demons looked to north and east, to west and south, turning over in his mind the treasures of his realm, but the voice of Kazir came to haunt him even there, singing of the empty earth and its desolation, singing of how the Prince of Princes, without humankind, would be only a nameless mole beneath the ground. And presently Azhrarn crushed the collar in his hands to a shapeless molten thing, and hurled it down into the streets of Druhim Vanashta like a curse.

Kazir woke in the witch's house near dawn.

"You have slept many days and many nights," said she, "though, no doubt it seemed but an hour or so you were in the Underearth."

All this while she had kept him safe and preserved his body in its sleep by means of her spells. Now, as he rose and shook off that prolonged slumber, the woman stood watching at the open door.

Up sailed the sun, the sky ignited like a lamp, and along the plateau a slender figure came walking with blowing hair the color of that sky.

"I see a girl with wheat-yellow hair," said the witch, "and a flower face."

Kazir went out at once and waited before the house, and Ferazhin came running toward him with her arms outstretched, laughing with happiness.

For a year then, Kazir and Ferazhin were together, and their days make no story, for they were good and joyful and without event. They had no wealth, it is true, and wandered together from land to land as the poet had always done, earning their food, he by his singing, she by dancing, for she found she could dance, like a flower in a field in the gentle summer wind. They had no palace of crystal and gold, yet their hall was wide enough, with its blue roof, its floors of grass embroidered with asphodel and its great pillars of trees. Both loved the world, each loved the other. She would tell him all she saw, he would tell her all the history of things which he could divine by touch, in a stone or a ruined wall. They coupled thirstily, as do the young to whom love is an uncharted river. They knew the perfection of content.

Then, one dusk at the year's end, a boy met them on the road.

He was very young, this boy, and handsome, with large dark piercing eyes. He came up slowly, as if uncertain. Then he said:

"Can it be that you are Kazir, the blind poet, whose voice cures sickness?"

"I am Kazir," Kazir answered. "For the rest, it is not my boast."

But the boy kneeled down on the roadway, and caught at the hem of Ferazhin's dress.

"Lady, I beg you to help me. My father is lying ill in our house and will let no one come near him—only Kazir he calls for night and day. He says there was a prophecy in his childhood that he should fall ill and die unless blind Kazir should make him well with a song. Therefore, persuade the poet to come to him and save him."

Kazir frowned. The boy's words troubled him. But he said: "I will come with you if you wish."

The boy leaped up and darted on ahead, leading them. Presently the road ran by a fine house with open gates of iron. In the outer court a fountain played, and by the fountain sat a slim black dog.

"Now, if you will, you must come in alone," the boy said to Kazir, "and the lady must wait in the court. My father will let no one in the house but myself, and even I am not permitted to enter the room where he lies."

"Very well," said Kazir, though somehow he liked this notion very little. Ferazhin, however, sat by the fountain serenely, and stretched out her hand to pet the black dog, but it was apparently shy, and ran into the house with the boy.

Inside, there were many steps, and a door.

"Father," the boy called out, "I have found Kazir." When no one answered, the boy muttered: "He is very weak. Go in and sing to him, and make him whole if you can, and we will bless you forever."

So Kazir stepped into the room. Yet he did not sing. It seemed to him that the place was empty, he sensed no invalid lying near, and suddenly the air was full of a dark strange incense. It reminded him of other scents that he had known only once before—when his soul walked through the streets of Druhim Vanashta.

At once Kazir turned about to leave the room, but something ran against his legs—it had the form of a dog but, touching it, Kazir knew it for what it was—demon flesh. Next moment a ringing nothingness came rushing into Kazir's brain as the shadowy drug filled his lungs. In vain he tried to beat it off, to reach the door, to cry to Ferazhin and warn her. Eagles of night smothered him. He sank down and lay as if he were dead.

Ferazhin started up in the court. There had been no sound to alarm her, yet abruptly she was afraid. Just then, out of the house came the young boy, the dog at his heels.

"Ferazhin," said the youth, "Kazir is dead."

And the black dog barked.

Immediately she knew them—one of the Vazdru in the form of a boy, while the inky dog—she stared into its coals of eyes and glimpsed Azhrarn. And the house was wavering all about her, like smoke. Now everything was gone, house, court, fountain and the two figures with it. She stood on a hill slope by a little stream, cold under the stars, and before her lay Kazir.

She ran to him. She did not stop to reason. She took up his icy hands, brushed with her fingers his closed lids. She felt no heartbeat, heard no breathing. "Now I know you are dead," Ferazhin whispered, and as Azhrarn had promised her, she felt her own hands grow stony, her own heart stop and her breath; her lids fell shut and she too lay dead beside Kazir.

But Kazir was not dead. He still lived, as the Demon Lord intended. Gradually the drug of Underearth left him, he stirred and woke. Then he felt the open hillside, the starlight. Remembering what had gone before, he called Ferazhin's name. She did not answer him. The blind man sat up and stretched out his hand, and so he found her. He held her in his arms and discovered at once how all the life was gone out of her.

He had known perfect happiness for a year, now he knew perfect sorrow. He understood the trick, no doubt; perhaps he thought again of the river of sleep and a journey to Azhrarn's palace, but then he rejected it, for Azhrarn would demonstrate no leniency now, since this was his revenge on them. Kazir imagined the soul of Ferazhin, her flower soul, lost on the foggy threshold of death, wandering alone, searching and calling out in vain for his. Full of pain as he was, he shuddered at what her pain and fear and loss must be.

There was a village over the hill, and presently men came along the slope, going home that way. When they saw the fair blind stranger holding the fair dead girl in his arms, they were touched with pity and distress. Before the moon rose, they had dug, by the little stream, a grave for Ferazhin and laid her gently in it and covered her up, and over her body their priest had spoken such words of consolation and prayer as he knew. Then they entreated Kazir to go back with them; any one of them would have been glad to house him and take care of him, but he would not leave the place of earth where she lay. When they begged him, he began to sing of his love for her and her love for him, of the perfect year and the despair that followed it. The notes overflowed his throat like tears, yet he did not weep, his sorrow was too cruel for weeping. Only the villagers wept and, understanding, left him to mourn alone in silence.

All night he sat by her grave. A nightingale perched in a tree and made music, but he did not hear.

Near dawn, he drifted into sleep.

He dreamed.

He dreamed of the sorceress he had met, who had sent him down into the Underearth to claim Ferazhin, the old woman with the ring.

"Well, so Azhrarn has outwitted you," said she, "and your wheat-haired woman lies in the earth. Come, where else shall a flower lie when its season is done? The Prince of Demons has his magic, so have you, the magic of your songs. You spent a year with Ferazhin, now wait by her grave a year, if you have the patience. Bring water from the stream and sprinkle it over the spot, clear away the weeds that grow there. Best of all, each day sing to her death-mound how you valued her. Be faithful in this, and who knows how your garden will grow."

Kazir woke again as the sun was coloring the sky; he felt it on his face, like the touch of a kind warm hand.

The villagers, concerned for him, had left a little bread and some milk in a crock. Kazir emptied out the milk—perhaps he drank it, perhaps only poured it on the ground. He made his way, guiding himself as always with his staff, to the lip of the stream. There he filled the crock and, carrying it to the grave, he spilled it, as one would water a flower. Then, sitting down beside the place, he began to sing again, the first of many songs to Ferazhin beneath the earth.

"He is sick, the blind one," the people in the village said. "His grief has made him crazy. He will not stir from the grave. He fetches water to it each morning, twice when it is hot. He has worn a track to the stream from all his passing to and fro. He has built himself a little hut of clay and leaves. He sings once every dawn, and once every midnight, to the dead."

Yet they had not forgotten the power of his music, which had made them weep for him. A man had an infant daughter who fell ill and would not eat, and he approached Kazir in the cool of the day, and pleaded that he come and cheer her with a story or a song. Kazir went. Kazir sang: the child laughed and became well inside the hour. After that, they often asked

Kazir to help them. Mad he might be, but poet and healer he
was, too. They grew very fond of him, and at times of plenty
would have heaped him with gifts, but he would accept
nothing, only a small amount of food, and the right to tend
the grave of Ferazhin.

Months passed. At noon, a shepherd going by the hut with
his woolly school all about him, called to Kazir: "Something
is growing where your lady lies."

Kazir reached out and touched the shoot softly.

"Ah, Ferazhin, my blind world's sun. . . ."

Soon the villagers began to talk afresh.

"There is a young tree pushing up on her grave. A tree all
silvery leaves. It looks a tree for flowers, but there are
none."

Months added themselves to months. Winds came and
went, warm winds or cold, shaking the leaves of the flower-
less tree, stirring the pale hair of the poet who sang beneath
it. The year was woven on the loom, finished and folded
away upon the pile of other years in the tall chests of Time.

That night the poet did not bring water to the tree. He wept
there and the tears fell down to nourish its roots as his songs
had fallen to nourish them.

At midnight there came an alteration. Hard to define that
change—he felt it like the turning of a tide. Kazir touched the
tree and found a dream struggling and swaying inside its
bark.

"One flower," Kazir murmured to the tree, "only one."

He did not see it, but he knew, the swelling of the silver
thing upon its stem, the splitting of that silver, the violet cup
within that folded back, petal upon petal, until the heart lay
open.

She had come to a dim pallid place. It was a place of
ghosts, the threshold of death and life. Why mysteries teemed
there she could hardly tell. Souls, half-formed, clamoring to
be born, souls, wild with fright or anger, bursting up like
gray fires to their freedom from existence.

Ferazhin stood quite still in the floating mists, and called
for Kazir. He did not answer her. No hand grasped hers, no

voice of sunlight lit up the shadows. Only the shades fluttered about her like bats.

"Kazir, Kazir," Ferazhin cried, but only the bat-wing voices sounded:

"On, on," they whistled, "follow us on this great and terrible journey!"

And others, dark souls still cramped by diseased bodies or cruel lives, hissed:

"Come, you cannot linger here. Here is No Place. Here you will forget everything, all you were and all you might be. Here your thoughts will die as your earthly brain has done already. Forget, forget, no one remembers you, and come."

But Ferazhin only wandered through the mists, entreating Kazir to find her.

No time passed in such a spot, yet a sort of time passed. Ferazhin did not fly upwards with the other travelers who rushed through that gate. She searched until she was all search, she called a name until she was all one calling cry, like a bird in the desert. She despaired and became despair. She did indeed forget everything. Forgot herself, forgot the way from the threshold, forgot, at last, even Kazir.

Then, into limbo, pierced an invisible thread like silken wire, which wound about her heart so that she recollected she had one. Slowly, yet inexorably, the thread began to tug at her, to pull her back toward that monstrous shifting door by which she had entered. Little by little, fragment by fragment, the thread drew her. It seemed she heard music and saw light, and she loved them, though she did not remember what they were.

Then came a great agony, and fear and joy. They overwhelmed her, drowned her, bore her away with them. She tumbled through seas of fire and flames of pain, she put on flesh like a scalding garment, and knives tore wide her eyes to a sky of black radiance.

She stood in the cup of a vast flower, as once before. She saw a man, as once before. Seeing him, finding him, she recalled everything.

Kazir put his arms about her, and lifted her down to him. They clung together as the stem of the tree clung to the earth.

What they said and what they promised in that moment who needs to be told?

But somewhere perhaps some dark door slammed like thunder in a city underground.

BOOK TWO:
Tricksters

PART ONE

1 The Chair of Uncertainty

There was a king in the east, in the city of Zojad; his name was Zorashad. He liked to raise armies, he had a talent for it. He seemed indeed to grow armies, as a field grows weeds. And strong weeds they were, of bronze and iron, and terrifying they looked when the sun flashed on their brazen marching and on their machines of war and the clouds of dust that rose before and behind. And terrifying they sounded when the clash of their metal was heard, the tramp of feet and rumble of wheels, and the bellow of bulls' horns and trumpets. The bravest kings and princes and their staunchest captains felt their battle-anger dilute to confusion in the vicinity. And certainly, Zorashad did not lose one battle, and sometimes had no need to fight at all. Great lords would genuflect before him in surrender without a blow exchanged. Not merely the armies, but he himself seemed to carry with him a huge sense of mastery—he was impervious and ruthless. Those who knelt at once he spared and took as vassals; those who resisted he would mercilessly overcome, and then he would put entire families to the sword, burn the royal palaces, raze the cities and lay waste to the land. He was like a dragon in his fury, rending and unreasonable. His passion was vainglory, but he was also rumored to be a magician.

This rumor was because of a mysterious amulet. No one knew how Zorashad had come by it; some said he found it in the desert in the desolate hall of a ruin beneath a fallen column, some that he got it from a spirit by means of a trick, others that one night, many years before, he had come across a dead animal on a lonely road, a creature that was like no other beast ever seen on earth and, guided by some instinct or prophecy, he had slit open the monster's gall bladder and found there the amulet, in the form of a blue stone, smooth and hard as jade. Whatever its source, however, the king took to wearing the amulet about his neck, and who could deny its efficacy? He was presently the ruler of seventeen lands, an empire stretching hither and thither, this way and that, till it reached on all sides the blue acres of the sea. It was related that even the lion would step out of his way.

As Zorashad grew in years, so his vainglory grew, and perhaps, weighted down by it, he became also a little mad. He levied massive tribute from his vassals, and had built for himself a temple, and here all his subjects were obliged to come and worship him as a god.

Golden statues of Zorashad were erected in Zojad and in every one of the conquered cities, and inscriptions in gold set in panels of snow-white marble beneath them. This is what the inscriptions said: "Behold with terror Zorashad, Mightiest of the Mighty, Ruler of Men and Brother of the Gods, whose equal is not to be found under Heaven."

The people marveled at this, and trembled, expecting any moment for the gods to strike the cities with plague or thunderbolt because of this blasphemy. But the gods, in those days, regarded the deeds of men much as men have always regarded the antics of very small children. So there was little danger from the serene country of Upperearth, where sublime indifference no doubt continued. Danger there was, but it had another shape.

It had become a whim of Zorashad's, when he sat and feasted at night with his lords, to have brought in and set facing him at the table, a tall chair carved from bone. This he called the Chair of Uncertainty. Anyone might sit in it, rich man, prince or beggar, freeman or slave, even the murderer and the thief might sit down at the king's table, eat the choicest fare off plates of gold and drink the finest of wines from crystal cups, and no one could restrain them or bring them to justice. That was Zorashad's decree. But at the end of the feast Zorashad would do to them whatever he wished—either good or evil, according to his mood; for this resembled, Zorashad declared, the uncertainty that the gods visited on man during his life, not to know whether pleasure or hurt, humiliation or triumph or annihilation was his lot. Some who sat in the bone chair might be fortunate; the god-king would give them precious metal or gems to take away. They would go out blessing him, glad they had risked their luck. A few Zorashad might have sewn up in the skin of a wild ass and driven braying through the streets under the lash till dawn. Others he would condemn to the axe. It made no difference what the guest's status might be, or his deserts. Sometimes the high-born or the virtuous died horribly while the murderer ran off laughing, with a cap full of emeralds. It was a chair to gamble in, and most of the gamblers were desperate men, who considered anything better than life as they were forced under their circumstances to live it. Yet occasionally, a sage would come, thinking he could outwit the king and so grow famous in the land. Several were the heads they left behind, spiked on his gate. Generally, it may be supposed, the chair of bone stood empty.

One evening, just after sunset, a stranger entered the city of Zojad, a tall man, shrouded in a black cloak. He passed as quietly as a shadow through the streets, but when he came to the doors of the palace where the guards stood with crossed spears, the king's hounds began to howl from their kennels, the horses to stamp and whinny in the stables and the falcons to screech in the mews. The guards, alarmed, glanced about them hurriedly; when they looked back at the street, the stranger had vanished.

He was in Zorashad's splendid hall. The brilliance of two thousand candles played over his cloak and could not pierce it. He came up the room, and the minstrel girls fell quiet to watch him pass, even the gorgeous birds in their cages of gold stopped singing: they put their heads under their wings as if they felt the approach of winter. The stranger halted before King Zorashad's table.

"I ask a boon, O king," said he. "To sit in the Uncertain Chair."

Zorashad laughed. He was pleased at this unexpected diversion.

"Sit and welcome," he said. And he called for basins of rosewater for the guest to dip his hands, and for the best roasts and vegetables to be given him, and for wines like ruby or topaz to be poured in his goblet.

Then the stranger drew back the fold of the cloak which had concealed his face. There was not one who saw him who did not wonder at his extraordinary handsomeness. His hair was blue-black like the night, his eyes like two black suns. He smiled, but the smile was somehow unpleasing. He lightly caressed the head of the king's favorite hound and it slunk away and fell down in a corner.

"O king," he said in his voice that was like dark music. "I had heard men risked their lives to taste the fare of your table. Do you mock me?"

Zorashad reddened angrily, but the cries of his lords made him look down at the plate his servants had set before the stranger. And there, where the roast and the tender shoots had lain, was coiled a sinuous slime-green snake.

Zorashad shouted. A slave snatched up the dish and threw its contents in the brazier; certainly he feared his king more than the venom of the snake. A fresh platter was brought, and the servants once more heaped it with aromatic food. Yet, as the stranger took up his knife, a smoke seemed to drift about the table, and suddenly there on the plate writhed a knot of angry scorpions.

"Oh, king," murmured the stranger, softly and with reproach, "it is true only desperate men will eat in your chair of bone, knowing death may await them in exchange for their meal, but do I seem so starved that I will relish these vermin, sting and all?"

"There is witchcraft in my palace," bellowed Zorashad, and his court turned pale, all but the stranger.

Dish after dish was brought, but none would the stranger eat and no man blamed him for that. All manner of horrors sprang from the plates, even the sweetmeats changed to pebbles and wasps. As for the wine, the goblet of yellow, upended, spilled stinking urine, the red was unmistakably blood.

"O king," said the stranger sorrowfully, "I had thought it your custom to mete out fates impartially, but I see it is your habit rather to slay your guests at the board."

The king leaped up.

"You have spoiled the food yourself. You are a magician!"

"And you, sir, are a god, or so I was told. Cannot a god defend himself from such silly tricks as any poor traveler might have about him?"

Zorashad, overcome with rage, roared out to his guard:

"Seize the man and kill him!"

But before one brazen foot could take a step, or one bronze-gloved hand could grasp a sword, the stranger said, most gently: "Be still," and not a man or a woman could move, and all sat in their seats as if their limbs were turned to stone.

A deep silence came down on the hall then, like a gigantic bird foldings its wings.

The stranger rose, and going to stand by the king as he sat shrinking yet frozen in his chair, bowed deeply and spoke in a caressing tone the words of the inscription.

"Behold with terror Zorashad, Mightiest of the Mighty, Ruler of Men and Brother of the Gods, whose equal is not to be found under Heaven."

Only the eyes of the petrified king could move. All through the hall only eyes were moving, darting like frantic jeweled fish as they followed the progress of the fearful stranger. He walked about the table smiling.

"I await, magnificent king," he said, "the axe of your vengeance. Pray get up and deal me my punishment. Am I so much your inferior that you will not deign to humble me further? Am I to endure forever the shame of your pity? Speak."

Zorashad found then he had once more the ability to do so. He whispered: "I see I have wronged you, mighty one. Only release me and I will worship you, build you a temple to touch the sky—bring you a ton of incense every dawn and dusk, and sacrifice always in your name.''

''My name is Azhrarn, Prince of Demons,'' said the stranger, and at the words, the two thousand candles flickered and went out. ''I am not worshipped, only feared, by men who are not gods. Under heaven, on earth or beneath it, I and I alone am without equal.'' Zorashad whimpered like a beaten dog. In the dim flare of the braziers, which was all the light left burning in the hall, he saw the Prince's hand come toward him and felt the magic amulet snatched from his breast. ''This is your power,'' Azhrarn said, holding it in his palm, ''this, and nothing else. This is what made men dread you, this is what made you love yourself.'' Then he spat on the stone and let it fall on the table.

At once a silver dancing flame sprang up where he had spat. The flame gnawed at the amulet; it glowed and seemed to grow white-hot and presently shivered in pieces.

There was uproar in the king's hall. Men, freed from the spell of stone, leaped to their feet and collided. Only the king lay in his chair like an old man sick with fever.

The stranger of course was gone.

That night there were many wonders. In the palaces of sixteen kings, sixteen omens. Many, lying asleep, woke up with a start to shout for their priests to read a dream. Ten spoke of a huge bird which, flying into their chambers, murmured to them in a musical voice. In five kingdoms a serpent sprang out of the flaming hearth like a coal and called aloud its message. And in the north, a young and very handsome king, walking sleepless in his garden under the moon, met a man in a black cloak, whose bearing was princely and who talked to him like a friend or a brother and kissed him before leaving him, with a touch as fearful and as thrilling as fire. And the substance of all these miracles on the night of the sixteen kings was this: The sorcerous amulet of Zorashad the Tyrant is destroyed, and his power is ended.

Vassalage to Zorashad had not been sweet to them. The heavy tributes had worn them out; their pride ached like an old wound. They banded together and soon fought with

Zorashad a colossal battle on an eastern plan. No longer was Zorashad a god. His hand shook, his face was white as paper. His brazen army slunk away and left him and presently he was slain. But his old cruelties were not forgotten. Like vultures the sixteen kings swooped on Zojad and razed it. The palace burned, the treasure chambers were sacked, and the Chair of Uncertainty itself was broken into splinters. The household of Zorashad they put to the sword, as he had put to the sword so many households. Seven sons and twelve daughters and all the wives of Zorashad perished on that night, even his hounds and his horses they slew, even the birds that nested in his trees, such was their hatred and their fear. Afterwards they rejoiced that they had slaughtered every living thing that had belonged to the god-king of Zojad. But one living thing had escaped them.

There was a child born that night, the thirteenth daughter of Zorashad. The mother the soldiers found and slew, but an old woman, a nurse, had snatched up the baby and run out with it. She ran along the great highway which led out of Zojad, between the statues of Zorashad the god. And as she ran, she cursed him. Near dawn her fragile heart cracked inside her and she fell dead. The child dropped from her hands upon the paving of the road. Both its arms were broken at the blow, and its soft face, scarcely formed, was ruined by the sharp stone and the brambles that speared at it as it went rolling down among them. By chance merely, its eyes were spared. It set up a feeble thin scream of agony, but only the wind heard, the wind and the jackals creeping towards the smouldering city.

2   King Zorashad's Daughter

A man lived in the hills above Zojad. He was a hermit, a priest. His dwelling was a cave, furnished with simple things, woven hangings of coarse plain cloth and a bed of matting and some magic too. The people of the villages round about brought him their sick to heal, or came to ask his counsel. Once or twice a year he would travel from place to place to speak words over their crops and pray for rain or sun, whichever they required. In return they gave him such small things as he needed—a bit of rope, an earthenware bowl, and every few days something would be left a little way from his home, a pot of honey or a loaf or a basket of fruit. No one came close to the cave. If they wished to speak to him, they would stand on the slope nearby and call, for, although he was a hermit, he did not live quite alone. Beasts would sometimes share his cave, the wolf, the bear, even the lion. He had no fear of them, the holy man, nor they of him. They came and went as they pleased, and their eyes met often, the golden eye of the creature with the dark quiet eye of the priest.

On the night that Zojad burned, the priest smelled the smoke and heard the distant thunder. He went up to the hilltop and saw the glare on the sky's edge. The moon was blue from the smoke, and once a large bird flew over it and its wings made a sound like bone-dry laughter in the air.

The priest watched all night on the hill. Near dawn he fell into a kind of dream or trance. He saw the smoke on the long paved road that led to Zojad and heard the jackals barking, and a horrible thin wailing rose up from the thickets at the roadside. The priest came to himself with a shock. He rose and hurried, compelled, down from the hills toward the city.

The sun was rising when he reached the road. It was quite deserted, no one had come from Zojad for a long while, not even the soldiers of the sixteen kings, who had still much business there. Three jackals had found the body of the old woman—but the priest noticed on the pavement beside them a golden anklet which they had discarded, having no use for it. Next he saw a fourth jackal, and this one had in its jaws the tiny body of an infant.

The baby no longer screamed. It was little better than dead, and dangled from the jackal's mouth like a disjointed doll. Nevertheless, the hermit-priest, with that curious understanding common to his kind, felt emanating from it the faintest flickering of life.

He stood quite still and said to the jackal: "My brother, I am sorry to deny you, but what you carry still lives, and therefore you have no right to it."

The jackal pricked its ears, and its eyes met the eyes of the priest. What it saw there, only the jackal knew, but it laid down the baby very carefully, shook its forefeet as if ridding them of dust or blame and ran to join the other three at their grisly but blameless feast.

The priest went and took up the child. He looked at its wounds and covered it over with his cloak and strode quickly homewards. There, in the cave, he tended it, set its poor broken limbs as best he could, although he knew its arms could never now grow straight, and doctored the terrible disfigurement of its minute face, and gave it a medicine to drink mixed with goats' milk. He worked skilfully and with compassion. He did not waste any time in lament or useless anger, though the state of the child might have moved anyone to either or both. He had a ruthless tenderness. He wept neither for the dead nor the living. He did what he could, and trusted that the gods, also, would do as much.

While she was a little girl, Zorashad's daughter was happy enough, though in a curious way, compatible with her surroundings and manner of existence. For life in the cave was calm, oblique and absorbing, and she learned there calm, oblique, absorbing lessons—the skills of the clean earth magic which the priest practiced. She learned too those channels of magic she must beware—sorcery, necromancy, all those avenues which men approached at risk of sanity, soul and ego itself, but she saw them only like a row of black doorways, forever closed, and had no desire to knock on them or find out keys.

During this time she was ignorant of herself, as only a creature lost in external things can be. Indeed, she was hardly conscious of herself—she was all ear and eye and thought. She had never seen into a mirror, never looked at her marred face; she had never wept in outraged horror at the scarred and twisted flesh, nor marvelled bitterly at the cream-smooth brow, the large eyes and copper hair which her perverse destiny had left her. Despite her crippled arms, her body was beautiful; she never noticed it, it made few demands. And though sometimes these arms, warped like winter trees, would gnaw and burn with pain, she never cried out in anger at the fate which made her suffer it. Through her short life she had suffered intermittently so, and there was always the gentle priest with his salve, and the leopard with its torn side wounded more sorely than she. All her days were elements, sun, snow, shadow, wind, clear water, blowing grass, the gathering of herbs, the making of spells, the serene hours of lessons. All her nights were warm dark red coals on the hearth, and golden coals of beast eyes smouldering softly.

Sometimes the priest would go on a journey and would not take her, but she did not mind this. He left her behind to care for their home, to tend any animals who might come there. She had never spoken to a human, save for the priest. He had made sure of that, knowing, without rancour, how the human tribe might treat her. When men and women came to the cave for aid, she peeped at them through the curtain with the fox and the bear, and only the priest went out. She had a sort of innocence, a sweetness, despite her deformities, that sprang from an uncrippled brain and an open heart. She had never been censured, ridiculed, reviled, hated.

One day, when she was fifteen, the priest was from home. He had gone to pray over the crops of the villages. At noon, when she was mixing herbs in the cave, she heard the sound of horses' hooves outside, and went quickly to look out from her hiding place. No one before had ever come when the priest was away, for the villagers knew the times of his absences and they feared the cave and the wild beasts. Yet these visitors had not traveled from any village or lonely farm. Even she, who had never seen such worldly magnificence before, recognized it instinctively when she saw it, and she was very awed.

Ten horses stood outside, fretting, white or ebony, and caparisoned in gold and silver. Each had a rider, all dressed in a radiance of silk, metal and jewels as bright as the moon, but the young man who sat his horse in front of them was to her like the sun itself.

She never dreamed that he would speak, supposed he would simply pass on, as the sun does, illuminating but not communicating with the world.

When he called out suddenly, it frightened her, for it seemed too real.

"You there, hermit," he cried scornfully, "come and heal us, for we are sick."

And the whole company laughed uproariously.

Zorashad's daughter stared out through the curtain at him, and a new sensation took hold of her. She guessed abruptly that he mocked the priest, and had come here only for that purpose, but this was a little thing compared to the fascination the sight of the young man exerted over her. All at once, his reality, his mockery even, excited her. He was wondrous, but actual. A part of the earth she knew. She became all joy, all amazement. She had asked nothing from the leopard, only to worship and tend him, and he had suffered her without flinching. Now she asked only to worship the young man on the white horse.

Compelled, unconsidering, unaware of self, all ear and eye and thought, she came out of the cave and stood on the slope, gazing up at him.

Her ugliness, of which she had never been told, was so

frightful that the young riders drew back in alarm. But presently the beautiful young man, who was a king and a king's son, realizing that she was, though vile and crippled, only human, halted and laughed again.

"Gods of Upper Air defend us!" he cried, "what apparition is this?"

Then, seeing her large eyes fixed on him, and becoming uneasy after all, he demanded:

"What are you staring at, you stupid monster?"

"At you," said she, "because you are so fair."

She spoke without apology or embarrassment, in her spontaneous gentle way. But one of the king's companions shouted:

"Don't trust her. She wants to blast you, my lord, to make you as hideous as herself. Surely she is a demoness, and has the ill-eye. Her arms are crooked as sticks."

At this the king took up his whip, and slashed her across the cheek and neck with it. Zorashad's daughter fell down without a word.

"One scar more will make no odds to that face," the king told her. "Go masked in future, or you'll sour the wine in the skin, and the milk in the cow, and break every looking glass in the land."

She had always been quick to learn; it had been her talent. Now she learned quickly too.

The king rode away into the woods with his friends to chase the deer with arrows, and Zorashad's daughter lay where she was, with the pain of the whip still raking her cheek, and the pain of that other whip, worse than the first, the whip of his cruel tongue, raking her heart.

This was how the priest found her when he came back in the dusk with the fireflies wooing his lamp.

He saw some great misfortune had fallen on her; no doubt he guessed well enough the nature of it. It had been only good luck that he had shielded her so long from herself. Besides, he was old now, and could not protect her for ever. He asked no questions, but stroked her hair a little while, then went in and made up the fire. Soon she followed him, and raised her dreadful face to his.

"Why," she said softly, "did you never tell me what I am?"

"You are yourself," he said. "What more need you know?"

"No, I am not myself, for always I thought myself the same as the rest of human-kind. Now I learn I am a monster, with an appearance to laugh and tremble at, and twisted limbs—a man came here today and told me so, and when he was gone, I looked at myself freshly, and I went to the pool and waited there till the ripples were still, and so I saw all he had said, and worse. If you found me at birth, why did you not kill me? Why leave me to suffer this?"

"That was not my choice," said the priest, "but yours. If you cannot bear to live as you are, you know enough to mix yourself a drink to end all sorrow, and I will not prevent you, though I should grieve at it."

At this the girl wept, for she loved life as do most living things who had known a little freedom and happiness in the world.

The priest comforted her, and said:

"Sit here, and I will tell you something of yourself. You are not whole, for you have no past, no reason to explain your burdens and your misery. This I will give you. Then you shall decide what is to be done."

So he told her everything, for he knew everything. How he knew it is not certain. Perhaps he deduced the story from the gossip of the villagers, the golden anklet which the jackals left aside, the royal robe the child was wrapped in. Perhaps he discovered it another way, a stranger way. . . . Whatever it was, he knew, and soon, so did she, all of it, from the time of Zorashad's mastery to the coming of the Prince of Demons, from the extinction of the amulet to the dead nurse, the disfigured baby.

When the priest had finished, she sat silently for a little. Then she said:

"So I am the thirteenth daughter of a dead tyrant. What of his city Zojad?"

"Zojad is rebuilt on its own ruins."

"Who then rules in the tyrant's place?"

"A king, the son of one of the sixteen kings who rose against Zorashad."

"This king's son," she said, "something tells me that the man who spoke to me today was such a one. Can it have been he who rules there?"

And the priest did not answer.

She was not as she had been, (how could she be?) though she took up once more the calm and useful life of the acolyte. She never spoke again of her pain, within or without. Her spontaneity was gone, and her joy. Her eyes now, looking at something beautiful, a leaf, a beast, a sky, were full of an empty and unrealized hunger. And also now, when the moon rose like a silver omen above the land, there was no longer worship or wonder in her face, and when the seasons added their veils of different color to the forests and the hills, she only said: "Now it is winter, now it is summer," never anything else. One more thing had altered with her. She had taken to wearing a mask of cloth that hid all her face save the lovely brow and eyes, and gloves on her ruined yet agile hands.

Then the old priest died, and part of her died with him, the most essential part of her, her sense of purpose. He passed with peace from the world, she was left anguished in it. She wept upon his wooden breast and presently buried him and stood in the comfortless silence.

In the months which followed, few came to the cave for healing, only travelers from remote villages who had not yet learned of the priest's death. On the very day of his burial, a woman had stood with a sick baby and cried for help on the slope. When the strange masked girl came out, with her red-hot hair and leaden tread, the woman ran back a little way and cried: "No, no, not you—where is the priest?"

"He is dead," said the girl, and automatically she added, because she had inherited his medicines and the duty, if not the actuality, of his compassion: "Is it the child? I can help him—" And the woman, sensing everything about her, even through the mask and the low voice—all the ugliness and the bitter unlovingness—made a sign against evil, and fled. This was like a wound, a new wound made in the old, not because the girl felt herself hated, more because she had failed the priest.

One day, she was sixteen. It was the turn of autumn. Then winter came.

All through the winter, she lived in the cave, Zorashad's daughter. Even the beasts did not come to her, they had forgotten the road. Only hurt and loneliness sat with her, and a sort of rage, inexplicable, deadly.

Each night she lay in the cradle of blackness, and soon a waking dream began to take her. She saw her father, Zorashad, clad in dark metal, riding through a vast city, the people falling on their faces before him in terror, while cressets of fire blazed from the roofs of palaces and temples. Presently the dream altered a little, slowly, and by degrees. At first she rode at her father's side in a royal dress, holding a beautiful porcelain mask before her own smashed countenance—a mask so thrilling and lifelike that it seemed to everyone that it was really her face, and she was renowned for her loveliness. Then, when the cruelest nights of winter came, turning the reeds along the margin of the pool to spears of jade and vitreous, her dream grew also more cold, more cruel. Now she rode in Zorashad's place, dressed in his iron, and masked in iron, a great diadem on her hair. She ruled Zojad, ruled all sixteen vassal cities, as he had ruled them; she was the king's daughter, Zorayas, queen and empress, and captives tottered after her chariot in chains, among them the young king who had mocked her. Everyone who saw her now, looking at the masked face which showed only the fine eyes and clear brow and strong hair, whispered that it was beauty she kept hidden, not ugliness. Zorayas was so fair that should she unmask, her wonderful looks would blast them like a lightning bolt.

One night, tossing beneath this glorious and torturing fantasy, she sprang up and ran outside and cried aloud in a voice like the cracking ice. "What shall I do?" she asked herself, and lay on the ground, her ear pressed to it, as if listening for some answer.

An answer came. Indeed, it seemed to come from the earth, or Underearth perhaps. She saw before her a row of doorways, fast closed, some with keys waiting to be turned in their locks, others with the keys lying in a great pile among the shadows. They were those doors of dark magic of which the priest had bade her beware, which, until now, she had never thought to enter.

But Zorashad's daughter put the image aside. She turned her head from it, she went back into the cave, colder than the cold night.

In the morning, a voice woke her, calling to her from outside the cave, calling for her help. It was the first voice she had ever heard which cried specifically to her in this way. Despite her reserve, her heart was lightened. Someone had learned of her presence here, that she had been the apprentice of the priest. Someone needed her kindness, entreated for it.

The need to be needed, to be necessary; a gift.

She went out, unsure, balanced on a thread, supposing that this might be the answer to her question.

A man stood among the frosty trees. He was a pedlar, his cart of goods close by. A swarthy man, with little bright eyes and a foxy smile. He bowed, more courtly than a prince.

"What ails you?" Zorashad's daughter said to him.

"Ah, lady, a snake bit me, back there in the forest—my boot took most of its teeth, but I think some poison remains. I came on very weak, and my head spins. But I heard a tale of a priestess here, clever with healing."

He seemed not to mind the cloth mask, nor to fear the cave, for he hobbled closer.

"I will help you," she said.

"You are to be blessed, lady. May I come into the cave?"

She was surprised he did not fear it, but neither did he seem to fear her. Close to, he was bigger than she had thought, and had a powerful presence, a kind of male smell and aura. She had been used to the priest, impersonal, without aggression. This man was not like that. She took him inside, and he leaned heavily on her shoulder, and slumped down on the mattress by the fire.

She fetched the salves and clean water quickly, and bent near.

"Which foot?"

"This," he said, and then he grabbed her.

It was too swift and took her wits. He slung her down, and when she wildly fought with him, he struck her and her head span as he had told her his was doing.

"Kind, sweet girl," he said, pulling loose his belt and tying her hands with it above her head in a trice, "a snake never bit me in the foot after all, it bit me here," and he showed her his groin. "See the swelling? Does it not grieve your heart? Look how it sticks out, and only you can cure me." She floundered and screamed, but he pushed her mask, all crumpled, off her face, into her mouth. "I do not mind them ugly," he declared, "though with such a face, you must be lonely. Did a bear gnaw you? Another bear shall gnaw you now." And he ripped open her garment and sank his teeth into the upper mound of her breast, so she screamed again, at which he struck her a second time, and all struggle left her.

She lay beneath him in a nightmarish, strengthless swimming of horror, agony and bewilderment. She could not find her voice, nor any strength to beat him off. He was heavy and determined, and well-practiced in this art.

He kneaded her flesh with his hands, which were never still, and scrabbled over her as if he meant to climb a mountain and must grasp for desperate holds. His mouth hung open and he gasped for air, but his eyes were in no doubt either of the ascent or of the summit. He slavered on her breasts and champed his teeth on them and forced his hot tool through the smallness of her maiden's gate in three great spasms of wild effort. She could not even shriek, he made the only noises that attended their sudden haphazard union. Having broken into her citadel with a bronze-beaked ram, he thundered up and down in the bloody dark there, and howled as his lust burst from him, and bucked and kicked, bruising her afresh as his hands clenched on her, till the last drop was squeezed forth.

He left her, chuckling and well-satisfied at his deed. She lay a long while, until the yellow light of afternoon muddied the forest. Then she dragged herself about, cleansing the wounds he had given her, applying the salves. She did not weep. Later, she walked slowly to watch the jade reeds rattle

by the frozen pool, the obsidian trees fade into a brackish
sunset.

Something of her had survived the three icy fires, the cruel
scourge, the desertion through death, the gouging rape. But
what had survived was an iron stick, and frost-bitten harder
than the frozen reeds and the cold trees. Though it had not
been what she looked for, she had had her answer. Presently
she returned to the cave.

She cleared out all the old litter of things, and sorted the
items she would require, and made such preparations as were
needful. For a long while, after the moon was down, she sat
and stared into the cup of her own brain, doggedly drawing
forth her will and knowledge.

Two hours before dawn, a clap of thunder sounded in the
forest; a rain of icicles fell down; a wind swirled gibbering
among the trunks of the trees. Zorayas had opened the first
black door of sorcery.

One hour before dawn, the pedlar, who lay asleep in an
abandoned hut at the edge of the forest, woke to find a twilit
woman at his side. She said, in a dulcet and winning fashion:
"I hear you have been suffering from a snake bite which
caused a swelling, here." And she touched him in such a way
that the pedlar became very interested in her. For some
reason he did not think to ask her how she had discovered
him, or how she came to know what he had said the previous
day to the idiot girl in the cave. Soon indeed he rolled the
stranger on her back and mounted her, and was entering when
something about the gate surprised him, for it did not feel as
it should. The pedlar glanced down, and roared with terror.
He was mounted astride a log of wood, and he had thrust his
phallus, this time, into the grinning jaws of a huge black
viper, which now, with a venomous clash, closed them.

In the lands all about, things went on as they had always
done. The fields were planted, the herds brought to grass, and
in the cities men toiled and took their shares of misery and
pleasure, and kings idled on their silken couches, and fair
women looked in their looking glasses and sighed admiringly.

And at the heart of it all, like the worm in the apple, the beetle in the woodwork, sorcery was working, eating out the pith: soon the apple would break open, the wooden beam fall down, and the lands start up in fear.

Perhaps some guessed—the hunter who saw lights flicker above the trees of the forest; the beggar woman who, going by the old priest's cave one day at dusk, witnessed a curl of smoke run in there and take on the form of a peculiar beast, with the body of a lion and the head of an owl. Stories were told now, about the masked witch in the cave, the sorceress. She had killed the priest, they said, and her friends were demons, the little, almost inconsequent demons of Underearth—the Drin—the dregs of that shadowy hierarchy below, who obeyed the will of powerful magicians, having no true initiative of their own. With the help of the demons, this witch had slain a poor pedlar, and in a most awful manner. What would she do next?

Even in Zojad, possibly, men had word of the witch. Maybe they laughed about her.

The pedlar had been inadvertently the catalyst. Now Zorayas' aims were guided by her dreams. Zorashad's daughter, the sorceress. She remembered the young king with his lash, his spiteful tongue, remembered he sat in the royal chair of her dead father. Her chair. This wrong went deeper than any wrong which came after, despair or rape; they were done with. The curse of ugliness and disinheritance remained.

On a night in high summer, when the young king sat at table in Zojad, the lights in the hall began to dip and dim, and up from its dish sprang the roasted bird that had just been set before him. It seemed to flap its wings, its eyes—made of two curving bits of quartz—fixed on the king. He jumped to his feet and down the bird fell at once. The king, anxious to seem unafraid, ordered the carver, jestingly, to slice the fowl into portions before it should fly off altogether, but the minute the knife went through it, out fell a ball of glass which, rolling from the table, smashed in pieces on the floor. And in the glass lay a scroll.

The court stood amazed at the miracle, but the king arrogantly bent and took up the scroll and read it. It said:

"What is one scar more, O king? I will tell you. One scar more to me is one crown less to you."

At once the king turned grey as dust, for he remembered immediately, though why he was not certain, that day a year before when he had lashed the crippled girl across the face with his whip. A dark horror overcame him. He scented sorcery as the rabbit scents the hound.

Yet nothing else happened that night, nor for five nights afterwards.

On the seventh night, as the king sat in his gardens, under the stars, a veiled woman came between the trees. He took her for a servant, until she drew close and whispered in his ear.

"Here I am," she said, no more, no less, but at the words the king trembled violently and cried out for his guard. Swiftly they came running, and found the king shaking in his chair and the veiled woman standing there beside him. "One moment," said she, and made three or four passes in the air with her gloved hands. Who can say what happened next? It is told that all the guard fell dead in their tracks, and blue-faced Drin sprang up from the ground in full armour and with swords, and stood grinning, ready to serve their magician mistress. Then she cast off her veil, and she too wore armour of black iron chased with silver, wild beautiful work these demons had made her, and on her face an iron mask, which had features of its own like those of a fair woman, and left only her forehead and eyes to be seen, and her torrential hair. With her iron glove she pointed at the king and what a change she made in him! He seemed to shrink, to shrivel, to curl up like a dead leaf—presently this was all that was left of him: a little dry lizard skulking on his chair, which abruptly darted down and away into the dark garden, and as it darted Zorayas mashed its tail with her heel.

Zorayas smiled inside her mask, her fiery disfigured smile, but the lips of iron were implacable and emotionless over her own.

She marched with her guard of Drin into the hall of the palace, and there she summoned the court of the king.

"Look well," she said, "I am your ruler now, and I will

rule you as my father ruled Zojad long ago, for I am Zorayas, thirteenth daughter of Zorashad. I do not claim to be a god, it is true, but I claim to have more power than any other in these seventeen lands that stretch every way to the blue acres of the sea. Serve me, if you wish, and prosper. Defy me, and see, I will replace you all with these my followers the Drin, the Little Ones of Underearth. Or you can search out your king in the garden, on four little lizard feet, which I will give you so you may run as he does now, before his broken tail.'' At this the Drin giggled and applauded, and the white-faced court prudently fell on its knees to adore her.

Thus Zorayas came to be queen in Zojad, and thus new statues were put up in the city to replace those which had been melted down by the sixteen kings. Yet never did she claim to be a goddess; her spells were enough indeed to put fear into men's hearts. And before long, armies began growing again like weeds in Zojad, armies of bronze and iron, and she had won back to herself those sixteen lands that had been lost when Zorashad's amulet was destroyed.

3   The Starry Pavilion

Many tales were recounted then of the Iron Princess who rode at the head of her army, and some were true and some were not. She was a mighty witch, she could take no wound, demons marched in the ranks behind her; she covered her face because one look from it would scald with fire or turn to granite or melt as with acid any who beheld it, though others said she was so beautiful no man could watch her and not lose his wits, and that one of her smiles could darken the moon and one frown could kill the sun.

In a year she had regained all that had been snatched from her, and more, and she sat in her sorcerous tower of brass, or upon the great throne of Zojad in her mask of iron, and ruled with a hand of iron, and if she was not happy, neither was she impotent on the earth, and she burned with a flame of pride that seemed as fierce as any joy.

And then there came a day when everything was done—her empire vast and unassailable, her fame assured, all her goals reached, her hopes satisfied, and there was nothing left—save an emptiness which rushed in like a cold sea and flooded her heart.

So she sat in thought, and out of the cold sea rose one last dream, a dream so foolhardy, so impossible, it lit up her world again with a brilliant light.

She had exacted all her vengeances—on the king who had mocked her, on the sixteen other kings who had slain Zorashad and taken her birthright; only one being remained who had paid her nothing in recompense for her years of doubt and humility and her ruined face. That one being, he who had begun it all with his own casual vengeance—the ruler of the lower lands, master of Vazdru, Eshva, Drin, one of the Lords of Darkness—Azhrarn, Prince of Demons.

At the impulse, the heart of Zorayas raced. Yet she did not boast aloud as Zorashad had done. She kept her own counsel, and only went more often to her tall tower of brass. And there, by the flashes of the blue and lustreless fire, she passed, night by night, in and out of those doors of Power that now were so familiar to her.

At last she stood in the tower and called up those demons who appeared on earth in the form of strange animals and monsters, the Drindra, the lowest of the Drin, and the silliest and most mischievous of all. Soon the octagonal room was full of grunting, whining, chattering things, which skittered away before the princess's iron finger.

"Be silent and attend," said she, "for I wish to ask you questions."

"We are your slaves, peerless mistress," fawned the Drindra, dribbling on her boots and licking the floor at her feet.

"No," said Zorayas stonily, "you are the slaves of your lord, Azhrarn the Beautiful, and it is of him I wish to learn."

At this the Drindra blushed and shivered, for they loved their Prince passionately and also feared him greatly. Zorayas knew she must be careful then, for asking lore of Underearth was very difficult since no demon could be constrained to tell anything freely, only answer truthfully when the questioner's guesses were correct, and even then they would, if they could, try tricks.

"It is known," she therefore began, "that there are certain special tokens that will summon demons of the Eshva and Vazdru. Can it be that there are tokens that will summon even Azhrarn the Beautiful?"

The Drindra chittered together and said:

"No, no, incomparable queen, nothing of that sort can be fashioned by mortals."

"Did I say tokens fashioned by mortals? I am thinking of

curious pipes of silver shaped in Underearth as toys for friends and lovers. Are there such, and can any call Azhrarn?''

"Yes," hissed the Drindra in mournful voices. "So it is."

"Then can it be there are any of these pipes on earth?"

"How could it be," chirruped the demons, "that such pipes should be allowed to reach the earth?"

"This is not what I asked you," cried Zorayas, and she struck her iron fists together, at which a bolt of steely fire sprang out like a whip and made the Drindra jump and spit.

"Be kind, sweet mistress," they whimpered, "you are right, and your wisdom glows like a precious jewel."

"How many of these pipes exist on earth? Seven?"

The Drindra wailed and would not answer.

"More than seven? Less than seven?"

"Yes."

"Three?" Zorayas asked, "two?" And then, angrily, "only one?" And the Drindra assented. "Where then does it lie? On land? Under water?"

"Yes!"

"Beneath the sea?"

"Yes!"

Zorayas gave a shout of derision, and the Drindra cowered.

"Yes indeed," said she, "I have heard tell of such a pipe—the serpent's head your lord gave to a youth who was dear to him, a hundred thousand years ago—Sivesh, who lies at the ocean's bottom where Azhrarn drowned him, with the silver pipe about his delicious neck, which is now all bones."

The Drindra lashed their tails and whispered: "Yes," like the steam from water thrown on hot metal.

Zorayas might have turned herself into a fish and swum down to retrieve the enchanted pipe, but it was very dangerous for a mortal, even a magician, to take on an animal form, or any form other than his own, for quite quickly he would forget his human values and reasoning, and begin to think exactly as the creature would think whose form he had taken. There were many tales of great sorcerers who, in order to avoid some calamity or to discover some secret, changed themselves into beasts, reptiles or birds of the air, and then forgot all their spells and even who they were, and so remained moving, slithering or flapping to the end of their days. Therefore Zorayas bound one of the Drindra by terrible magics, and forced it to fetch her the pipe, which it was very loath to do.

"Rest assured," said Zorayas, "I wish only to honor your Prince, not to anger him, for indirectly he is the cause of my present good fortune."

So, bound as it was, the Drindra fled down through the waters of the sea to a place where milk-white bones were lying on the sand. Here the ocean creatures had gathered in wonder a thousand years before, and the sea-maidens with their ice-green tresses kissed with their cold lips the colder lips of the dead youth, touched with their cold pointed tongues the two gems of his chest, the threefold treasure of his loins. But Sivesh did not stir. Only the currents combed his hair, as once demon fingers had combed it, and his wide eyes were full as with tears of tragedy and despair. Eventually the sea folk abandoned him, and the water erased him and left only his bones—and the serpent pipe about his neck. This the Drindra snatched off, gibbering, and fled back to Zorayas' tower of brass, and cast the pipe down at her feet with the seaweed still tangled on it.

Zorayas took up the pipe, and gazed at it, an hour or more.

She had a curious pavilion built in the great gardens of the palace, with walls of jet-black granite. There were no windows in these walls, and the floor was laid with bricks of pure gold, yet the ceiling of the pavilion was strangest of all. It was made of a dull and inky glass that reflected no light and through which nothing could be seen, and here and there in it were set pale diamonds, sapphires, zircons in the exact positions of the stars. So cunning was the workmanship of this ceiling that, looking up from inside the pavilion, you would think there was no roof at all, only the night sky with its little fires overhead. At one end of the chamber, facing the double doors, hung down a thick cord of velvet.

Here in this pavilion, by this cord, Zorayas sat with the serpent pipe in her hand, while the moon rose and the bells of Zojad tolled out the hours of the night. Presently the moon sank, and they rang the last quarter before dawn. Then Zorayas set the pipe to the little incision in her mask, and blew it.

There was no sound. At least, no sound that could be heard on earth. Then suddenly the air was full of a brazen thunder, and in through the double doors burst a lightning. Zorayas reached and twitched the velvet cord to the left and the doors clanged shut again. The lightning meanwhile resolved itself into a shape like a huge dragon, with molten lava licking from its mouth like twenty tongues.

But Zorayas only said:

"Be still. Exalted one. I am protected from your fiery breath by my spells. Will you not permit me to see you, as did my father Zorashad?"

At this, the dragon seemed to melt and fade, and there in the pavilion stood a tall and wonderfully handsome man, with a black cloak like wings.

Zorayas looked at him, and her senses were confused at his beauty, as were all mortal senses, but also her heart leaped with triumph.

"Lord of Shadows," said she, "forgive your handmaiden that she has entreated you here. By accident I found this pipe, and knowing from an ancient fable that it would call you, how could I resist the chance of looking on your form, O Prince of Princes?"

She knew the vanity of Demons, and had addressed him exactly as she should. Azhrarn seemed neither grim nor questioning, only a little amused.

"You must also know then," he said, "that, having summoned me, you may ask one request of me."

"All I ask, O Incomparable Magnificence, is to gaze on you and give you my thanks, and to return you this pipe which is rightly yours."

And she went down to him and handed him the pipe, which he took, and the touch of his hand was like a cool flame even through her glove, which made her poor twisted fingers sing in pain, and every scar on her ruined face throb, and the scars the pedlar had left upon her breasts and between her thighs were seethed in fire. And just then she heard the bell sound in Zojad which betokened the rising of the sun.

What a burning gush of fury and joy she felt. She laughed aloud at it, out of the fire.

Azhrarn had all this while been watching carefully for the dawn lighting of the sky, but no light fell through the black glass roof which looked precisely like the sky itself. However, hearing a bell, he said to Zorayas:

"I am intrigued at your courtesy, Iron Lady, but I think the sun is near, the light of which is to me an abomination. Therefore, I must leave you."

"Must you?" said she, going back to where hung the velvet cord, and taking it in her hand. "O Azhrarn," she murmured in a smiling voice, "my father Zorashad was a fool and set himself above you, and him you destroyed. I am his daughter, and in that destruction I lost my birthright and much more besides. Due to my own skill in magic, I have regained many things, but one thing I could not alter, and for this one thing I will, after all, exact a boon from you."

"Speak then," said Azhrarn, and now he seemed impatient.

"I would see," said Zorayas, "one of the Lords of Darkness face with his glory the glory of the earth's sun."

Perhaps in her triumphant mockery she mistook, but it seemed to her the wonderful countenance of Azhrarn grew paler.

"Have I not told you," he said, "that I abhor the sun."

"Abhor or *fear*, great Lord? I think you go in terror of its rays, which, if they should touch you, would reduce you to powder or stone or some such other lifeless and unlovely thing."

Then such a look of malign shadow passed over the face of Azhrarn that even Zorayas held her breath.

"Accursed of all women, do you suppose you will go unpunished for your insolence? Fear the night, fool, daughter of a fool."

And turning, he went toward the closed doors.

"Wait!" cried Zorayas, and gave a little twitch of the cord to the right.

A crack sprang open in the roof of cunning glass, and through it a solitary golden beam shot like an arrow into the golden floor below. Azhrarn stood still and stared at it, and his cloak beat about him of its own volition like a terrified bird.

"I have learned," said Zorayas softly, "that to a demon, even to the Prince of Demons, the light of the sun is Death. I have learned too that even though he may travel as fast as the lightning flash to his domain, the rays of the sun will still strike him as he passes, and that, even if he wrench up the ground itself, to pass to the lands below in that way, gold is not a metal to his liking, and will take him longer to disperse. Thus, should he attempt to open the earth in this pavilion, he must work slowly because of the gold bricks in the floor, while I can open the roof wide with another tug of the cord, and let in the sun like rain to cover him."

No one knows then what Azhrarn said or did. Perhaps it was so fearful that even writing it down, the words would scorch holes through the paper and those who read them go blind. No doubt he threatened Zorayas with all manner of horrors, and no doubt Zorayas assured him that even should he slay her she would still drag open the glass with her last strength.

At length Azhrarn grew very still, and stood in the darkest half of the chamber. While the sun arrow pierced the floor before him. He was at her mercy, the mercy of a woman of earth; the thought obliquely fascinated rather than angered him. He saw in it, too, possible avenues of escape. Besides, she had not yet opened the glass roof, this moment was the enjoyment of her pride, and the pride of mortals often destroys them.

After a while, Azhrarn said to her, in his most gentle and thrilling tone:

"You told me, daughter of Zorashad, that you had regained many of those things which your father's death lost you, all but one thing which you could not alter. What can it be, brave and intelligent maiden, which your vast power could not encompass?"

But Zorayas did not answer, only played with the velvet cord. Azhrarn smiled to himself. He knew very well that his voice, flattering and praising her, was the sweetest sound she had ever heard, and that, for all her ideas of vengeance, she could not bear to silence it just yet.

"It is well known," he therefore murmured, after a moment or so, "that demon-kind will make bargains. Should you decide to leave your ingenious roof closed and permit me to return to my kingdom, I could offer you vast power, enough to suit even your splendid nature."

Zorayas smiled, though the iron mouth did not.

"My armies, O Prince, are legendary, and avoided over the whole earth. Already I rule seventeen lands. In another year I could rule double that number if I wished. As for my other powers, you yourself are tasting them, are you not?"

"Indeed, wise maiden. I see my error. Nor is it any use to offer you the riches of the mines," Azhrarn said lingeringly, "the rubies and diamonds and emeralds at the earth's core?"

"I have jewels enough," said Zorayas. "You see, *I* wear none. But if I wished, I have so many slaves that in a year I could triple the number of gems in my treasury. Look up, at the costly brilliants you mistook for stars, O Prince."

"Indeed, insurpassable maiden. There is no bargain I can make with you after all. You have everything mortals yearn for—power, sorcery, wealth. Though why you do not yourself wear jewels puzzles me, and also this habit of masking your face and hands—and at this, Azhrarn saw Zorayas stiffen in her chair and her grasp tightened on the cord. "One request," said Azhrarn. "At least, O fair and noble one, let me look on the face of my vanquisher. Such beauty you must have that it will outshine the very sun you threaten me with, as even your beautiful eyes do now."

Zorayas gave a cry; it was full of pain and anger. Azhrarn needed no more; he stretched out his hand and the iron masked cracked right across and fell in pieces. Zorayas shivered, and with her free hand she hid her misshapen face.

Azhrarn laughed. Even in that extreme moment, the workings of the mind of the Prince were far from simple. No longer did he feel any animosity towards the poor grovelling dangerous creature on the throne. He was agreeably provoked by her learning, her cunning, her daring; he saw too, in a

woman of such power and warlike thoughts, a way to make
some delightful trouble in the world.

"O best of women," said Azhrarn in his most musical and
endearing tone, "I note there is, after all, a bargain I might
make with you. Open the roof now, and I, perhaps, may
perish and you may be revenged, and will then live out the
rest of your short life emptily, shut forever in your mask.
Men will bow before you and fight in your armies and tell
how you belittled Azhrarn, one of the Lords of Darkness, and
all your days neither man nor woman will tremble with desire
for you, kiss your lips, sing of your love. You will remain
cold as ice till the tomb eats you and the worm takes his
pleasure where you have had none." When he said this, the
girl shivered, though her hand on the velvet cord did not
falter. "There is another way," said Azhrarn softly, coming
nearer. "No magic in the world can remedy your ugliness,
but I, and I alone, have the power to make you beautiful.
More beautiful indeed than you have ever dreamed, more
beautiful than any other woman of earth, before or to be. I
can make you so lovely that whoever looks at you will ache
for you; men will happily die if they can lie one hour with
you. You will no longer have need of armies or slaves for
cities will open their gates in order to worship this face which
now you dare not show. Kings and princes themselves will
toil in the mines of earth to lay treasures at your feet in the
hope of one touch of your mouth."

Zorayas stared at the Demon for many minutes, and eventually whispered:

"If you can do this, I will let you go."

Then Azhrarn went round the chamber, avoiding the arrow
of the sun, and he took Zorayas' crippled hands, and the
gloves burst open and a scalding needle ran through her flesh
and into her whole body, and when she looked down, her
arms were straight and free of pain and white and smooth as
ivory, and her hands as graceful as doves, and her breasts like
flowers. Next he laid his palms against her face. The fire that
seemed to come from them was so awful it made her scream
out, her skin was like a land shaken by earthquake. Then the
fire died, and she saw the Demon stand smiling at her in a

way he had not smiled before, a smile almost of an awesome and indecipherable tenderness. She put her own hands to her cheeks, and felt the difference there.

"Go and find a glass," said Azhrarn.

And she obeyed him, for what the Prince of Demons promised, he abided by, and the bargain had been made.

Beyond the pavilion in the garden there was a little pool, and going there, holding aside the reeds with her white hands, Zorayas looked at her face as she had looked only once before, in the forest. What she saw was a beauty surpassing the gorgeousness of the leopard, more poignant than the plumage of the spring, like the moon, the sun, a beauty only a Demon could invent, a beauty to cast down the world. And she rose up, throwing aside her iron garments, clothed only in this miracle, and went back into the pavilion and closed the door on the daylight.

The floor was broken wide, and there Azhrarn stood with his passage to the Underearth safely before him, yet he, even he, had stayed for one last look at her.

And Zorayas gazed at him, and kneeled before him and said:

"Now kill me, my Lord, and I will die adoring you, and beyond death I will tell them, if they listen in the mists that wrap the world, that you are King of all the kings, my beloved and my master, whose curse to me is sweeter than the song of the nightingale."

Then Azhrarn raised her in his arms and laid his mouth on hers, smiling still that what he had created seduced him.

"You have seen yourself, daughter of beauty. Do you imagine that I would destroy anything I had made which was so fair?"

And thus the flesh of Zorayas, which had known only the hurt of old wounds, a lash, a rape, the rasp of iron, knew loveliness in itself, and the embrace of Azhrarn upon itself and within, the seal of dark night upon her morning.

PART TWO

4   Diamonds

Two brothers sat at chess in a high palace tower, while beyond the jasper lattice of the window, a vermilion sun went down.

The sun dyed everything with a soft blush, the crags and dunes of the desert country, the shining river with its tree-tasselled banks, the walls and high towers of the palace. Even the faces of the two young men were painted with its color, lending them a superficial likeness. For, though brothers, they were dissimilar, Jurim, the younger, being fair and yellow haired, the elder, Mirrash, of a stern and smoky darkness. Nor were their temperaments matched. Jurim was a poet and a dreamer, Mirrash a strategist who did not trust the world. Their father, an aristocrat of ancient family, had died and left his lands jointly to both sons, that each might contribute, from his opposite values, a complementary whole, since, differences apart, they loved each other well. Into their joint keeping also he had put the astounding hoard of diamonds which had been the source of his fame and wealth; half the hoard to each of them.

These diamonds. They were everywhere in evidence about the palace; upon the handles of chests and doors, inlaid in the mosaic paving. The cornices of the roof were set with diamonds, and the eyes of the twenty amber lions that mounted up the stairs between the cedars, and diamonds as small as peas flashed in the fountains, brighter than the water.

Indeed, it was a curious sight, to come from the barren

111

desert to the shining river, and see reflected there and going up beyond the bank, an equally shining house of many towers, sparkling with gold and priceless jewels, night behind it and its face to the sinking sun.

Tempting to robbers, one might suppose, such a house in the midst of the wilderness. Not so. The diamonds, renowned for their flawless beauty, also possessed a curse. Whosoever stole them would perish. It was this simple. The thief would discover the gem burning his pocket, his pouch, his coffer, his hand. The fine white daggers of its radiance would alter to the murky hue of old blood. In the night, the thief would feel strangling fingers at his throat, the gripe of poison in his belly, a stabbing like a blade in his heart. He would die with a blue face and many regrets. So the story ran. A few had disbelieved it, put it to the test, wished they had not, and were buried. Only as a sincere gift might the diamonds be received in safety and enjoyed.

Jurim had pondered sometimes on the gift of diamonds he would hang upon his bride, when he found her. There had been many beautiful girls, round breasts, antelope eyes, heavy silken tresses, but for a wife he would have one who was, to these wayside lilies, an orchid. He had heard a name whispered, he had not dared think of it too long. She was a queen, ruler of twenty lands, more lovely than loveliness, who paved her road with the broken hearts and bones of men—Zorayas, who, they said, had lain with a Demon in a starry pavilion. Zorayas, who could not be as maleficent as men asserted, for men's pictures of women were always too much of one thing, too little of another. Jurim, mere prince of a desert estate, could not aspire to an empress-queen, but to think of her, it amused and pleasantly pained him, like the dreams forgotten with dawn that left, nevertheless, their shadows behind upon his brain.

The sun was almost gone, a pink glimmer at the edge of a blue night. Then it seemed to be rising again.

"Look," said Jurim to his brother Mirrash, "either the day is coming back, or those are the lights of a caravan."

"A caravan which has lost the way, then," said Mirrash.

Soon enough, they heard the music, the silver bells, saw

the fringed swinging canopies, the flower decked beasts drawing the chariots, the warm lamps glowing in the dust, and they smelled the rising scent of incense and jasmin.

"It is more like a bridal procession than a caravan," said Jurim wonderingly, and his heart beat fast remembering his dream.

Presently the unusual caravan reached the gates. The servants and guards there seemed struck with amazement. A man ran into the tower, bowed low and cried:

"My lords, a strange thing. It is a lady from a far city. Her entourage has lost the road and begs for shelter until morning."

Jurim stood in silence, but Mirrash frowned.

"Who is she, this lady from the desert?"

"She prefers you do not ask her name," the servant said.

"And have you seen her face?"

"No, lord. She is veiled in a milky gauze down to her knees, but her robe is fringed with lapis lazuli and gold and her hands have emeralds on them, and she speaks as a lady does, as if she had silver in her mouth. Truly she is neither a robber nor a lewd."

"I think I guess what she is," said Mirrash. "For some while I have been expecting her. I wish we might turn her away, but she is cunning and a sorceress. No, let her in. Give her royal chambers and find food, but, for your own sake, avoid her eyes. For my brother and myself, we are away on business, you understand, and cannot greet the lady."

The servant went out, plainly afraid.

Jurim said; "Forbid yourself if you like, my brother, but not me. I am intrigued by her veil. What can she be hiding? Perhaps she is ugly and deserves our kindness."

"Once she was ugly, if the legend is true," answered Mirrash. "Now, few may look at her and keep a whole mind. She is Zorayas, the witch queen of Zojad, the doxy of demons and a scourge of men. No doubt she has heard of diamonds, too."

"Zorayas," murmured Jurim, and he paled.

He knew it fruitless to argue further, but in the quick soil of the romantic, his brother's warning put down no root. Zorayas and the dream were already in blossom there. In

Jurim's life there had come, so far, no huge calamity, no accident which would have shown him the nature of evil, and that Mirrash was wiser than he.

The lights and pipes of the entourage poured into the palace. A harp began to play a wistful melody in a chamber hung with silks that had diamonds stitched upon them. Here a veiled woman sat, all in white, toying with a rosy pomegranate and a golden knife.

Jurim entered the chamber, bowed low, and sent the servants out. He smelled the scent of sandalwood, jasmin and musk. He trembled, explained who he was, tried to see through the veil. The stranger laughed. One white arm appeared, its bones and flesh seeming sheathed in a skin of velvet. A gold bangle sang as it struck another of jade. Above was a white shoulder, burnished and succulent as a fruit, its pallor emphasized by one serpent of dark copper hair that slid back and forth, sometimes dipping again within the veil.

"Come and sit by me, lord prince," said the woman. "Should you like me to unveil? I will, if you desire it."

Jurim sat by her and requested that she would, and the woman brushed off the veil like smoke from her face and body.

Such a vision seared out upon Jurim, it was like lightning shattering a cloud. The blood drained from his heart and left him half dead and barely sensible. Her beauty was like death. It ate him away and filled him with itself. He could think of nothing but her beauty, see nothing else.

She touched his lips with hers. He tried to seize her. She pushed his hands gently away, and he could not resist her.

"I am Zorayas," she said, "and you are very handsome. But if we are to be friends, you must give me a gift."

"Anything I possess is yours," he said.

"The diamonds in this room," she said, "I counted them, there are fifty. Give me those."

Jurim ran to the walls. He tore the diamonds from the silks and heaped them in her lap. She drew his head to her breasts and caressed him, and presently she kissed his burning forehead, and she sighed: "How I love your hair, which is like gold, and your body which is strong like a stag's. How eager

you are, but first, will you give me the diamonds that hang
like grapes from the ceiling of the hall?''

Jurim ran to the hall. He was blind and deaf to all but her,
could only smell the scent of her, feel the cool rounded
litheness of her. He cut the diamonds from the ceiling, and
brought them to her. He let them fall about her in a rain and
buried his face in her hair.

She drew him down. He arrowed through the torrent of
her, foundered in the deep sea-cave of her loins. But there
was no end to the lure, no depth to the cave. The tide
returned to the mouth of Zorayas like flotsam.

Mirrash, meantime, had looked for him and found him
gone.

At the stroke of midnight, Mirrash went down silently and
listened at the door of the stranger's chamber. And there he
heard the voice of Jurim, pleading and promising. And every
so often another would whisper, and then at length Jurim
groaned with pleasure and could not keep back a cry like a
woman's.

Mirrash waited in the shadow. After a while, the chamber
doors were opened, and Jurim and Zorayas came out, walking softly as lovers. The face of Jurim was white, and his
eyes swam in blue hollows. But Mirrash averted his head
quickly, so that he should not see the appalling beauty of the
woman's face.

They went about the darkened rooms as if about a market,
and Zoray selected what she would have, diamonds large as
cups, and little faceted diamonds that blazed even in the
shade, and Jurim would tear and dig them from their places
and put them in the apron she had made of her skirt, and they
would laugh as if at some childish game. Eventually they
reached a room where the diamonds were clustered thick as
bees.

Mirrash stood outside the doors.

"Brother," he called, "remember. The hoard is only half
yours. You cannot take my half without my consent, and
your treasury is almost empty."

Jurim started, like a man waking from a dream.

Zorayas called sharply:

"Who is that scratching at the threshold? Is it a pet dog or cat that dares not come in? If it be a man, let him put terror aside. I am only a woman and will do him no hurt."

But Mirrash knew the danger too well, and kept out.

"Your pardon, lady, I cannot stay. I seek only to remind my brother that any gem he gives you that is not his to give will carry the curse to you as surely as if you had stolen it. And now, goodnight."

"These are sensible words," said Zorayas, though her voice was cold. "Pray keep tally, Jurim. I dislike the diamond curse. Give me nothing that is not yours."

Mirrash went to the great library, and puzzled there over books of sorcery and ancient writings, to no avail. He heard Zorayas' laughter like bright birds in the palace. And near dawn another of those despairing cries of sensuality that filled his heart with angry dread.

Dawn rose from the desert and turned the river to wine.

Zorayas stood upon the balcony and summoned a shadow from the air which gathered up her store of diamonds and bore them away in a curl of fire.

"Your gifts to me will soon be safe in Zojad, and I must follow them at once," Zorayas said to Jurim, stroking his hair. "Give me a lock of this gold too, to take with me. I shall not want to forget you too quickly."

"And I cannot bear it if you forget me," Jurim said. "Stay with me. For one more day, if no longer. Just one day. What is a day to you that means so much to me? One day and one night." And he embraced her.

"Ah, no," said Zorayas, "I must return to my city. I fear I have wearied you too long."

"No, No—" cried Jurim, holding her fast with a look of anguish.

"Yes and yes," said Zorayas. "Besides, I am unwelcome. Your brother is in a rage and spurns me. He denies you access to his share of the diamonds, and all yours are gone."

"I will entreat them from him. He will not refuse."

"Go, then, entreat him, my golden stag. But be hasty."

Jurim ran to Mirrash's chamber; he flung himself on his knees before Mirrash.

"Loan me a portion of your store of jewels, my brother, or she will leave me."

A look of loathing and distaste passed across the face of Mirrash, but he put the look aside.

"She will leave you in any event. Let her go, and thank the gods for her departure. She is a demon."

"I cannot bear that she should go."

"She has unmanned you," Mirrash said. "But, in truth, it is her common practice. You are no worse than the rest, Oh, my brother," he said, raising Jurim to his feet, "tell her to begone. The wound will heal. She is slow poison, lady death—"

Jurim said: "You refuse me then? It is your right. Only say."

"Yes, for your life I refuse you."

Zorayas only smiled when she heard.

"Well, I have half the prize. If you would see me again, sweet, you must send me all of it. And my kisses will be the dearer for delay."

She stood upon the parapet and a gilded chariot appeared from behind the sun, drawn by black dogs with wings. The sorceress stepped in the chariot and was borne away, and her entourage after her.

The grief that took Jurim then was terrible to see. He grew, in less than a month, pale and thin, a shrivelled grasshopper, who had been handsome and strong. He could not eat or sleep or rest, but paced about the palace all day and all night, and leaned on the pillars and walls from weakness and wept. He did not reproach Mirrash for withholding his share of their father's treasure, but Mirrash felt his brother's despair and illness as though they had been his own, and finally his resolve broke down.

"Come then, my poor brother, take all I have and all the palace has and give it to her, and ask her to come back to you." But his heart was cold iron in his breast, for he knew she had no pity, and her favor would only last a little while.

It did not even last so long.

Jurim went with a great caravan to Zojad; Zorayas took the gift from his hands, three hundred diamonds of many sizes. Then she bade him return to his desert, she would visit him presently. Jurim pleaded with her and she grew angry. She said he was not as she remembered but shrunken and ugly. Her soliders were set upon him. He came home beaten and bloody upon a bier and, catching hold of Mirrash's hand at the gate, he gasped: "Is she here before me?" and later, as he lay on his bed: "will she never come?"

"If her face matched her nature, she would not be fair," said Mirrash.

When he was a little recovered, Jurim would lie by the jasper lattice of the high tower, staring westward, watching for her. Sometimes the dust would swirl and take on the color of the sunset, and he would lift himself and cry that she was near.

There were no diamonds left to Jurim or to Mirrash, Zorayas had them all, all but one single blue diamond that was the ornament on the gate to their father's tomb.

As he lay by the jasper window, this diamond began to haunt Jurim. At last he begged Mirrash to take the gem and go to Zojad with it and request Zorayas to take pity on him.

"Our father will forgive me. He would not have me die of this love, which will otherwise kill me."

"Can you not try to fight this malignant spell?" Mirrash said. "She will give you nothing of herself any more, but she will bleed us dry of all our wealth—has she not reduced us sufficiently already?"

But he saw it was a sickness and a spell indeed, a worm in the heart of his brother, Jurim had grown so frail now, he would surely die. If this last action would comfort him, maybe give him strength to survive a little longer, then Mirrash could not deny him. And perhaps, though he had searched his father's library in vain, he might find some clever mage in the witch's city who would discover a cure for this malady of deadly love.

Mirrash took his brother's hand and pressed it, and told him he would do as he wished and to trust in the gods. Then Mirrash dug out the diamond from the tomb gate and hid it in a cloth bag about his neck.

5   A Love Story

The palace had fallen somewhat into disrepair. The source of the wealth of this house had been the diamonds, and they had been the luck of it too. Now leaves blew about the marble floors, and mice ran up from the granaries where the grain had become low and of poor sort. The landworkers had left the green fringe of the river, fearing poverty to come, and the fields ran to rank seed and the winds destroyed the good crop. Many of the precious things of the palace had been sold, and the stables of fine horses were empty, so Mirrash must travel on foot to the city.

He took no one with him on the long hard bitter road. He drank from rock fountains and little streams, and ate the dry fruits of the valleys like a common vagabond. No robbers molested him, he looked too wretched to be worth their trouble. He carried only two things with him: the hidden jewel and a little cake of salt.

After some days he reached Zojad and walked there through the broad streets and between the great statues till he came to Zorayas' palace.

At first they would not let him in, travel-worn as he was.

"How dares a vile beggar disturb the courtyard of our peerless queen?"

"Only tell her," said Mirrash grimly, "that the brother of Jurim is here, from the diamond house."

When these words were relayed to Zorayas she had him brought immediately before her. Not only for his talk of diamonds, either, but because she was curious to observe him, this prince who wisely had kept away from her till now.

She wore a dress sewn all over with diamonds, and diamonds in her ears, but the headdress on her copper hair was made from the skull of a lynx.

"Well, come close, and look at me at last," she said. But Mirrash had not been idle as he waited at the door. He had rubbed the cake of salt into his eyes to make them smart and water, so that still he should not be able to see her.

When she noted this, she was peeved at his intelligence, for she liked well the effect of her beauty, and would have been interested in its action upon Mirrash.

"What ails your eyes, Prince?"

"Tears, shed for my brother who is almost dead of you."

"I do not require his death. I do not ask it."

"No, lady. You ask for diamonds, of which, I hear, there were already plenty in your halls before you sought our house."

"True," she said, "but I will be denied nothing. I wanted your jewels because they were reckoned hard to get. And besides, they are the best gems I have ever come on for clarity and lustre. Nor any curse with them, either, since every one was a gift."

"A gift given by a young man in the prime of his youth, fair and vigorous, as you should know. He offered you all he had, of his wealth and of himself."

"It was not enough. As to his looks, I have been honored by the Prince of Demons, after whom all men seem only as ships without sails. But you mentioned diamonds?"

"Yes," said Mirrash, "I have one here. See," and he showed her the blue gem from the tomb. "This last jewel is mine, and I do not mean you to have it, lady, for you are already adamant and transparent enough."

"Well, one more or less is nothing," said Zorayas, "with princes as with jewels."

"As I thought," Mirrash answered, "you have no charity in you."

"Go ask the snow and the wind for charity, you will get none from me. Go and put out the sun with your salf-cake tears."

*   *   *

Walking from the mandragoran presence of Zorayas, Mirrash believed his brother as good as dead. But he went, nevertheless, and sought a much-respected sage in Zojad. He told him everything, and how Jurim would leave hold of life when he heard of Zorayas' ultimate indifference. But the much-respected sage merely blinked his vague proud eyes and said: "Every man dies soon or late. Bow to your destiny. You must accept the burden and the grave. My fee for this advice is one silver piece."

"The only fee you will get is my fist between your eyes," said Mirrash, "and you may take your advice and eat it," and he went instead to a temple and there told his story to the priests. They listened solemnly, but when he was done they only narrowed their hard greedy eyes and said: "Bring us a piece of gold and we will pray for your brother to our god."

"I have no gold with me," said Mirrash, "and if you will not pray without, your god is welcome to you and you to him." And he went away.

He walked the streets till dusk. Then he sat down for very weariness outside the door of a shoddy little tavern.

As he sat there the stars danced out like blue fire-flowers in the sky with a slender moon, and presently a man came shuffling down the street with a red lantern.

Pausing before the inn, this man began to shake his lantern and call for custom. He was muffled up but clearly was an old story-teller, and his price was a black penny.

No one came out of the inn to him, and he seemed about to turn away, when Mirrash stayed him and gave a piece of money to him.

"You are the first in this city who does not want diamonds or silver or gold from me," said Mirrash, "and your wares are dreams, of which never before did I have any need. But now I could surely do with a dream, a tale where all ends happily, or at least justly. Do you have such a one?"

The story-teller squatted down, set his lantern between them, and opening the lid, threw in a pinch of incense. He tapped his shadowy bearded chin with his bony finger.

"I will tell you the story," said he, "of Taki the Drin and the lady snake."

Lulled by the pleasing incense, the warmth of the lamp and the presence of the old man, Mirrash leaned his tired back against the inn wall, and listened.

"Down in the Underearth," said the story-teller, "where the sun or moon never shine, yet where it is always as bright as day, there lived a little Drin in a house of rock. His name was Taki, and he was very ugly, as indeed all the Drin take a pride in being. He was a maker of jeweled images, which sometimes he would give to the Vazdru princes, but mostly he left them in his house where he could look at them and speak to them. It is a known fact that there are no feminine demons of the class of the Drin, they are the spawn of stones and the whims of the demon lords. Sometimes a beautiful Eshva demoness will consent to lie with a Drin in exchange for some necklace or ring he has made, or a mortal woman who is ugly herself. But generally the Drin conduct their loving among the reptiles and insects of the Underearth. Taki, however, preferred the company of his images, for he loved most the glint and glimmer of gems and fine enamelwork.

"Then, one day, as Taki was walking through the forest of silver trees that lie to the north of Druhim Vanashta, the city of Demons, he saw a snakess sunning herself in the sunless air upon a bank of crystal poppies. This lady snake was like no other he had ever seen. Not creeping and dull, but slinking and mellifluous, and all her skin was like the marvelous layers of a cameo, now agate black, now emerald, now smoky shining pearl, and her eyes were like two topazes, and her tongue thrust like a flickering sword from the red velvet sheath of her mouth. Taki stared in wonder at this new glint and glimmer; from a wobbling of his joints and a beating of his heart and a dryness of his mouth he was aware he loved her. 'Beauteous lady snake,' said Taki, 'you are all I have ever dreamed of. Come to my house of rock with me and I will give you silk to lie on and dishes of cream to eat, and a ruby to wear about your long throat that a queen once wore.' But the snakess grimaced and turned her jeweled head. 'Be off, foul dwarf. Everything you say is a lie.' 'No, I assure you,' cried Taki. And he ran home and, filling his arms with silk and satin, gems and metal, he bore them to the snakess in the forest. 'Is that all you offer me?' the snakess snapped. Taki rushed at once to bring her more. At last, when the riches were piled as high as the trees, the snakess nodded, and permitted Taki to carry his gifts inside her burrow in the dark soil, and here she instructed him to crawl about, hanging up drapes and fixing gold pendants into the walls. When this was done and Taki turned to her eagerly, she said she was faint with hunger, so Taki ran out again and fetched a dish of honey and cream and another of fine black wine. When the snakess had appeased her hunger and thirst, she leered at the Drin, and told him to wait in the antechamber of her burrow while she prepared herself for the night. With a joyous heart and urgent loins, Taki paced about the antechamber (bent double all the while, for the roof was low), until suddenly an enormous black cobra entered. 'What oaf is cluttering up my mistress's apartment?' demanded the cobra, and seizing Taki in his jaws, he bit him terribly and thrashed him with his tail and soon slung him from the burrow and slammed the door.

"Taki crept away, and was for a long while very ill from the cobra's venom and his beating. When, after much time had elapsed, he returned to seek his love, certain there had been some mistake, he found the lady snake and the cobra entwined in the forest in a most definite fashion, and, looking up from their slitted eyes and pausing in their labor, they laughed at Taki and called him names until he fled.

"A frightful thing is love. Taki mourned and pined in his house of rock, his tears flooded the floors and his groans were so powerful they assumed the form of bats and flapped about the place in swarms. Finally, a miserable artistry took hold of him, and he began to make an image of his beloved, exactly life size, and resembling her in every detail. The image was of ivory and heavy silver, and decked with emeralds and jet. In the eyes he put topazes and garnets in the mouth. It weighed a great deal.

"Meanwhile, the beautiful snakess had come to think herself somewhat hasty. After all, no doubt she had not exhausted the treasure hoard of Taki. She would go back and entice him further, till he had no more to give. Then she could laugh at him indeed.

"The snakess set out for Taki's house with three black mice walking on either side of her to hold a parasol over her head, and a white mouse walking before to throw down paper flowers.

" 'Taki, dearest!' cried the snakess at the door, 'Taki, beloved. I have come to visit you!' But Taki was sobbing in a cellar and did not hear. The snake therefore glided into the house, sniffed haughtily at the furnishings and hissed greedily at the chests and boxes, and told the mice to swallow all the jewels they could see and never mind how she would retrieve them later. Inevitably, after wriggling about for an hour, the snakess came into the room where the jeweled image stood which resembled so exactly herself. Now, the image was incredibly lifelike, for the Drin are clever at such things, and as stunningly lovely as its original. The snakess was vain and loved herself before all else. Seeing the image, she gasped and a pang shot right through her, fang to tail. Forgetting everything, she stretched up and, festooning the image with her enamel body, she coaxed and crooned to it in amorous accents. Naturally, it felt as cold as she to the touch, and she was quite convinced it was her double, her sister, her predestined lover. But the image did not, of course, respond. In a paroxysm of frustrated anger, the snakess lashed with her tail, and the image began to topple. In another moment it had fallen smack on the back of the lady snake and crushed her to death.

"The three mice, stuffed with pearls and peridots, dashed out, but they met a raven on the way, who questioned them closely. The raven promptly called all his friends to a snake dinner in Taki's house, and it earned him the reputation of an immaculate host for many seasons.

"As for Taki the Drin, he encountered a centipede in the cellar, a wild young thing with some interesting notions about legs. He emerged from his seclusion much recovered, and swept the strange white bones from his house with a bemused forgetfulness, and put the fallen image away in a closet. He remembered the snakess only occasionally, though the ravens toast her succulence to this night, as they perch on the battlefields of men.''

The storyteller, having concluded his tale, added: ''Maybe not a joyous story, but at least a just one. You should perhaps give it some thought on your long road home.''

Mirrash caught the storyteller's sleeve and asked him who he was.

''A rich man once,'' said the storyteller, ''but my two sons gave all my wealth away to a beautiful snakess. Now I expect one of these sons will have to join me on my road, where the mists are thick. The other is stronger metal. But let him recall my story when he puts the diamond back in the gate.''

The old man moved about, and was gone up the street before Mirrash could collect himself. To be sure, then he ran to pursue him, but he could not find him at the corner, though the way ahead was straight and the walls of the alley sheer, nor was there any glow from the lamp.

''Can it be my dead father who came to advise and to warn me?''

It seemed to him also that just at the turning of the street, there had been two figures in the light of the lamp, one old, one young. . . .

A servant met Mirrash at dusk some days after, before the palace, and told him Jurim was dead. He had been lying by the jasper lattice in the tower, looking for his brother's return, when a black shadow had squeezed in there, and dropped a single diamond at his feet. And the shadow had cried: ''My mistress Zorayas is generous. Since you will never look on her again, she returns you a part of your gift—buy a farm with it, and grow fat.''

And when Jurim heard these words, he rose as if he were strong again, went to the hall and took down his father's sword and fell on it.

It was not far to go, only a little way from the wall, to the grave by the river. Mirrash did not weep at the fresh-turned earth and the poor stone marker, although, in the days of their wealth no prince but had a tomb hewn of marble, inlaid with gold and precious gems. Mirrash knelt by the spot. "Oh, my brother," he said, "oh, my brother, Jurim."

When the night burned its cloak in the sunrise and the day came to show him the desolation of the river fields and his neglected home, he went into the palace, to the library of sorcerous books a second time, and closed the door.

6   Love in a Glass

Many had died for Zorayas' sake, in one way or another. Some risked themselves on fearful enterprises to gain her attention, and perished, some slew themselves at her disfavor, and some she slew herself, for expedience, revenge, or even for amusement. Azhrarn had made her beautiful, and beauty went to her head like strong drink. Azhrarn had set his seal on her, and something of his fascinated wickedness, his delight in the sport of tangling the plans of mankind, had permeated her bones.

One new death meant nothing. She would have thought no more of Jurim, or his taciturn dark brother, if she had not begun to hear a strange story, which angered and interested her.

She had achieved some knowledge of the speech of birds, a frugal bizarre tongue, to human ears more like the conversation of dainty mad people than a language. Zorayas would sit beside a crystalline pool, admiring her reflection in her silver mirrors, while handmaidens combed her hair. And she would listen the while to the chatter of swallows, sparrows and wild ibis as they drank at the margin of the water, among the rushes of thin beaten gold. Presently, in this manner, she learned of an error she had made.

"Who is that bird in the water?" demanded a sparrow, new to the clear pool, and pecking wildly at its reflection.

"Splash!" cried another, throwing water over itself.

A third preened dolefully on the marble bank and said:

"There sits the queen of Zojad, who does not know she has been cheated."

"Cheated of what? Of a worm?" cried the first sparrow.

"Of a diamond."

"What is that?" asked an ibis.

"Diamonds are the things which fall from the sky to make everything wet," said a swallow. "But men catch them in jars."

"Tomorrow I shall lay an egg," said the ibis inconsequently.

"Mirrash has cheated Zorayas of Zojad," said the third sparrow. "He kept from her the one diamond, which was worth all the rest that she has, the blue diamond from his father's tomb-gate."

"Worms are to be found near tombs," said the first sparrow, "but I suppose no one will thank me for this generous instruction."

"My egg will be larger than any egg ever laid before," said the ibis.

"The diamond of which Mirrash has cheated Zorayas is worth all the diamonds of the earth," said the third sparrow and, ruffling his feathers, he flew away.

"Such rudeness," said the swallow, "but I forget why."

It seemed to Zorayas that the sparrow which spoke of the diamond had been unusually lucid. She wondered if Mirrash himself had sent the bird, some final boast to her that he had refused her the last gem and the best.

"But he may alter to me," said Zorayas. "We shall see."

True, Mirrash had not looked at her, had not allowed the irresistible spell of her beauty to enslave him. True, he would be particularly on his guard against her now. She remembered his cunning with the cake of salt. But she would not rest till she had what she wanted, the last diamond, and his submission. She did not like men to defy her, she, who once had suffered from men so cruelly; like some disease, she had set herself to curb them in her world, to cauterize and make them harmless.

Zorayas saw she must return to the desert palace by the shining river, but not in her former guise. Not a milk-veiled lady under a fringed canopy, accompanied by bells and music

and the scent of incense. Nor would she return as she had
gone away, a sorceress in some supernatural conveyance
drawn by unlikely beasts. This time, Mirrash should have no
warning.

A storm roared across the desert. Dust rose into the sky.
The sun became a red blur, the shining river grew dull as
unpolished bronze, and the trees groaned in the wind.

Someone knocked on the gate of the palace, of which all
the shutters were closed and bolted. Someone struck the iron
of the gate, and wept, and cried for help. At length a porter,
on the instructions of the steward, opened the gate a crack
and dragged into the confine of the inner court a dishevelled
creature. A poor dancing girl she seemed to be, lost from
some caravan, her cheap finery in rags, her body scored and
bleeding from the harsh beating of the sand, her face ob-
scured by dust and tears and cascading dusty hair of the
deepest black. She huddled in the court, kissing the feet of
the porter, and next the feet of the steward who had rescued
her from such a vile death in the storm.

There were few servants left in the palace, most were gone
as the riches were gone. The old steward conducted the
dancing girl to a secluded room, showed her a couch and
ewers of water, and had bread and wine put before her. The
girl thanked him again and again.

"Pray tell me," said she, "who is your master, that I may
also bless his name."

"My master is Mirrash, upon whom grave sorrow has
come. He would profit from any blessing, great or small."

"And is his heart heavy with grief? Some dear one lost,
perhaps? Good sir," said the girl, modestly lowering her
gaze, "I look a poor sight now, but only permit me to bathe
and tidy myself, then let me attend the bedchamber of your
lord. I have learned many curious arts of love as a part of my
trade. Maybe I can console him, if only for an hour or two.
Do not deny me for it is my dearest wish. If you think it
proper," she added, "I will demonstrate firstly to yourself
what I am able to perform."

The old steward was past the age for such exercise, and

suggested he would be content to watch the dancing girl at her bath. This was agreed on, and the steward was extremely gratified, for though he never quite glimpsed her face through her hair, he had an excellent view of everything else, and the girl was unusually and compellingly beautiful. Presently he grew affable, and let her persuade him that she be taken, unknown to Mirrash, to his bed, there to await the prince.

'Certainly,' thought the steward, as he stowed the succulent damsel in the bedchamber, 'I shall get a reward for this.'

Mirrash had for some months spent the larger part of every day in the great library of the house, though at other times he shut himself in a cellar room of the palace, which he always kept securely locked. From this room had issued occasional strange sounds and musky odors, and a flicker of weird lights. Tonight also, Mirrash came late from the cellar to his bed, and it might be supposed the eager dancing girl was growing weary of the delay.

The lamps burned dim. Mirrash entered the chamber, threw off his garments and lay down in the bed. No sooner had he done so than he felt a sinuous touch and started up.

"Do not be alarmed, my lord," said a sweet voice next to his ear. "I am your slave, here to serve you gladly from the well of my love."

At this, Mirrash lay back and said:

"Whoever you are, you are welcome to my life."

Then the girl, encountering his face in the red gloom of the lamps, gave a start, for the eyes of Mirrash were bound with cloth.

"Why, my lord, is this some game?"

"Indeed, no," said Mirrash. "I have gone blind."

The caressing hands of the dancing girl were still.

"Some new trick," she muttered. "How can this be?" she added.

"I have thwarted a powerful sorceress," said Mirrash, "Zorayas of Zojad, perhaps you have heard of her name? The demons love her, and for sport attacked me and blinded me."

The gentle fingers of Mirrash's companion had roused and were already on the bandaging.

"Come my lord, let me see. I have a little cleverness in healing. Perhaps I may aid you."

"No, on no account," said Mirrash, drawing away. "Do not trouble yourself."

At this, the girl turned her attention to other areas of the prince's body, but he sadly told her: "Kind maiden, this, too, is useless. Not only have the demons rendered me sightless but also impotent." Yet the girl, finding things quite to the contrary, assured him he was mistaken. "Ah, take no note of such outward signs, this is how the demons torment me. The vessel is filled to overflowing, but no sooner shall we begin to drink than I will find the wine is mysteriously vanished without trace, and the vessel flaccid and empty."

"Now, my lord," chided the girl, "let us not be overly pessimistic. Perhaps the demons have relented in their spell."

No doubt this was so, for, after some further urging, the sword found the sheath, and Mirrash enjoyed her lustily.

Zorayas—who, but she? Even the expedient storm had been her conjuring—was not inclined to join her enemy in his passion, but awaited her moment, demonstrating such cries and movements as he might think feasible under the circumstances. At length, as the supreme instants of congress overtook Mirrash, Zorayas snatched the bandaging from his eyes.

Thus, despite his evasions, at the height of his pleasure, he must behold her and the adhesive enchantment of her face, framed now by red copper hair, the black wig flung aside.

Mirrash moaned and sank down, and cursed himself, and her, and then gazed again at her, and entreated she would forgive his curses, declaring he would be glad to die for her.

"That is not necessary," said Zorayas, "but some small token. . . ."

"Anything I have is yours, as I am."

"The thing you would not give me, the blue diamond you boasted of, worth all the rest."

Mirrash stared at her. His dark eyes were bloodshot and wildly swimming. It delighted her to see him so utterly reduced.

"The diamond is in the gate of my father's tomb. Take it. Only let me kiss your mouth again."

"Later, perhaps," said Zorayas. "For now, the diamond will suffice."

They rose. He led her down and through shadowy gardens where the storm had died, beside a shimmering pool, to the marble portico of the mausoleum. Here on the iron gate, something flared with a cool blue light. A great diamond, and something else beside.

"Now what is this?" asked Zorayas, white as ivory and red as wine in the dark. "Some other trick? Come, I know you cannot lie to me now."

"Lie to you? I would rather cut out my tongue." He fell to his knees before her and clasped her ankles.

"When you showed me the diamond in my palace, it was without a setting."

"Yes," he said, "I prized it from the setting, this oval mirror, tall and broad as a man, which hangs upon the tomb gate."

Zorayas stepped past him, and went to inspect the object on the gate, and noted it was a polished oval of blue metal, as long and as wide as he had stipulated, with the diamond burning at its center.

"A mirror, you say," Zorayas questioned. "I can see no reflection."

"That is but the case, and the jewel is set in the case. The mirror is within, but no one may look on it. It was my father's glass, a magic thing he found in an ancient temple. Even he never opened the case to glance at it."

"Why not, pray?"

"It was the toy of demons," Mirrash said, crawling after her, and pressing his lips to her heel. "The glass is said to reveal an ultimate truth. No man dares chance such a sight. But, lady, let me extract the jewel for you, and then—"

"Leave it be," said Zorayas, frowning. "Are men yet so craven? Demons are wise, but humanity need not fear them if humanity will be courageous. I shall take diamond and case and mirror too. For if no man dares look into the glass, *I* dare to do so. Come, cease grovelling there, and fetch it down for me, unless you are a weakling."

Mirrash obeyed her. He staggered under the mirror's weight,

but set the case, firmly closed, at her feet, and then tried to kiss her mouth which also remained firmly closed. She thrust him from her.

"You are only a dog," she said. "Do not be less than one."

"Lady," he cried, "do not trust the mirror, it will harm you. Let me lie with you again, I am on fire—pity me—"

"You are not worth my pity," said she, "you are a fool."

She snapped her fingers. There came a rushing sound. A chariot drawn by black, snake-headed swans swept up and bore both her and her prize away.

Mirrash stood alone in the garden. Soon he went to the pool. A little sparrow, trained by magic to speak certain words, ruffled its wings as Mirrash bent to the water and bathed his eyes. The bandage had been a ploy. Before entering his bedchamber he had dropped inside his eyelids a certain ointment that blurred and distorted his sight. All things this night had appeared as hectic inchoate monstrosities, now elongated, now bloated, as if seen through a warped crystal. Even the wondrous face of Zorayas had appeared so. Though her touch had fired him and her body pleasured him, that devastating submission her face exacted had missed him like an arrow shot wide.

Truly, he thought, her face had resembled her nature tonight. Would his brother Jurim had seen her in such a fashion.

Zorayas dug out the diamond and hung it about her white throat. She did not delay to investigate its powers; she had become too interested in the hidden mirror that had framed it.

She made certain preparations. She was proud but not stupid. She sensed already a great force of energy in the oval of blue metal, power striving to pierce the case and enlighten whoever could confront it. An ultimate truth. Who did not hanker after such? It could make her name more terrible than even now it was. And in her own eyes it would also enlarge her. Zorayas, the most beautiful and the wisest woman of earth, the lover of the Prince of Demons, the possessor of an Ultimate Truth. Like many before her, and since, whose confidence had withered in their earliest years, even the

bright bricks of success had not built a stronger house for her.
Within, in the lowest region of her soul and mind, unknown
to herself, she was still a small voice crying for another glory
to salve her hurts. She must better the best, none must
withstand her, she must conquer what others dare not face,
drink seas and trample mountains. She would never rest till
death, the last battle, made mockery of all her victories.

She went to her tower of brass. She ringed it within and
without with spells and talismans and occult symbols. She
burned aromatics and sprinkled the floor with wine and blood,
and drew there the signs of power. She purified her body,
bathed and anointed herself, and spoke words of protection.
She stood naked, the beautiful sorceress, her long hair empty
of jewels, falling about her like a burning briar.

She eased the hinges of the blue metal case with oil, she
slid a slender knife between the case and what lay beside it.
She freed the clasps.

She moved back, and let the tall mirror, the height of a
man and as broad, containing an Ultimate Truth, fold open.

Unblinking, arrogant, she stared into the cold sheen of
glass.

And saw—

Merely her reflection.

Zorayas' mouth whitened, she clenched her hands. She
snarled.

She had been *cheated*.

Then, despite her rage, something caught her eye. What
caught it was the pure miraculous loveliness of the image in
the mirror, her own. Zorayas hesitated. Her hands slackened,
and she let out her pent breath in a slow sigh. How beautiful,
how beautiful she was. She had never fully seen before her
own perfection. There had been the silver mirrors, highly
polished, showing her enough to marvel at, there were the
crystal pools where she might lean to glimpse her glorious
face between the gold reeds and the alabaster flowers, as once
before, at the first, she had leaned to glimpse it. And yet, not
one of those reflections could compare with this, not one had
shown her so much. Her whole self, clad in visual music, a
mirage of flame and ice, metal and silk.

Zorayas laughed, stretching forward, her anger quite forgotten. No glass had even been this clear or this accurate. Eyes laughed back at her like dark flowers against a sunrise, a mouth laughed like a rose. Her body, an orchid on its slender dual stem, the hollows flushed with a glow as if of candleshine, the penciled line between limbs and torso, the round brush strokes of the pelvis, the fox that crouched at her groin, and above, the white innocence of the breasts with their twin citadels of knowledge.

Ah, the gift of Azhrarn the beautiful, this feast of beauty. Zorayas seemed to fall towards the outstretched arms of the creature before her, which silently beckoned and received. Her palms touched the palms in the mirror, her belly melded to the form of the white pelvis, her breasts flew to the mirror breasts, a meeting of doves. She pressed her mouth to the glass and, for a moment, felt a warm vibrant texture against her body, a mouth that hungrily offered itself to hers.

With a cry, Zorayas threw herself back.

An ultimate truth? Perhaps she had discovered it. That she loved herself, if none other. And then she perceived a new thing. That the mirror, which reflected her so well, reflected nothing else of the chamber, not a ray, not a shadow, not a hanging, not the symbols on the floor nor the smoke-wreathed sigils of the walls. Only Zorayas did the mirror show. Only she.

Zorayas thrust at the case of the blue metal and it slammed shut. She took up her mantle, and fled from the tower of brass.

Three days and almost three nights passed before Zorayas returned to the tower. During those three days and nights she did many of the things which it had become her practice to do. She rode with her hounds—she hunted men rather than beasts, those slaves foolish enough to offend her—she travelled her gardens and her pleasure rooms, pausing to caress a gemmed book, a jewelled wrist. She called together the scholars and astrologers of Zojad, and argued and debated with them. She had actors perform a play for her, and one who amused her she lay with and another whom she did not like so well she hung from a rafter by his ears and his tongue.

She had grown cruel and luxurious. Hardship had taught her, a Demon's couching had ensured the rest.

She purchased eighty flamingoes to clothe the pools of her garden. She ordered a feast at which every course was a different color, the red baked meat of crabs and rosy fish and red wine in ruby goblets, white meats with almonds and white wine in porcelain cups, green cakes of angelica, grapes and candied cucumbers and green sherbets in emerald thimbles. And one course for her enemies, a blue course of poisonous cyanose wafers and undiluted indigo in drinking vessels shaped like sapphire skulls.

But all the while she did these evil and exotic things, she was remembering the closed mirror in the tower. The memory skimmed across her brain like a bird, crawled in and out there like a serpent. She inspired, in those three days and nights, no beauty to equal what she had seen in the glass, nor did she inspire quite such fear, not with all her games, as the fear that had clutched her vitals as she fled her own image.

On the third night, she called musicians to play for her. The song reminded her of a woman's body gracefully dancing. White peacocks walked in the garden, their whiteness recalled another whiteness of flesh. Zorayas clapped her hands. Her collection of beasts was brought. She went to the huge gilded cages. Spotted panthers with eyes of green bronze, tigers of cinnabar with eyes of orichalcum. And in the eyes of each, a tiny reflection.

It was a terrible craving in her she must satisfy, to look once more in that tall glass. Maybe her fancy, her own magic, had invested it with qualities it did not possess. Yes, no doubt, that was it. If she visited the tower of brass, opened the case of blue metal, she would see simply a large and lustrous mirror, flattery to her exquisite beauty, but no more.

The moon had set. She climbed the stair of the tower in darkness, went in at the door of the sorcerous room in the dark. The case of the great mirror glowed like a still blue lightning. Zorayas crossed to it, freed the clasps, stood back to let it swing open.

She did not need a lamp. The mirror shimmered, glimmered. Something wondrous looked out at her.

Zorayas smiled, she could not help herself. The image in the mirror smiled.

Zorayas caught her breath, the image likewise.

Irresistibly drawn, Zorayas took three steps towards the image; the image took three steps towards Zorayas. They gazed, lips parted, eyes wide. The hands of the image slid downward, and parted the fastenings of the golden dress. Two white moons rose from the golden silk. The image in the mirror whispered: "Come nearer, beloved. Come nearer."

Zorayas stared, at the image, at her own hands—still by her sides; her own breasts—covered by the silk. The image had done something she had not. The image had spoken.

"Who are you?" Zorayas cried, "and what are you?"

"Yourself," whispered the image. "Come to me, my beloved. I seethe and pine and ache for you, beloved of beloveds."

Zorayas trembled. Her eyes filled, she could not breathe. Before she knew it, she had run half the distance toward the mirror, her arms outstretched. A few steps more, and she could press herself again to those familiar valleys and hills, that fragrant landscape which she knew better than any land she had conquered, better than any lover she had ever lain with. But she forced herself to a halt, before the hands which reached out to her could touch her own.

Zorayas ran again from the sorcerous tower, and locked the door behind her. She wept. It was with a sense of desolation rather than of escape or fear that she descended the stairs.

She flung the key of the tower door into a deep well.

Mirrash had made the glass, made it especially for Zorayas. It had been forged in cold fires and shaped with burning words. Mirrash had become a sorcerer, letting the ancient books teach him, dedicating himself to his task. It was not so much vengeance he sought, as to rid the world of the wickedness of Zorayas. Jurim was dead, but there would be other Jurims, that Zorayas would prey on, if she remained. He had puzzled some while over the tale the story-teller had recounted, puzzled too if the story-teller were really some phantom messenger, broken loose from the limbo of souls in order to warn and advise, or merely a wise man, cunning and well informed.

At any rate, the tale had been apt—beauty abusing what worshipped it, beauty seduced by its own vision, bringing itself to death.

As the snakess had come on an image which exactly resembled herself, so Zorayas should come on one, in a mirror. And the mirror would not be mortal. The mirror would draw life from what looked there, the mirror would live, in its own way, and would desire, love, yearn for, plead with, compel the object of its life.

On the night she had come to him, he had predicted Zorayas' behaviour and so outwitted her, but now he was not certain he could guess her mind. He did not know how long he must wait. Zorayas was strong-willed and powerful, perhaps she could resist the mirror's spell.

The palace in the desert fell into decay. The shining river was clogged with weeds and shone no more.

Perhaps Zorayas would exercise her spite upon the giver of the gift—

But Zorayas had forgotten Mirrash. She had forgotten everything but one thing. Her actions had become those of a doll on strings, yet she did much. She conquered five more lands, riding at the head of her armies. She had built for herself enormous citadels, mansions and statues. She turned from human lovers and lay with beasts. A third of a year a lion was her lord; his mane was plaited with jewels; in his eyes as he mounted her, she saw reflections.

One night, she wished Azhrarn would come to her. She burned rare smokes, and spoke certain words. She dared not summon now, could only cajole. Perhaps he would have come, the Prince of Demons, if he had been aware of her beseeching. But he had turned from her to other things, turned from her perhaps for a few days, a few months of Underearth—a mortal's lifetime—and looking back, he found her gone.

Time wearied Zorayas. Though she had the face and body

of her youth, she felt an old woman, exhausted and bored by
the world. It seemed there was nothing she could not do, and
nothing indeed she had not done. No enemy could withstand
her, no lover deny her, no kingdom defeat her. Perpetual
success beat her to her knees. Now the small voice of uncertainty within her did not cry for victories to salve its hurt; it
murmured: ''What worth was all this labor, that has not eased
me?''

She had no love for life, had never truly had any. In fact,
she would have been happier with less, striving and sadness
had made her strong where power had sated her.

The last flickerings of her determination to survive died in
orgiastic banquetings, in sorcerous madnesses that dyed the
night sky green or the blue hills red, and grew the tails of
monkeys upon the rumps of men, in strange excursions over-
land on a ship with wheels, or across the sea in a big-sailed
chariot drawn by dolphins.

At length the ultimate ennui descended on her.

She lay like one already dead. Seven days she lay on her
couch. And then one memory quickened her.

Zorayas called three giant men, her slaves. She took them
to the tower of brass and instructed them to break in for her
the locked door.

It did not take long, she had always realized it would not.
The act of throwing the key into the well had been a gesture.

When the door gaped, Zorayas sent the slaves away, and
went up alone into the room.

The mirror opened. There could be no doubt. The image
stood naked, wrapped in its dark red hair, motionless. The
eyes of the image were closed. It made no sign, no movement. It looked like a marvelous icon, as though it were
dead.

''I am here,'' Zorayas said. ''You are all I seek, and all I
wish for.''

She unfastened her mantle and stepped from it, naked now
as the image.

The lids of the image raised themselves slowly. A dawn
broke upon the magical face. It raised its arms, the arms of
Zorayas: ''Come to me then.''

Not running this time, nor holding back, Zorayas walked towards the mirror until breast met breast, limb met limb, palm touched palm. For an instant she felt the cool resistance of glass, then the glass seemed warmed and melting. Warm eager hands encircled her, squeezing her more closely to a warm breathing form. Her own hands swam and fiercely clasped a smooth slenderness. Mouth fused with mouth and thigh with thigh. Zorayas abandoned herself to an ultimate truth of matchless ecstasy that dissolved her in its fire—

The slaves in the garden turned at the weird glare in the sky. A rose-colored sun was being born inside the upper room of the tower of brass. It swelled and brightened, became an intolerable whiteness that pained the eyes of all who saw it. A shattering explosion followed.

After the thunder and terrible light had faded, those who crept to the tower of brass found only a stump of charred metal. Nothing else remained. Not a tile, not an amulet; not even a fragment of glass, of bone, or of woman's hair.

Mirrash came to the palace where formerly had ruled the queen of Zojad, now so mysteriously vanished from the earth. Some said she had been carried off by the Drin, others that she had abandoned her wickedness to become a traveling holy woman.

There was bickering in the city and in the palace. The kings of many lands were on the march once more, anxious to break the yoke beneath which Zorayas had held them. There was some further trouble too, for in the night a lord, who had appropriated one of the large diamonds which Zorayas had won from Jurim, had been found horribly dead.

As the ministers squabbled on the steps of the tall throne, where once they would have drawn their very breath in anxiety of the woman who sat there, a dark stern man entered the hall. How he got by the guards no one knew, but discipline was lax, and the soldiers were deserting in squadrons.

"I am Mirrash," the stranger said. "I hear someone has died already of the diamond curse. You will have more deaths unless you listen to me."

And he reminded them of the bane the diamonds carried,

that only those to whom the jewels had been sincerely given might enjoy them in safety.

"My brother gave the diamonds to Zorayas, but she has gone away. If any of you to whom they were not given should attempt to keep them, they will kill you, one by one."

As always, somebody scoffed and said he scorned the curse, and took a diamond collar and put it around his neck. Mirrash shrugged, and soon the man was discovered, blue in the face and unequivocally deceased.

Then they were in a hurry to give the gems back to their rightful owner. Diamonds poured into the casks and boxes Mirrash had brought with him, the casks and boxes were loaded into carts, and mules and outriders attached to them.

Presently Mirrash, with all his family's hoard of treasure restored, got on to his new horse, which Zorayas' steward had insisted he take, and rode away towards the desert, grimly smiling, with his back to the setting sun.

BOOK THREE:
The World's Lure

PART ONE

1   Honey-Sweet

She was so beautiful, and so gentle, that they called her
Honey-Sweet—though her name was Bisuneh. Her hair grew
to the ground; it was the pale delicate greenish-yellow of
primroses. She was the daughter of a poor scholar, and they
lived in a city by the sea. Honey-Sweet Bisuneh was soon to
be married, to the handsome son of another poor scholar.
While the fathers had muttered in the library over antique
volumes, the daughter and the son had wandered in the shady
garden among the roses and beneath the burnished leaves of
the ancient fig tree, and first their hands had touched, and
next their lips and their young bodies, and presently their
hearts and minds. There followed various promises and pledg-
ings, various exchanges of gifts. Since weddings were expen-
sive, foxy prostitutions of art took place—one old scholar
composing a lament on the death of a lord which brought
tears to the eyes, and considerable silver; another old scholar
dedicating his translation of some long dead poet to a prince
in a white palace, which brought gold. Both the scholars'
wives were dead. They looked at their children fondly, this
invasion of youth and passion in their dry houses scented only
with the dust of books.

It was a month before the wedding.

Beautiful Bisuneh and two pretty friends sat in the twilight
garden, under the ancient fig tree. Overhead the stars grew
bright, and far below the sea rippled like the back of a dusky,
slowly swimming crocodile.

"I know a spell," said one pretty friend. "It will show how many children you will have." The other friend was afraid, did not like spells. "Oh, it is a simple thing. A few words, a lock of Bisuneh's hair, a pebble thrown."

Still the friend was reluctant, but Bisuneh was curious. She wanted, she declared, three tall sons, and three slender daughters. No more, no less.

So, under the dapple of the fig leaves and the stars between, they made their magic. It was such a small one. Generally it would have gone unnoticed. But to a demon, the slightest whiff of magic was like a lure.

One of the Eshva was not far off, adventuring on the night time earth, idling by the dark waves of the shore. He scented the spell like a well remembered flower. The Eshva were the most oblique of all the echelons of the Underearth, and the most inclined to dream and to romance, and this one no different.

In his male shape he climbed the shore road, clothed in the gathering night, now floating in the air. He reached the wall of the garden, looked through a crack a bird could scarcely have found.

He observed two pretty girls, one radiant girl.

A pebble leaped and rang on the stone paving.

"Why," said the first pretty girl, "there are no children here at all. And yet, wait—yes. One child. A daughter!"

"Only one," wailed the other pretty girl. "Can it mean Bisuneh will die? Or her husband will die?"

The first girl slapped her angrily.

"Silence, fool! It means the charm has failed. What is this talk of death?"

But Bisuneh solemnly shook her head. "I do not fear. It is just a silly game. Three days ago I visited the wise-woman who lives on the Street of the Silk Weavers. She told me neither I nor my husband should die till we were very old, unless the sun should sink in the east, which is surely to say nothing can harm us, for who can suppose the sun will ever do that?"

Then the two friends laughed, kissed Bisuneh, and put white flowers into her hair. Another laughed also, beyond the wall, silently. But no one was there, only a smooth black cat running away along the shore road, with a flash of silver eyes.

The Eshva entered a room of black jade, threw himself down before a shadow there, kissed its feet, and the kiss bloomed like a violet flame in the shade.

The Eshva raised his glowing eyes. Azhrarn read this within them: A walk in the dream of the earth, the world of men, and a shape there formed like a maiden. Her skin was like the white heart of an apple, her hair a fountain of primroses.

Azhrarn fondled the Eshva's brow and neck. He himself had been a long time from the earth, many months, perhaps a mortal century.

"What else is she like?"

The Eshva sighed at the touch of Azhrarn's fingers. The sigh said this: Like a white moth at dusk, a night-blooming lily. Like music played by the reflection of a swan as it passes over the strings of a moonlit lake.

"I will go and see," said Azhrarn.

The Eshva smiled and shut his eyes.

Azhrarn went through the three gates, black fire, blue steel, chill agate. As an eagle, he flew across the purple plain of the night sky; a smear of dead crimson marked where the sun had long since fallen. He came to a city by the sea, to the small garden of a small house. The black eagle settled himself upon the roof. He watched with his brilliant sideways bird's eyes, now one, now another.

An old scholar drank wine under a fig tree. He called: "Bisuneh!" A girl stepped out. The scholar patted her hand, showed her an entry he made in a huge old book, at a place where the page was sign-posted by a pressed papery flower. Light from a window spun the color of green limes in the girl's fair hair. The eagle watched motionless, beak like a curved blade.

"See, here is your mother's name, and mine," said the scholar. "And here is your name and his, the man you are to wed, who shall be my son."

The wings of the eagle softly stirred, no more sound than the breeze made in the leaves of the fig tree.

Presently the old man and the girl went in. A lamp began to glow in a window near the roof, and then went out. The girl disrobed, clad only in her hair, lay down in her narrow bed and slept.

In her sleep, a wonderful scent drifted to her. She heard tapping far off on an open shutter, a noise like leaves walking. A voice sang into her ear, pleasant as velvet. Bisuneh started awake. She stole to her window and looked out.

A dark man stood below in the garden; she could not make him out. Wrapped in her hair, in the shadow of her window, he seemed to her also a shadow. Only his eyes, catching some mysterious light, gleamed.

"Come down, Bisuneh," he called softly. His voice was like no other she had ever heard. She almost leaned out to him, almost turned to seek the door and the stair and the way into the garden—but a cold drop fell into her brain which said: Beware. "Come, Bisuneh," said the stranger below. "I have loved you a long while, I have traveled many miles to find you. One glance of your eyes is all I ask, maybe one compassionate chaste kiss from your maiden's mouth."

The flesh of Bisuneh answered the voice as the harp would answer when the musician takes it up; her nerves and her instincts impelled her towards the door or to leap from the window down into the stranger's arms. But she would not.

"You must be some evil spirit to summon me thus," she told him. She slammed the shutters closed and bolted them. She opened a little casket and drew out a necklace of coral her lover had given her, and she spoke to it, and soothed it and kissed it, using it as a charm against any wickedness the night might threaten her with. Very soon she felt a delicious tension slacken in the air. Slumber overcame her. She fell asleep with the coral necklace in her hands, and in the morning thought her fear a dream.

It amused Azhrarn to be thwarted by this startled virtuous girl. The first time, it amused him. Her strength of will, her foolish sensible disbelief in him, delighted him. The first time, delighted him.

He returned at dusk the next night. There were guests in the garden, merry-making. Later they went away, and the girl stood alone staring out towards the sea, with the coral necklace round her throat.

Bisuneh, smelling the perfume of the lilac colored roses, musing, suddenly noticed a woman standing on the shore road. She seemed to evolve from nothing, this woman, yet, becoming distinct, appeared more vital and more real than anything else. Bisuneh could not take her eyes from the woman. She was impressive, imperious, her hair was blue-black, and her eyes brilliant. She had no modesty, no timidity or reserve. She came straight to the garden wall, and, gazing at Bisuneh with her strange mesmeric gaze, she said: "Let me tell your fortune, little bride."

The voice of the woman was deep and melodious. She reached across the wall and took Bisuneh's hand, and at her touch, Bisuneh's heart began to pound, she could not tell why.

"I hear," said the woman, "you fear men. This is unfortunate, since you are to be wedded."

"I fear no man," faltered the girl.

"One you feared, last night," said the woman.

The girl paled, remembering.

"It was a dream."

"And was it so? Come, why did you fear him? He meant no harm to you."

The girl shivered. The dark woman leaned across the wall and lightly kissed her. It was like no kiss this shy girl had ever known. The kisses of her lover, the deep hunger of youth, had not moved her as did this brief brushing of the lips. Yet, at the kiss, she felt again the recollected alarm of the previous night, her senses tugging one way, her reason another. She snatched free from her hand, her mouth.

"Who are you?" she asked, knowing somewhere deep within herself and failing to comprehend her own knowledge.

"A reader of fate," said the woman. Her face had changed, become remote and cruel. "You are stubborn, and stubborn-

ness angers the gods. Still, you have been promised a cheerful old age, have you not? Unless the sun sinks in the east.''

The woman turned and walked away, but there came a
great swirling of sea wind that billowed her cloak, and abruptly
she seemed to vanish.

The girl ran indoors. She took an amulet from a box; a
holy man had given it to her mother. She hung it about her
neck, and prayed that demon-kind would cease troubling her.

The woman had been Azhrarn. He could put on the form of
anything, being what he was. The girl had refused him twice
now, and in two guises. Mortals did not refuse Azhrarn.
His voice, his eyes, his touch produced an alchemy that
thrilled their nerves, infatuated them, outlawed their wills.
But Bisuneh struggled, and her struggle had ceased to enter-
tain him. Her virtue had become a silken sheath to rip, her
beauty a cup to drain.

There was one last trick. It pleased him. He had seen her
betrothed in the garden among the guests. Now Azhrarn
fashioned for himself an exact semblance of this lover, and
knocked on the shutters of her window an hour after midnight, wearing the semblance like a cloak.

She crept to the window, afraid. In a whisper she asked
who it might be. She heard a voice she knew. She opened the
shutters, he caught her in his arms. The joy of his strength
fired her as even her love for him had not done before.

"I can abstain no longer," he said. "Will you make me
wait till we are wed?"

"No, I will not make you wait, if this is what you wish."

There was no lamp alight in the room, the chamber was
black. She recognized his hands, his arms, his body, his
mouth, yet did not recognize them; it was all new, a refind-
ing. And it disturbed her, his coming here, the deception, the
cool impetuosity, as if planned.

The moon was rising from the sea. Moment by moment it
silvered the rose petals in the garden, the trunk of the fig tree,
the tiles of the house. Its single eye stared in at the open
shutters. Bisuneh, as she began to drown in the waters of
desire, as her lover lowered her to the bed, caught abruptly,
unexpectedly, the black glitter of a pair of eyes—

No, this could not be. They were the eyes of her betrothed, veiled with the vulnerable lusts of men. But yet again, beyond the eyes, beneath them, surfacing as a black shark surfaces from the waters of an innocent sea, another pair of eyes looked down on her, invincible and wide.

Bisuneh thrust free of the tide that drowned her. She flung herself from the bed and clutched the useless amulet. In the gloom, her lover stirred, and his voice was altered.

"This is the third time you have refused me. Do you guess who it is you have refused?"

"A Demon."

The moon filled the chamber with a white shining. Bisuneh saw Azhrarn standing before her. She hid her face from his beauty and his stony glare. She had lost her value for him. He was bored with her. It only remained for him to destroy her, in the way of demons, the stale remnants of a feast that now he would disdain to sample.

"Honey-Sweet," said Azhrarn, "your days shall be bitter hereafter."

She did not see where he went, but he was gone.

Bisuneh dropped down in a faint.

Bisuneh became pale and silent. She would tell no one her foreboding. She went to the temple often to pray. But time went by with no violence or menace in it. She began to think again that she had dreamed it all. Brides were subject to such fancies, so she had been told, in the last days before their nuptials. Bisuneh recalled the wise-woman's prophecy: A happy old age unless, impossibly, the sun sank in the east.

The day of the wedding arrived, dusk fell, there was a procession of torches, flowers scattered. The son of one scholar and the daughter of another were joined, and borne away to a feast in the house of the boy's father, where their wedding chamber had been prepared.

Many gifts had come; two silver vases, twelve drinking cups of finest porcelain, a great carved chest of cedarwood, sweet yellow wine from an excellent cellar, a damson tree in a pot which next year would bear fruit, a mirror of burnished bronze. But one gift no one could account for. And though it was exceedingly beautiful and obviously of enormous cost, no one would admit to sending it. It had been found by the groom's father in the porch of his house when he rose at dawn, a huge tapestry, an evening scene of woods and water-falls, very lifelike, worked in a hundred varying shades of gorgeous colored thread. The father, meaning to keep it a surprise for his son and daughter-in-law, had had an inspiration at sunset, and hung it ready in the chamber where they were to spend their wedding night, on the drab wall where there was no window, and very sumptuous it made the room seem.

Presently the bride went up from the feast and quickly enough the groom followed. There were good wishes and certain jests. They shut the door, the two lovers, having glanced about politely and from gratitude at all the riches there, the bowl of purple grapes, the jug of wine, the embroidered cushions, the wonderful shimmering curtain on the wall . . . The lamp burned low, they barely saw anything, and besides, had eyes only for each other.

They lay down in passion, forgetting all else.

Midnight came and went. Below, most of the wedding guests departed. The streets of the city grew subtly quiet in the last hours before sunrise. Here and there a cat prowled, a dog padded, here and there a robber sidled, and a string of girls with withered hyacinths in their hair, having sold their bodies for a few pieces of money at some lord's banquet, walked dolefully homeward to their hovels, arm in arm. And something else was abroad, too, something not clearly seen. It scuttled into the shadow of the wall of the bridegroom's father's house, eddied up a creeper there, so to the upper story. A window stood ajar. The strange night shape paused, peering in. It was like a little dwarf. It carried something over its arm.

A Drin. Azhrarn's messenger, this work being too crude and ugly for an Eshva to achieve. And over the arm of the Drin, a patchwork drapery, like the flaccid skin of some creature, yet set together wrongly, part bristled, part a dull sheen of scales, part a matted fringe of hair. Surely it could not be that somewhere someone had selected the hide of a boar, its chest and forefeet only, the tail of a giant lizard, scaly and reeking, the severed head of a wolf, and combined these three with the stitches of a spell, the rivets of an enchantment?

The slithering dwarf darted over the sill into the bridal chamber. The dwarf grinned at two lovers still entwined, fast alseep. He rolled the young man aside, ran his squat drinnish fingers over the lean torso and strong loins, stared and poked at the girl's milk-white figure bound by ropes of yellow hair. But dawn was near. The Drin sensed its coming as the horse scents fire. Quickly he flung down over the youth's body the hideous amalgamated skin. Azhrarn's second gift—the first being the tapestry upon the eastern wall, where he had influenced the old man, unawares, to hang it.

The vile skin writhed as it settled, seemed to take on life, then lapsed, covering Bisuneh's bridegroom totally. Now a shiny tail twitched where the hard-muscled legs had been, a boar's muddy belly and forehoofs and barrel neck jerked where the young man's breast had quietly breathed. The handsome face, sated and serene, was replaced by a wolf's grizzled and nightmare face with lolling tongue and yellow teeth.

The Drin was gone. The first rose patina of light appeared on the eastern horizon. The glow of dawn spread over the house, and washed in eventually through the western window of the lovers' room.

Bisuneh opened her eyes. Drowsily she noticed the gentle luminosity of the western window, looked where it fell about the chamber, a glow here, a flush there. Looking, she saw the tapestry at last, hung on the eastern wall, catching the window light. How marvelous the tapestry was, the woods of many-leafed trees, the plashing falls, so lifelike she could almost hear them. Above, a sunset sky, the tired sun declining, that darker sun of evening that cannot be mistaken for the fresh pallor of dawn.

Gradually something horrible began to suggest itself to Bisuneh's half lucid mind. She could not think what it might be, for she was happy, tranquil, and the tapestry exquisite. Then she remembered. Upon the eastern wall a sun was going down—sinking, as in the wise-woman's curious foretelling—in the east.

Inevitably, as she started up, Bisuneh's eyes sought the young man beside her. And found a monster.

She screamed until the two fathers and the guests remaining in the house came running. And still she screamed, as the rest of the company stood stricken with nauseous terror, screamed till the thing on the bed stirred, and tried to speak her name, and grunted and barked, and would have pulled itself forward on its two stumpy hoofed feet, dragging its reptilian tail uselessly behind it, save that a man struck it down, then another and another, till it lay motionless.

They believed that the monster had come in at the window and devoured whole the bridegroom, intending next to ravish or devour the bride. Finding no blood or trace of its grisly feast, merely increased their horrified awe. They were doubly terrified now, for the monster appeared dead, its black ichor spreading where the blows had struck it down, and they feared some obscure retribution from a source more abscure— for clearly the creature must be of demonaic origin. None thought for a moment that it was a changeling. Not surprisingly, for none could see in it a vestige of the youth it had been, the handsome and wholesome son of the scholar. And as the frightful skin had grown into and absorbed his own, it might be supposed his brain and his heart were similarly refashioned into some sub-human travesty.

The bride's screams had sunk to whimperings, and the women led her away, themselves in tears. The neighbors who had gathered to gawp when her cries had roused them, were sent off with lies. Rather than thinking to ask help from the city, the wedding guests and the two fathers were at one in their desire that the atrocious matter be kept secret, and not merely from fear. They were ashamed at this contact with horror, felt obscurely it must be the punishment for some sin, collective or particular. The dead creature they loaded in a covered cart. Drawing lots, it fell to the wine merchant's two strong sons and the three strong sons of the mason to take the cart with its contents, under the mask of darkness, to the city limits. There, among the rocky hills, in a barren gulley seldom visited by men, they tipped the tell-tale stigma away and cast down burning straw to be certain of the work. It never occurred to them the thing might still live; it did not stir, it seemed quite dead, its stench could easily be interpreted as the fetor of decay.

But perhaps something so ensorcelled and deformed could not die.

As the five young men were hurrying homeward, they heard a faint echoing intermittent howling in the gut of the rocks behind them. The mason's sons glanced at the sons of the wine merchant. No, it was not their concern, the noise was only thunder. They told each other this until they believed it, by which time the sounds had long since died from their ears.

Bisuneh lay sick in her father's house a long while. It was feared she had lost her wits. They brought her flowers to cheer her, and gentle Bisuneh tore off the flowers' heads. They brought her a singing bird in a little cage, but she opened the door and let it free and a hawk spied it in an instant and slew it in the sky, and when she saw that Bisuneh only nodded, as if she had expected nothing else. She cut off her beautiful hair, she shed no tears, she said no word. She was saving herself, letting her hatred and her bitterness swell inside her. She did not know this, it was her instinct.

The physician whispered to her scholar father.

"She must not continue as she is. You must take her away to some other place. Her womb is tenanted. She is with child and does not care. She will die and the child will die."

Bisuneh drew no comfort from the prospect of this child, the last vestige left to her of her lover. She was sure the child would perish and she with it. She understood quite well who had harmed her, and why. She grew thinner as her womb increased.

One night her hate was ready. She knew it, and woke knowing it. For the first time in months, Bisuneh spoke, and the force of her hate overflowed her words. She did what no mortal dared to do, she did it, hoping for death. She cursed

Azhrarn. Having done so, she sank back exhausted, and
waited readily for death to follow.

In those days a curse or a blessing was like a bird. It had
wings and could fly. And the stronger the blessing or the
curse, the stronger the wings and the farther the bird could
go.

The curse of Bisuneh was very strong, for everything in
her, who had once been named Honey-Sweet, had turned as
bitter as gall. And the bird of the curse, which was of a color
never seen by mortals save with an inner eye—the vivid color
of pain and the dark color of brooding—flew unerringly
towards the earth's center. It had no eyes, the bird, yet it
could see, and no voice. It got through into the Underearth by
way of chinks and crevices smaller than a mote of dust, yet it
was quite large enough that when it had passed between the
towers of Druhim Vanashta, and gone in at an emerald
window, and perched upon the shoulder of Azhrarn, he both
saw and felt it.

Azhrarn smiled. Perhaps winter smiles when it bites dead
the leaves on the trees.

"Some mortal has cursed me," said Azhrarn. And he
shook off the bird into his hand, and looked at it, and saw the
pattern of the brain that had formed it and presently the skull
and the head and the face behind which the brain lay. Then
Azhrarn kissed the bird's icy wings. "Does she not realize,"
said Azhrarn, "that no curse comes home to me, who am the
father of all curses?" But her foolhardy hate pleased him. He
had punished her before through others, could do it again.
"Little bird," he said, "misguided little bird."

2   Shezael and Drezaem

At the time of the earth's flatness, the soul did not enter the body of a child until some days before its birth. The embryo grew in the womb, a plant, without thought or motive, until the moment that the elected soul flooded invisibly into the sleepy chambers. Presently, the unborn child, inspired by the arrival of its soul, would begin to scent its life, and at length contrive to be birthed. Sometimes no soul was ready for the child, in which case the pangs of labor were merely the body's rejection of inanimate matter, and the baby born was lifeless.

But a soul was ready for the child—a girl-child as the charm had discerned—in Bisuneh's womb. One perfect amorphous soul bathed clean in the abstractions of the misty limbo that lay beyond the world, one soul half female and half male, as in those times all souls were.

The road of the soul was life. But on the threshold of smokes that lay at the entrance to that thoroughfare, a dark shape stood with a dark sword in its grasp, barring this soul's way, while other souls flashed past like meteors.

The soul was afraid, as a child would be afraid since it was to a child it had been going. It did not know that one of the Eshva stood before it, nor what the sword portended, nor even why it should fear.

But then the sword swung, and the soul was cloven in two parts. There was no pain, but a sense of bewildered loss, also divided. Each portion of the soul was aware separately of its

157

plight. Then the female half of the soul, dashed on by unreasoning forces, was swept and tossed into the portals of warm human flesh, and sinking there into red-darkness, assumed the posture of the embryo, while its desolation melted from it with the rest of its memories, the residue of its incorporeality. It slept.

The male portion of the soul, swirling with its anguish, was wrapped within the womb of a black flower. The Eshva, this prize in his hand, listened attentively at the gate of life. And somewhere he heard a woman's lament begin, a woman wailing at the still-birth of her child.

The Eshva darted through the unworld on to the earth. He rushed through air, erupted out of it upon an empty plain where thin sheep were grazing, and there, in a stone shepherd's hut, he found the woman sobbing on her bed, while the husband stared in the wicker cradle at his unliving son, born dead a few minutes before.

The Eshva smiled, standing in the doorway.

"I must bury him," said the man. "He would have been a fine boy. Hush, my wife, there is nothing to be done."

The Eshva laughed—soundlessly.

The man looked up in alarm, in rage.

"Who dares mock human sorrow?"

The Eshva came into the hut. He brushed the lids of the man's angry eyes with his fingers so they fell shut. He breathed on the woman so she lay back, quite drugged with the deliciousness of his breath. Then the Eshva went to the cradle, opened the baby's mouth and crushed the black flower within it. The male half of the soul was shot into the child's body like juice squeezed from a fruit.

The Eshva scattered the bruised petals of the black flower upon the baby's now breathing body. The baby began to bellow and cry.

As the shephard and his wife opened their eyes in amazement, a black dove flew from the hut.

Bisuneh's child was born. How beautiful it was. It grew each day more beautiful, each year more beautiful. A girl child, slender as a stem, white skinned, her mother's hair of pale primroses yet paler still—the ghosts of primroses—eyes like grey pools between dark silver rushes.

How beautiful the child was. And yet, how strange. She did not speak, she did not hear what was said to her, at least, she *would* not speak, *would* not hear. Her tongue and throat were sound, her ears were sound, also her eyes, though often she would appear blind, staring at a void, walking silently past the hand of the mother or the grandparents or the friends, not from malice, but as if she truly did not see . . . Poor child, poor Shezael, Bisuneh's daughter. Was she a half-wit or a cripple? Was she possessed?

"I know where the evil has come from," said Bisuneh listlessly.

No one spoke of it. No one chided her or assured her it was not so. Once or twice a traveler had come from the rocky hill roads, and recounted tales of strange howlings and moanings and rumblings from a steep gully or a deep cavern.

"The child lives, but she does not know me," said Bisuneh. "When she is older I will enter some sisterhood of priestesses. I have no use for this existence of mine."

Bisuneh had become more withered and more plain as the years went by. As if in contrast, the child bloomed and shone. If the child had loved her, Bisuneh might have healed from her wounds, but beautiful Shezael, the half-souled, stared at a void and walked by silently. Fifteen years Bisuneh waited. On Shezael's name day Bisuneh kissed her old weeping father farewell, and kissed the forehead of the beautiful child, and went away to a far desert. Here, in a fane of stone she ended her days, a shaved priestess of a grim unloving order.

Shezael perceived her departure without giving any sign.

She saw this only as she saw all else, like movement through a screen, something unrelated to herself. Hers was the female portion of the soul, the negative portion of passivity and stasis, of the obscure and inconclusive, which, unbalanced by the masculine counterweight all other souls possessed, produced this utter inertia.

The grandfathers were both old, two old scholars, unworldly, troubled. They would not live much longer. Maybe they should wed Shezael to some kind youth who would not mind her—she was unusually beautiful, and many would be glad of a silent wife.

Across three lands, mountains, quantities of water, the stone hut stood upon the hill and the thin sheep tugged at the unwilling grass.

The shepherd's wife washed garments in a narrow stream. She kept one eye for the sheep and for the boy. He was supposed to be watching the sheep, this son of hers, but she could not trust him. Something might distract him, he would leap up with a sort of fury, fling a stone into the air for no reason. His temper was violent. He was brash. He would crush a butterfly, unthinking, beneath his fist; he had slain two of the precious flock one day, by beating their heads together with enormous force, and braining them. It was not from cruelty, it was a strange insensibility, a kind of blindness. The shepherd's wife sighed. Who did not know her son was addled, and also violent? Mad Drezaem they called him in the village. Since his eleventh year, the men had been afraid of him, and the women ran when he came near. They would have liked to murder him for sure, the villagers, if they could get at his back, but he was too strong and too quick for them, his instincts sharper than a fox's though his mind was dull. Yet they would slaughter him like a mad dog if ever they got the chance, and he only fifteen and, despite his wild ways, as handsome as a prince.

The shepherd's wife sighed again, looking at her son. He was still now, but it would not last. And that hair of his, so fair that it was like the color of the silver-grey bark of particular trees, and the unnerving beautiful eyes of him like hot bronze, and the strong brown limbs of him lithe as a leopard's—and he was as destructive and unpredictable as one. For the third time, the shepherd's wife sighed. She did not think of the adage of that district that declared: When a woman sighs three times, it bodes ill for someone.

The boy was staring, animal like, alert for nothing in particular, tensed to spring at shadows. To Drezaem, the world was a jungle, he knew neither fear nor law. When he harmed a thing he would feel the brief surprise of regret, but it never lingered. His thoughts were always racing. He must leap this way and that to keep up with them. He loved to fight or to couple, straightforward, brutish deeds. Some nights he would rise with the moon and run till he dropped—a long while—over the burned barren countryside. He had learned to swim as a dog learns, by falling in water. He had learned nothing that did not come as easily and suddenly as that river.

His was the male portion of the cloven soul, the positive portion of action and volatility, of the flagrant and the unswerving which, unbalanced by the female counterweight all other souls possessed, produced this unmitigated ebullience.

Abruptly there came the alarming note of the big ram's horn, sounded from the village only in times of urgency.

The shepherd's wife started up, flustered, did not move, only called for her husband. Drezaem, however, roused by the clarion, vaguely aware of its significance, was already bounding towards the village.

There was a new sight in the street there, to be sure. One hundred men in armour of shining bronze, soldiers of the king of the land, and a plumed king's messenger in silks and gold.

The messenger read from a scroll. He spoke of danger, loyalty, death and reward. He spoke of the king's decree, that the ten bravest, most vigorous youths from every town, and the single bravest and most vigorous from every village be sent forthwith to a certain mountain beyond the king's capital, there to offer themselves in combat with a dragon. Already five hundred youths had perished, but no matter. The king's magicians foretold that a champion should finally come who would slay the frightful beast. Then should vast riches be heaped upon him. In any case—the messenger here gestured to his brazen escort—to refuse to provide the required young man would be to invite disaster.

To Drezaem most of the speech went unheard, the threat unrecognized. But he grasped the words 'combat,' 'dragon,' 'vigor.' He was about to rush forward when he found the men of the village had already seized him and were offering him frantically: "This is the bravest one, no doubt of it—slew a wolf in the spring, tore it apart with his bare hands—look at his eyes! Crazy to fight and to kill.''

Drezaem laughed. The captain of the soldiers beheld his fine white teeth, his hard body, his eyes like a lion's. Usually there was reluctance and trouble, this made a pleasing change. Within a few minutes the soldiers had marched off, Drezaem with them, running freely behind the messenger's horse. By the time the shepherd and his wife arrived in the street, the dust had settled, and their son was lost to them for good.

It had happened like this. The mountain that lowered seven miles beyond the capital of the king was old almost as earth itself, and a molten cauldron lay at its core, though snow crowned its peak. One night the mountain stirred in its millennial sleep, and stirring, woke another thing that dwelt there. The dragon also was old, old nearly as the mountain. It came of that menagerie of villainous perverse things left over from the beginnings of time. The color of the dragon was scarlet, the color of blood, but its mouth and tongue were black; even its teeth were back, though adamant as ossified wood. It had two short horns, and the bone at the tip of its tail was bare, as were the bone ridges along its spine. Yellowish, ugly, naked bones they were, too, sharp enough to split a man, which they had frequently done. It was the length of four stallions, snout to hindquarters, the tail an extra.

It emerged on the fertile mountain slopes, among the groves there, and the obnoxious breath of it destroyed the trees, and the animals which came in its way. Where it passed it left a trail of blackened, twisted, unrecognizable litter. It ate men. It needed a man for every day of its life, a strong tall man, juicy and young. It needed heroes, or at least those forced to imitate heroes.

The king did not actually believe that any would ever come who could destroy the dragon. The conscripts he sent to the mountain were fodder, a bribe, to keep the dragon from his city. If a day arrived when all the available peasant youths had been devoured, then the soldiers of the king would have to pick marked chequers from a dish, and whoever the chequers elected would have to go to supply the dragon. Thus, the soldiers worked diligently to find heroes among the farflung hovels and cots of the land.

Some were dragged screaming or insensible to the city, shovelled on to the mountain clad in ill-fitting armour, died with only a squeak or a curse to mark their passage. Some went roaring, puffed up with bravado, believing the lying prophecy meant themselves, till the dragon's teeth met in their vitals. Now a different kind of hero entered the city gates. He did not speak, he laughed, jumped to wrestle a dog, struck at a bird in the air. He did not stare at the splendor of the metropolis, did not narrow his eyes at promise of reward. He turned impatiently from the armour they showed him. He pointed at the mountain, grinned and raised his brows in query. They conducted him, and he raced all the way, galloping over stones and chasms, whooping, to meet the dragon. The soldiers stared, a couple wept. The dragon coughed on the slopes, and the soldiers hid themselves.

It was the heat of the day, and the dragon was drowsing among a wood of dead trees blasted by its breath. As things had turned out, it had found a man to eat already, a murderer who had been driven up on to the mountain by a vengeful crowd. So the dragon was not hungry or alert, not looking out for a meal, though still dangerous enough.

Suddenly the dragon heard an odd clamour. Not cries of terror or bellowings of challenge, but a clear merry yelling, quite out of keeping with the slopes as they had become.

The dragon yawned, and belched lively, and looked about.

Between a gap in the blasted trees, a wild youth appeared. He was neither crawling nor swaggering, he was not armed or dressed in armour. The dragon was used to three reactions in men at the sight of itself. The first reaction was to run, the second to fall prone and senseless, the third was to advance cautiously, muttering threats, sword lifted.

But the youth with the greyish fair hair and the blazing eyes did none of these things. Just as the dragon was lazily bestirring itself, lumbering to its feet, the youth came running, took a huge flying leap, and landed square on the dragon's forehead at the narrow point just between its two stubby horns and the area where its jagged backbone commenced. This was not strategem on the leaper's part, purely instinct, the bald spot being the only feasible place to land.

The impact jarred the dragon's brains. It shook its head. Drezaem, again from instinct only, grabbed the dragon's two horns to stop himself from falling off, and at once the fierce thrilling pleasure of violent action surged through him, and he began to pull and strain with all his considerable young might at what he held.

The dragon bawled. Its foul poisonous breath gushed out—missing Drezaem who was perched above and behind it—while its odor sent him giddy and thereby maddening him further. He was fifteen, but of unnatural strength, a strength reinforced and made positively supernatural by his lack of fear and finesse. He hauled upon the ugly bone protuberancies and, in another moment, had snapped and uprooted them from their sockets.

Black blood gushed from the two ghastly wounds, blinding the dragon. It boomed with agony, a discomfort increased by the fact that Drezaem was now using the dislocated horns to beat it over the skull.

Roaring and blind, the dragon burst from the wood, and ran head-on into the side of the mountain, which broke its neck for it.

Drezaem was flung off but was soon on his feet again, rattling the horns together insanely and jumping back and forth over the dragon's back.

Hearing these unusual noises replace the more usual ones of the dragon tearing its victim limb from limb, the king's soldiers eventually stole timidly up to see.

When they discovered the outcome of the fight, they banged their shields together, and carried the dragon's corpse and Drezaem shoulder high to the city. Indirectly, this wondrous half-wit had saved their skins too. They meant to make him a hero indeed.

The king was surprised but not displeased that someone had slain the dragon after all. As his soldiers had foreseen a day when all the peasants would be used up, so the king had foreseen a slightly more distant day, when everyone—soldiers, peasants, courtiers—would also be gone, and only he left to

flee the monster's hunger. At the prospect of fulfilling his decree, however, he was not pleased. To heap treasure upon an ignorant clod, and an imbecile to boot, was not to his liking. However, he noticed the steely glint in the eyes of his soldiers, how his captains' hands rested on the hilts of their swords. There had always been another possibility in regard to feeding the dragon; that his loyal army might revolt. The king perceived he had best give in.

He showered gold and precious stones upon the young madman, who grunted, toyed with them, put a pearl between his teeth and laughingly cracked it. The soldiers scowled at the king. The king led Drezaem to a mansion in the grounds of his own palace. He showed him the scented fountains, the peacocks. At last the king opened a door of ivory, and revealed twenty-five lovely maidens clad in rainbow gauzes through which their limbs and breasts gleamed like silver.

"Ah," said the king, "I see we have made some progress."

The maidens gave faint shrieks as Drezaem burst among them, but they were all taught. At least he was beautiful, if rough and impetuous.

Drezaem became the king's champion. He did not really know what he was. He was only aware that there was endless carnal delight to be had beyond the ivory door, mountains of food upon his table, and a continuous supply of men to fight.

Several champions from foreign parts were sent against Drezaem. Always some monarch thought he could do better. A saffron giant came from the north, tall as two men together. He swung Drezaem aloft, but Drezaem grasped the giant's wrists in an impossible grasp, using both arms and legs for the work, and ground them till the giant screamed for mercy. A grey giant came from the west, but Drezaem ran round him in circles till he howled, at which Drezaem jumped for his throat and throttled him. When there was a battle to be fought, Drezaem would race before the captains, without horse or armor, and then throw himself upon the enemy with blood-curdling happy yells, wreaking destruction on every hand.

Sometimes he was wounded. He never noticed till he fell down from loss of blood. He was so vital, however, that none of these hurts incapacitated him for more than a few hours. As for his women—there were a hundred now—the ivory door swung open and shut all day long and all night when he was home, and when in the field, pretty girls were dragged from their parents' care to satisfy the king's champion.

The soldiers revered him.

"What matter if he never speaks, what matter if sometimes he flies into a sudden rage or fit, knocking over wine jars, flinging tables in the air? Look at his fine muscles and his clear eyes, look at that ivory door opening and shutting! My, he is a champion and no mistake."

He was seventeen. He looked like a god, acted like an unpredictable animal. Yet, even in his rages, he seemed joyous, overbrimmed with life.

One day a minstrel came by the camp. The king's army had fought a battle, and won. The king's champion was in his gold embroidered tent with three squealing wenches.

The minstrel sang for coppers. He had seen a girl in a far city, a strange dumb girl with silver eyes and ghostly primrose hair; he sang of her, for she had struck his fancy. He was a dreamer and somehow had come to the truth without guessing it, for in his story he called her—as poetry merely, an invention—the half-souled.

The soldiers, sentimental after the battle, liked the song. Imagine their astonishment when the flap of the champion's tent was flung wide, and the unmusical champion came forth, his face desolate and his eyes streaming tears.

Without a sound, he fell to his knees before the minstrel.

They were all afraid, as if at a portent. The champion wept, but did not seem to know why he wept. No one dared question him, in any case anticipated no reasonable reply, for he never spoke. Presently the champion raised his head and, seizing the minstrel's little harp, he tore out its strings. And then, with an awful wordless crying, he ran away from the camp into the empty plains that lay beyond it.

Shezael had continued a virgin, unwed. Despite her beauty, her oblique wits deterred suitors. Somehow, they were afraid of her. Had she not been born of a cursed marriage? Few knew the facts of Bisuneh's wedding night, yet rumor abounded—the bridegroom had mysteriously died, but of what, and for what reason, seeing he had been healthy and youthful? No, the taint, whatever it was, must have passed to the daughter. Best let her alone.

Sometimes she would sit in the window of her grandfather's house. The old man was slow and tired. Alarmed at the cost, he paid a servant woman to be the escort of Shezael, to purchase and mend her garments, and take her to walk about the city by unfrequented byways. This servant was good natured, but a guardian watchful for the safety of her charge. Sometimes she would lead Shezael to the temple, and would pray there for the girl to be healed of her bizarre affliction, while Shezael would gaze expressionlessly at the blue tinted air.

Three months after Shezael had become seventeen, the servant woman took her for one of these unsatisfactory visits to the temple and in the holy place they came on the wandering minstrel they had met there half a year before. He appeared to be thanking the gods for his safe return to the city, but when he saw the servant and her charge he hurried up to them.

"Were I but a rich man, did I but lead a settled life," said he, "I would wed this maiden gladly. Though she is bedimmed, she is more lovely than a lotus."

"Be off," said the servant, but she did not mean it. The minstrel, for all his roguish trade, was no rogue, but gentle and amiable. Presently they sat to talk in the temple porch, while Shezael stood gazing at the clouds, the flowering trees, the ocean.

The minstrel told his adventures. How he had sung in poor inns and busy markets. Of the robbers who had beset him but let him free in exchange for a song or two, seeing they were starved of culture and he mostly penniless, of the wonders of a town where the richer streets were paved with slabs of jade, and another town by a lake where trained birds could imitate all manner of noises, barking dogs and lowing cattle and tinkling bells—yet could not sing a note. Last, he told her of how he had made a song about the sad beauty of Shezael (the woman scolded him, looking pleased), and rendered it in the war camp of a king. "And then," declared the minstrel, "a young madman strode from a tent and snatched my little harp and tore loose all the strings. What a thing, you may say," said the minstrel. "But there is worse, for I have had to fashion a new harp. When I restrung the old, I found the seventh string was tangled with a single long hair from the madman's head—a hair of fine greyish blond, near enough the color of the string itself. Try as I might, I could not get this single strong hair free from the seventh string of the harp. And now, listen." And taking the instrument from his pack, the minstrel plucked all its strings, one after another. Six had a clear sweet tone, but the seventh, where the single hair was tangled, *groaned*.

The servant clutched his arm. "Ah! Throw it away! The harp is possessed."

"Wait!" whispered the minstrel, "look at the girl."

Shezael had turned. Her face was changed. Intent and serious, she stared at the harp, her eyes focused, her lips parted. And suddenly she laughed. Not a fool's laughter, the laughter of sheer joy, which there is no mistaking. Then, coming straight to the minstrel, she lifted the harp from his unresisting hands. Turning about once more, Shezael began to walk away, as if at last she had learned the road home.

The woman was alarmed. The minstrel was curious, moved, yet not amazed. He had half expected something of the sort, had come every day to the temple for a month, meaning to meet Shezael and her guardian for the purpose of proving some weird magic he had sensed in the air.

That night, Shezael placed the harp beside her bed. It was the narrow bed her mother, black-fated Bisuneh, had slept in. Shezael did not disturb the strings of the harp, but she looked at it till her eyelids fell shut.

Her existence had been like a dream, her dreams sometimes more acute than her existence. Now she dreamt with a vivid clarity. She became another.

She was a shepherd boy, she had killed a wolf, no, it was a dragon. She was a king's champion, she slew giants. She was called Drezaem. She was a youth, tall, sun-burned, handsome, with eyes of bronze. She was a warrior, yet she fled into the empty plains. She lay near dead in the cruel heat of the day. Sometimes she roared and moaned and wept from an intolerable, inconsolable sense of loss she did not understand.

Shezael woke as the sun woke, her cheeks wet with tears, without sorrow.

She rose and dressed herself. She smiled upon the garden from the window. She plucked a rose and left it on her grandfather's knee where he slept in his chair, a chrysanthamum and left it on the pillow of the sleeping servant woman.

Shezael knew her path as if she had read it from a map.

She took the path unhesitatingly, without a second thought. Hers was the female portion of the soul, obscure, sensitive to occult things.

The path led her through the morning city, through the tall gate, along the highway, into the wide world.

She knew her way by instinct, yet blindly. She had not foreseen or reasoned that it lay across three lands, a range of mountains, many wide rivers, a great lake. Neither was she conscious of dangers or necessities. She set forth without provisions of any kind. She set forth as the metal pin flies to the magnet, the tide to the beach, for she had never possessed human logic or caution, obscure Shezael. Only the tug of her lost half-soul drew her.

She left the city and the sea behind, and quickly came on a deserted track. Night fell and Shezael did not heed it. When she grew very weary, she lay down and slept on the bare earth, and started up at the first ray of dawn and went on. Several days she walked, without food, only once or twice pausing to drink when a stream ran beside her path. A growing weakness barely impinged on her thought, but at length she could go no farther.

It had happened that a slave-dealer had chosen this track to reach the nearest town. His men found Shezael lying by the roadside, and set up a clamour. The slave-dealer called them off. He liked the look of the girl, who would make an excellent pleasure-slave. He forced broth between her teeth and lifted her into one of the carts.

It was a journey of four days, and took the route Shezael must in any case have traveled. Perhaps because she sensed this, Shezael neither cried out nor attempted to evade them. If she was aware of her captors, it was only as a helpful agency, bearing her towards her goal.

They reached the town. The market ran up into rich streets lined with white mansions, and every fourth paving stone was made of green jade. The slave-dealer set Shezael on a rostrum. The bidding began quickly, but tapered off as the buyers noticed the girl's peculiar emotionless staring. At length a young nobleman stepped forward.

"This girl is witless and dumb. Anyone can see." The slave-dealer remonstrated. "Then tell her to speak," said the nobleman.

This the slave-dealer did, loudly, and to no avail. The crowd of potential buyers began to mutter and turn away. The dealer raised his whip, but the young nobleman caught his arm. "No matter. I have too many chattering women in my house as it is. I will buy her."

Money changed hands and documents were signed. The nobleman led Shezael to his chariot. When they reached his mansion, he conducted her inside, and showed her a marble room hung with rose velvet, and had slaves bring her food and wine.

"This chamber shall be yours. These slaves shall be yours. I set you free, you shall be my beloved, but I will not own you." The nobleman took Shezael's hand. "I heard of you in a song, a maiden with such hair and eyes. But can you be as the minstrel said, 'half-souled'?" As it transpired, it was not only in the king's war camp that the minstrel had sung his song of Shezael.

Shezael had been gazing about her, gradually becoming more agitated with the need to away. Yet, when the nobleman spoke those words, she looked at him with a terrible profundity. The nobleman realized he was in the presence of another's destiny, and so forceful was this aura of fate that he could not withstand it.

When she walked from the room, he did not stop her, but he accompanied her. "You must not leave here as you came,"

he said. "Clearly you are making a journey of great need, but
to travel alone will put you in the way of danger again.
Come, I will give you my chariot and the three white geld-
ings that draw it and a groom to drive them, and bread and
drink so you shall not starve."

All this was done. The nobleman, as if in the grip of a
spell, did not regret the loss of his coins, only of Shezael, and
her he did not hinder. He swore the groom to protect her also.
The three white horses tossed their heads.

"Which way must I go, mistress?" asked the groom.

But the nobleman said: "She looks towards the mountains—
go that way. And do not return to me till she is safe."

The chariot journeyed swiftly. It raced along ancient tracks,
and crossed the mountains in two days by the wide pass. But
in the valley below robbers beheld it.

A bow twanged. The groom pitched over the rail, dead
from an arrow in his breast; a robber jumped into the chariot,
seized the reins and checked the horses. Another seized Shezael:
"Here is a fine treasure!"

Next the chief of the robbers came. He cuffed them aside,
and lifted Shezael in his arms and examined her. Eventually
he said: "This is the witch-girl the minstrel sang of," and he
set her down gingerly. Instantly she turned and began to walk
away, leaving the chariot, the dead groom, the dumbfounded
robbers. Superstitious, they did not go after her. They had a
robber-god which they worshipped in a cave. His creed declared: "For every fifty travelers robbed and slain, let one go
free. The gods care for excess in nothing."

Shezael came to a broad rushing river. The ferryman caught
her back from the brink.

"By my life, you cannot walk on the water, lady. I must
ferry you across, and you must pay me." But, looking in her
eyes, the ferryman said: "Why, you are the maiden the
minstrel sang of. You shall be ferried for nothing."

The next river had a bridge. Fruit trees grew along the
track now, and berries, which sustained the wandering girl,
for she plucked them absently, as she had been taught to
pluck the figs from the tree in the garden of her grandfather's
house.

Shezael passed, unseeing, through five villages. In the fifth, a woman ran and brought her a loaf: "You are the maid in the song. Good fortune go with you in whatever you are seeking, for surely you are magic."

She had crossed into the third land, over mountains and waters. She passed along a road, and would have seen, if she had looked, the king's capital shining in the distance and, seven miles beyond it, the snow-capped mountain where the dragon had eaten men, and perished at the hands of Drezaem.

Finally Shezael entered a town on the shores of a vast lake. Here on the quay, beside the silken water, an old lady was slowly walking up and down with her servants, and on a golden leash she led a green bird, which now and then would bark vigorously.

"I see a child with beautiful hair," said the old lady. "In a moment she will fall in the lake. Go, one of you, and bring her to me."

Shezael was brought to the old lady with the barking bird.

"Yes, as I thought," said the old lady. "She is the maiden of the minstrel's song. And truly, I believe she is half-souled, as he said. Can it be she is searching for the other half? Well, she shall have a boat to aid her over the lake. Go under the auspices of the gods, my child. And beware the snares of night."

Thus Shezael came over the lake and reached the empty plains where Drezaem wandered in his melancholy anger.

5   Night's Sorcery

Drezaem had lived in the plains many months. He had
survived by braining snakes and rodents with a heavy stone
and eating them raw, not thinking to make a fire. For drink,
he found subterranean streams in the caves where he crawled
to avoid the midday heat. On this limited sparse fare he had
become gaunt. His hair was more grey than fair now, his eyes
huge and savage. His heart was leaden, he did not comprehend what caused his grief, had forgotten what began it.
Some nights, under the cold stars he would howl with anguish, and even the wolf would fall silent, in uneasy respect
for his cries.

There came a night like any other, ebony bright with a
silver sweat of stars. As the moon rose, a tall man came
walking over the plain before it. His cloak was black, but his
hair blacker; blacker than both, his eyes.

Drezaem had mislaid the notion of men, except as enemies
to fight and slay. He surged up, snarling. But the black haired
man dissolved into a smoke, which came and wrapped itself
about the youth. The wild beast faded at the touch of the
smoke. Drezaem's eyelids drooped, and the murder in him
slept.

"Now," said the black eyed man, handsome as the night,
standing at the young man's side, "you shall be my son, and
I will make you glad again. For you have lived too long, my
infant, like a jackal of the plains."

Drezaem raised his head. His eyes met the stranger's eyes.

Through the layers of confusion and mist that clouded his perceptions, the eyes of the unknown man pierced like two black flaming lights.

"Look here," said Azhrarn, the Prince of Demons, pointing at a massive pile of featureless granite about a mile off. Drezaem looked.

The night shuddered. Every surface of the plains resounded as if to the chord of an enormous harp, and the pile of granite was altered. A palace stood there now, a marvel of glinting melanic crystal and polished jet, with towers of silver, roofs of brass, windows of turquoise and crimson which blazed with lamps. Before it lay gardens carpeted by dark velvet moss, avenues paved with jewels, black trees sculpted into fantastic shapes, lavender fountains and purple pools. Clockwork nightingales sang with ceaseless sweetness in the arbours, black clockwork peacocks with green and blue, real and seeing eyes in their fans, patrolled the lawns.

"You are in my cave, Drezaem," Azhrarn said. "You will live by night, as the moon does. This palace I give you. But you shall lack for nothing."

Azhrarn guided the young man through the gardens into the palace. A banquet was already prepared and lay ready. Drezaem needed no encouragement to gorge himself as he had done in the palace of the king. Perhaps he noticed this was even better. When Drezaem was satisfied, Azhrarn said: "There is one last thing you crave. I will remind you. A girl with silver eyes and primrose hair. Even this I have not neglected."

Then Azhrarn took up a ewer of alabaster. He opened the lid, and spoke certain words, and upended the ewer into the air. What poured forth was a cloud and a glow and a perfume, and these things resolved into a gorgeous woman.

It was not Shezael, indeed not. It was not Azhrarn's plan that the soul he had divided should be reunited in any form. Demonaic vengeance had the habit of becoming a game. Azhrarn, in some magic glass of the Underearth, had seen Bisuneh shrivelling in her wretched fane, and turned his eye after on the half-souled daughter, and he observed that weird, random forces were intent upon her salvation. Intrigued by the sport, Azhrarn had set himself to thwart them.

The woman poured from the alabaster ewer was one of the Eshva. Her shape was surpassingly beautiful; she was, too, part of the jestling of Azhrarn. Like all demon-kind, her eyes were black, not silver, yet the lids were painted with silver, sparkling with silver. Like all demon-kind, her hair was also black, yet in this black hair were masses of flowers, not garlands but actual growing plants, sprung invisibly from the strands of hair and from the roots of it. Pale, pale flowers of greenish yellow, tiny, ever-blooming primroses clustered thick in those dark tresses as dew upon a leaf.

Drezaem gasped. This loveliness struck even his unwoken senses, as the eyes of Azhrarn had fathomed his muddy brain.

The name of the Eshva woman was Jaseve. Before, the young man had tired quickly of a single body, a single face. But the demons were not of that order, men did not tire of them, nor women either.

Jaseve drew Drezaem into her arms that were like desire itself.

Azhrarn was gone. Drezaem lay with the demoness upon a couch of incense. He bared her breasts that were like mounds of snow, she bared his breast, gold from the sun; he uncovered her loins' black wooded valley even here spangled with yellow flowers, she uncovered him also and rested her lips against the burning tower his passion had built for him.

The sun was not rising in the sky, but in the body of Drezaem. The chariot of the sun, drawn by its scarlet horses, plunged and thrust through the tunnel of the mansion of Jaseve. But the horses did not, on this occasion, slip their rein. The eternal time of demons overmatched the human lover. He rode forever, a white arched bow upon the white crescent of her flesh beneath him, rode till he was molten, rode till he was fire. Only after many aeons of agonised bliss did he pierce and shatter the sun, and fall with its fragments many further aeons down into the ocean of Jaseve.

As Azhrarn told him, Drezaem lived now by night, as the moon did. He woke as the daylight fled and the stars solidified in the ether. He would feast then, take his ease. A thousand unseen servants would tend him, provide whatever he had a wish for before even he could think of it. When he felt the urge for battle come on him, giants and warriors would appear at the brass gates, ranting challenges. He would slay them all gloriously—or seem to—they were illusions. Such red meat catered to his former tastes. For his other appetites, Jaseve was there. The sound of her step upon the marble floors was enough to stir him. Gulfs of pleasure, chasms of victorious violence, these blandishments ensorcelled him five nights. And when the five suns that followed those five nights were rising, Drezaem would fall upon his royal bed and sleep till the last color again left the sky.

In this way he never saw what became of the palace as the sun crested the plain, never saw what became of his royal bed, the roses crushed beneath his back, the giants' heads piked upon his gate. For these splendors and atrocities were the things of night. The sun struck them and they faded into air, all but certain solid clockworks made by the Drin. Trees dissolved like ink in water, towers wavered into smokes, peacocks lay in tarnished heaps. The only walls then about the sleeping youth were the barren tiers of the granite, his only shelter a rocky archway. Jaseve was gone to Undereearth to avoid the day. Drezaem lay alone in a sorcerous stupor until the dark should come again, and Azhrarn should come again and remake the palace about him, and Jaseve pour from the alabaster ewer with the primroses growing in her raven hair.

Five nights Drezaem woke and orgied, five days he slept like the dead.

And on the fifth day Shezael climbed the pile of granite and found him.

She was thin and pale. The journey had been weary, terrible. The empty plains were formidable beneath the unrelenting hot sky, and after sundown, the cold winds blew. Her clothes were in rags, her feet and her hands were bleeding, yet she had noticed none of it; her pain and exhaustion meant nothing to her. The goal was still before her. Her instinct led her without hesitation. The severed soul within her was like an unhealing wound.

Seeing the granite stack in front of her, she had known

how close she was. Her heart had seemed to burst. She ran to
the rock and pulled herself among its steeples, and there she
found him, the man who she had dreamed she was, the man
whose flesh contained the other half of what was hers.

And at once she was soothed, comforted. She had no rage
or bitterness in her, and so her answer to the sight of him was
not to harm or to snatch, but to love. She knelt beside
Drezaem in love. She kissed him, his lips, his eyes, his
hands. The portion of the soul within him sensed her, but, as
the Prince of Demons had arranged things, so Drezaem slept
too deep to wake.

Throughout the day, Shezael sat beside Drezaem among
the granite.

The sun went down. In the dusk, a black wolf padded over
the rock.

He was not like the other wolves of the plains, which had
not come near Shezael. The eyes of the wolf scorched into
the brain of Shezael where few meanings had penetrated. The
wolf was Azhrarn. His gaze hypnotized and overwhelmed.
Shezael could not fight him, and did not try. He forced her
from the side of Drezaem, from the granite place, though the
portion of the soul in her was torn like a mortal hurt. Azhrarn
drove her away into the empty night.

Far from the spot, Shezael saw a radiance of lamps woven
into the sky. Shezael stood alone and weeping on the plains.
She thought: 'My beloved is there. What am I to do?'

She had begun to reason.

Shezael returned, over the track her own bare bloody feet
had made when the black wolf had compelled her thence. She
came to a gate of brass with a variety of hideous heads piked
above it. Beyond the gate lay a garden and a palace, and she
knew Drezaem was there.

Shezael set her hand on the gate, but at once a wall of blue
fire burst up all around the garden, and from the fire sprang
terrifying shapes that drove her off with whips.

She lay down in a cave, immobile as a stone, though her
blood and her tears mingled on the rocky floor.

*   *   *

She did not go back till the sun had gone over the sky and almost down again. She kneeled beside Drezaem where he slept. She had a girdle about her narrow waist of twisted strands of colored silk. This girdle she now wound about the wrist of Drezaem.

"I knew him from a single hair tangled in a harp string. When he wakes he will know me from this girdle I have worn so long. He will know me, and then we may not be parted."

And she kissed him and stole once more away.

Night came, and demon-kind. Drezaem stirred upon a heap of satin, hyacinths for a pillow. And as he stirred, Jaseve stepped near, and she saw the ragged girdle wound about the wrist of Drezaem, and in a moment she had pulled it from him and thrown it in a brazier of green fire which consumed it.

Night passed in riot. Dawn walked across the plain.

Shezael wept.

Then again, near sunset, she sought the place where Drezaem lay sleeping. She took a sharp stone and cut off a lock of her pale hair and hid it within his shirt.

"He will surely know me from this lock of hair, and then we may not be parted."

But when the sun was gone, and Drezaem stirred upon a heap of velvet with asphodel for a pillow, Jaseve came and smiled, and searched his clothing till she found the piece of hair and, before he woke, the demon-woman had thrown it in the brazier.

Another night, another dawn. Shezael in the afternoon, looking on the man who slept among the rocks.

"Perhaps you will not know me then. Perhaps the half of the soul which is yours has grown silent. There is no other thing I can leave you. I will come no more." Then she leaned and kissed him, his lips, his eyes, his hands, and she went away to the cave and lay down there, as once Bisuneh had lain down, expecting only to die.

Night dawned black.

Drezaem stirred upon a heap of furs with violets under his head. Jaseve stood over him, and searched diligently, and found no girdle, no lock of hair, nothing of Shezael's.

But there was one thing, something so small one woman never knew she had left it, while the other woman, even with demon cunning, never saw.

A silver lash from the eyelid of Shezael had fallen among the lashes of Drezaem as she kissed him. And when he woke the lash fell in his eye.

The lash did not discomfort him, but it did strange things to his sight. The miraculous palace trembled and grew shadowy, the delicious form of Jaseve took on a gleaming awful look, as if phosphorous were brewing in her bones. And suddenly a feeling of inconsolable loss rushed upon Drezaem, and he knew he had felt the despair of it before. He put his hand to his eye and rubbed it, and the silver lash slid on to his finger. As soon as he touched it, he knew what was amiss with him. His half-soul pounded on the gate of his heart and his flesh, and he cried aloud. "I must find her."

And then, too swift for all those snares of the dark to trap him, he ran into the plains, ran without understanding how he guessed the way, straight to the cave where Shezael was lying.

Later, Azhrarn strode across the plains. He strode until he made out two figures seated on the rock beneath the open sky.

Behind him, the sorcerous palace was gone, Jaseve poured like a rare wine back in the ewer. The peacocks spread their fans no more on the earth, and the clockwork nightingales lay unwound in the workshops of the Drin.

Azhrarn called to the two on the rock:

"Turn, Shezael. Turn, Drezaem, I am here."

And turn indeed they did, without hesitation. Azhrarn saw them in the clear radiance of the moon.

They were beautiful as two things can only be beautiful which flawlessly make one whole thing. As their hands fitted together, so did every part of them seem fitted, the angle of each limb, the curve of her cheek, her breast, against the straight symmetry of his. Drezaem's hair was silver, Shezael's eyes were silver. Her hair was floating gold, his eyes were burning gold. What had been bestial in him had grown calm;

who had been inert in her had grown vital. The expressions that passed across their faces were identical, and would always be.

The imbalance of each, counterweighted by the other, had become the most exact of all balances. Negative aligned with positive, the divergent paths coalesced. Iron was silk; silk was iron. What emerged was serenity, wisdom, power, magic—the unique perfection.

Neither was afraid—how should they be? They watched Azhrarn with a detached sweetness. They had the look of gods, or of God; the soul unseparated, complete. They were two beings, yet they were one.

Azhrarn wrapped his cloak about him. He was much taken with this sight. It pleased him, for an instant, more than wickedness.

"Too fine to sunder twice," he said. "For what it is worth in the world, go with my blessing."

PART TWO

4   The Anger of the Magicians

Between the rocky hills, an old track led to the city and the sea, but it was rarely traveled. For a hundred years or longer, men had avoided this road, since, even at the brightest hour of day, they declared, you might hear a monster howling there in the rock beneath your feet, and who knew but that sometime it might not get out and eat you? The mighty magician, however, he of the black and green silk coat and the ruby ring the size of a gazelle's eye, he, over whose head a menial held a fringed parasol as he rode in an open carriage drawn by six black horses from whose bridles dripped pearls—he was not daunted in the least by tales of howlings and eatings. Even the servants of the magician laughed.

"This is the Great Kaschak," they said. "Suppose there is some monster concealed under the road. Suppose it emerges. Then you may suppose Kaschak will eat *it!*"

So the magician set out. He had a mind to reach the city and its seaport before sunset, and had chosen the track for its swiftness. He had come to this land to work a healing miracle for a king's eldest son, and now, this miracle performed, he wished to take ship for his home.

The old track was dusty and here and there stones had fallen. The magician cleared the stones away with a momentous word or two that dissolved them in smoke. An hour after noon, the magician's party came to a dry well.

"It is time the horses were watered," said Kaschak. He struck the side of the hill and a fountain burst from it and formed a pool for the horses to drink at. Just then, from the mouth of the dry well, there rose a mournful ululation.

The servants of the magician showed no fear, for they trusted his powers. Kaschak himself went to the well, and leaned there to listen. Soon enough the fearsome noise came again.

"I believe I should like to see this creature," said Kaschak. He called for an unlit torch, and blew on it and it took fire. Then he lowered it some way into the well and left it suspended in mid-air while he peered down through a magic spyglass to see what was to be seen. "Ah," said the magician presently, "as I thought. A human translated by the fabulous method of a demon into a curious shape." (The glass revealed such information.)

Kaschak snapped his fingers and sparks flew from them. The sparks spun about and formed a net which poured itself down the well.

A vile clamour was heard, a scraping of hoofs, a scrabbling of teeth, a slithering smack, a slavering bark. Up from the head of the well drifted the torch, and went out. Next came the sparky net with, rolled and tangled and kicking and writhing inside it, an awful beast.

The front half of the beast was a boar, the back half a giant lizard's tail. Its head was a wolf's.

It floundered and bellowed and howled, swiveling its eyes and gnashing its lupine jaws. It had wandered for a century or a little longer through the crevices and caves that undermined the hills. It could not die, sealed forever within the scabbard of a demon's whim. Blows had not slain it, nor the fall into the gully; the burning straw had scorched and roused it, but not killed. For sure, it had forgotten its beginning, that once it had been a man, handsome, virile and young, who had lain down upon the body of his beloved bride to slumber, and woken imprisoned in the hellish form the Drin had made at Azhrarn's direction. Bisuneh's lover, still trapped in misery, while she had been dust for eight decades or more.

Kaschak saw all this, or sufficient of it. He was not a man of pity, but neither was he unjust. As the foul, stinking horror tumbled and groaned in the sorcerous net, Kaschak sent his servants hither and thither, to fetch this chalk and that powder, to take this amulet from the chest and lay that one back. In the middle of the afternoon, Kaschak began his spell. It was not concluded till the sun itself began to tire and sink down upon its distant bed of blue hills. The thing in the net had undergone many transformations and had lamented beneath them. Now, as the red light left the sky, a wrinkling movement went over the back of the beast. As a serpent crawls from its expended skin, so something now crawled from the wrinkled, three-fold hide.

It was a man who fell exhausted at Kaschak's feet. A man no longer with any appearance of youth, without a vestige of good looks or vitality in him. But still, a man.

He could not remember his name, had forgotten it as he had forgotten his earlier life. He had a vague memory of being cheated, cruelly deprived of joy without even an omen to prepare him. His recollections were merely of dark dripping underpasses echoing caverns bursting with his sub-human cries, filthy holes where he had hidden from meaningless terrors. Kaschak gave him food, wine in a vessel of yellow jade.

"You shall serve me two years to repay my trouble. I will call you Qebba—the much-spoken-of—for so you have been in these parts."

"Qebba" did not argue, with the employment, with the name. His face was the grey bony face of a man dying of hunger who can never be filled. He regained human speech only slowly. He consented to ride on the footboard of Kaschak's carriage. Sometimes, forgetting, his tongue would loll and his eyes roll frightfully. Those who glimpsed him when the carriage passed through the city thought him a lunatic, and marveled as to why he should accompany the Great Kaschak.

It was late, but the ship had stayed for the magician, seeing he was who he was. On the quay, Kaschak made an obscure gesturing. The fine carriage became the size of a walnut; he put it in his pocket. The six black horses, a drip with pearls, became six pretty, white-spotted black beetles. He put them in a comfortable box and, flanked by his servants, cheered by the astonished and captivated crowd, he went aboard, and Qebba with him.

The seas were calm, with a following wind. Two days from shore they came to an island, a forbidding place of black obsidian cliffs that stretched, seemingly without relief or break, into the sky. Here the ship's boat nosed on to a gravel beach, and the magician and his servants were put ashore. This gaunt outpost was no less than Kaschak's home.

The ship sailed on like a scarlet gull. Kaschak struck the impervious obsidian wall of the cliff, and a huge doorway, invisible before, folded open to let them through, grinding shut behind them. Beyond the cliff wall, the island was not as it had appeared—barren and bleak—but one glamorous garden of curious sort.

Rose trees grew in the magician's garden, tall as tall pines. Their blooms were of the palest green and the most transparent purple. Pink willow trees leaned beside the rosy pools that tasted of wine. On the blue lawns lions gambolled— they were the color of fresh cream with hyacinth manes— they ran to the magician and playfully licked his hands like dogs. Owls with round emerald eyes sang melodiously as young girls.

The magician's house was of green porcelain, with a roof of vari-colored glass to let in the light. An avenue of black trees with fruit of pure gold led to the doorway.

Qebba stared about him, bemused by the garden as by all that had happened to him.

"A word of warning," said Kaschak. "In my service you will necessarily learn some magic. Do not seek to learn too much or use carelessly what you come to know. Above all, never pluck the golden fruit of these trees."

The magician's house was no less a wonder than the garden. Diverse beams of color from the glass roof above dyed the rooms, shining on many items of precious metal. A huge water-clock of brass and silver, and in the shape of a galleon, told the hours. At dusk the lamps mysteriously lit themselves.

In a hidden chamber, behind two great doors of black lacquer, the magician practiced his arts. The handles of the doors were in the form of two hands of white jade; to open the doors one must needs clasp these hands in one's own, and twist them. This Qebba noticed the most trusted of Kaschak's servants do on particular occasions, when they were summoned to aid in some experiment. But Qebba himself was not admitted. He did not think to enter the room unasked, but it was reputed to be an awesome place.

Qebba's tasks were strange. Watch for a large bird in the noon sky. Count how many times it circled the magician's house before flying away and write the number on parchment. Go to the twelfth pool, pluck a reed, crush it in a mortar, spread the paste of it on the doorposts of the house. Every ten days, Qebba was told to climb up on the roof and polish the glass there—it must be very thick for it did not crack beneath his feet. Or he would drive the lions, which fed on grass and wild yellow grapes, to another part of the garden.

Two months passed. Qebba was neither happy nor unhappy. He fulfilled his duties, ate his meat and bread and slept in his allotted place. Occasionally he glanced at the doors of black lacquer with the white hands in them, but did not think to enter, did not really think of anything at all. Even now he would forget sometimes, loll his tongue, try to drag his hind limbs, as he had been forced to do when the tail of the lizard was fixed behind him.

One morning Kaschak summoned him and said:

"Go to the black trees in the avenue, Qebba, and pluck a golden fruit."

Qebba turned to obey, then hesitated and said:

"But master, you told me I was not to."

Then Kaschak laughed and went away. He had been trying Qebba, to see if he could trust him still. That afternoon he called Qebba again and said: "Here is a golden sieve. Go to the second pool and fetch me wine-water in it."

Qebba did not argue this time. Though it was a sieve, if the magician demanded it to be filled, then filled it would be. And sure enough when Qebba dipped it in the second pool, none of the water ran out of the holes. He carried the sieve to Kaschak, and Kaschak smiled and said: "As I thought, your years as an enchanted beast in the thraldom of demon-kind have instilled in you some aptitude for thaumaturgy. Come now, you shall enter my workroom." It was a fact that Qebba had acquired unrealized powers, as the magician had suspected from the first. All his tasks had been a test. The circling bird was invisible to an ordinary human eye, the magic reed would not have ground to paste for any man. Under the feet of another, the glass roof would have smashed at the initial step, and few could shepherd the blue and white lions. As for the last test, who but one gifted with sorcery could hold fluid in a sieve?"

So Qebba entered the chamber behind the doors of black lacquer.

A window was there that showed, not the garden beyond, but a hundred different places about the world, whichever the magician conjured to appear. The room was dark, yet everything in it might be seen. On a stand of brass stood the bleached skull of an ancient Magus, which could be made to talk when Kaschak required it. In a crystal jar with a stopper of agate was a tiny woman the size of a man's middle finger, and though she was tiny she was very fair and her hair was like a russet leaf folded about her. When Kaschak tapped the crystal she would dance lasciviously.

Amid these curiosities, Qebba began to learn strange arts, and Great Kaschak was his tutor. The manner of the teaching was bizarre, involving fast, fire, solitude and blood. Qebba's brain, slow in all else, moved swiftly at these lessons. And at his growing powers, a thrill ran through him. Yet always he looked to the magician for guidance, called him "master," kissed his ruby ring and was grateful. He was the child, Kaschak the father. This pleased Kaschak. He foresaw innumerable possibilities in this apt pupil, without danger to himself. The gifts of Qebba, coupled with his ingenuous dullness and malleability, made him the most perfect and most useful aid and servant. He did whatever Kaschak asked, all but one thing.

"Go, pluck a golden fruit in the avenue," said Kaschak.

Qebba answered: "You told me I must not."

And Kaschak laughed.

But even the wise are foolish.

It was the third time Qebba had heard mention of the golden fruits. Once he had been young and happy and quick of mind. Now some buried thought stirred in him. That night he dreamed he plucked golden fruit galore, and it rained down upon him, and, as each fruit touched him, it felt like the warm kisses of a lovely girl, and the glow of gold was like the glow of her hair in lamplight.

Qebba woke with a cry, and, barely knowing what he did, he ran into the night-time garden, into the avenue of black trees, and reached up one hand and grasped what grew there glittering.

At once a snake appeared, wound in the branches, a spotted snake of crimson and green, which seized Qebba's hand in its jaws. But Qebba knew by now a spell to defeat beasts and flying things and reptiles, and this he spoke, and the snake withered and shrank into a twisted cord of green and red silk, and slid into the bushes.

Then Qebba grasped the fruit again, but this time it became as hot as fire and scorched him and he could not keep hold of it. But Qebba had learned a spell of cooling, and this he spoke and the fruit was cold once more.

Then Qebba took it in both hands, and tugged it, but the fruit would not come away from the tree. So Qebba spoke a spell of loosening, and the fruit fell.

Qebba examined the fruit as it lay on the blue grass of the lawn. He did not know what to do with it now it was picked. But after a moment he heard a rustle inside the fruit as if something moved there, and presently a sort of scratching as if something would come out.

Qebba became alarmed, but stronger than alarm now was a

sense of urgency. Lamps were floating from the magician's house, floating in the air with no man to hold them up, and close behind, Kaschak would be walking, come to see what went on at midnight in his garden.

So Qebba spoke a spell of opening, and the golden fruit broke in two pieces, and from within them drifted a gauzy smoke.

Who would dare invite such a smoke? To some it might be healing, but to others, bane. Breathed in at the nostrils, it seemed to fill the eyes and ears and brain. To a man who knew many things, it would reveal many more, to a man who knew little it would reveal too much. Its name was self-knowledge.

Qebba breathed in this potion and staggered up, dropping the two pieces of the broken fruit, clutching at his skull. He had remembered everything—his past, his name, his youth, his love, his loss, his direful sojourn in the hills of rock—and he had reasoned that a hundred years were gone, that all he cared for had passed from the earth. He was alone, and cheated. He had borne the brunt of supernatural malice, without guilt. Men had mocked and reviled him, beaten, burned and cursed him. And now, even here, one sought to make a dolt of him. He had put aside Kaschak's justice, mislayed how he had reverenced him and felt calm in his presence as a frightened child found by its father. He thought simply that he had been duped once more. He knew himself, and he was brimmed with anger, hatred and a thirst to inflict hurt upon the world, as the world and its denizens had hurt him, poor Qebba, who would not own his former name even though he recalled it at last, poor Qebba weeping in the magician's garden.

The magician had come. His shadow fell slanting from the light of the floating lamps across the back of Qebba—one more burden that he would not bear.

Qebba started up, throwing off the shadow.

"You sought to cheat me," Qebba cried. "You have made me a worm, and laughed at me behind your sleeve. Once too often you mocked my foolishness. See, I have discovered it all. I am clever; you were careless to teach me so well. I am a magician too.''

The magician Kaschak said a word that should have bound Qebba more tightly than rope, but Qebba writhed and spoke another word, and the spell slipped aside. Then Kaschak paled, and gnawed upon the large ruby in his ring. For sure, Qebba had learned excellently. Kaschak saw, belatedly, that he had been too certain the beast was tame.

''Come,'' said Kaschak in an easy winning tone, ''your prowess pleases me. You were my servant, but shall be my brother. I saved you from a living death, do not be rash. This may turn out for the best.''

But Qebba grimaced, showing his teeth. There was yet some wolf in him.

''One deceived me before. He came by night, as you do, but him I did not see. I do not want the lying kindness and the gifts of men, nor of other than men. I am armed now.'' And he turned and strode away across the garden.

At that Kaschak was afraid, as he had not been afraid for a score of years. And, summoning his power, Kaschak flung a thunderbolt after his rogue apprentice, to slay him. But the smoke of self-knowledge had greatly heightened Qebba's abilities. He heard the thunderbolt and, spinning about, he flung one of his own, so the two met in the air and exploded with a blue flash. Qebba laughed. ''Now I know you fear me,'' said he, and he ran from the garden.

A single lion stood by the cliff gate, lashing with its tail and snarling. Qebba struck the lion dead with a shining lance he fashioned of air, and passed through the gate and on to the gravel beach. Despite his new-found skill, he had no power over the ocean, for the seas were of another kingdom than the earth, and had their own rulers and their own laws. But Qebba took from his belt a shaving of wood he had picked up, and tore a scrap of cloth from his sleeve, and said the applicable words, and threw them on the water. The cloth and the wood became a little ship and Qebba stepped into it and sailed away from the island.

And Kaschak watched him go in the magic window behind the lacquer doors, and his heart was full of anger and unquiet.

Qebba sailed seven days until he came on a rock in the sea, about the length of four men lying head to heel, and about the breadth of three men in the same attitude. Here, because beauty and comfort were forever soured for him, Qebba set up his home, sheltered by the point of the rock and certain arrangements of stone and cloth. For food he gnawed the sea wrack that grew there and fish that the tides washed up. When he thirsted he made rain fall from the sky into his cupped hands.

Then began a grim and deadly battle of two intent wills and two inventive minds. The strength of Kaschak lay in his mage-craft, but Qebba's ultimate strength lay in his unremitting, senseless, steely hate. As a man struck by misfortune will blindly turn and strike a chair or some other object to hand, so Qebba, unable to strike back across the years at what had truly injured him, now struck at his former master.

At first, Kaschak sought only to defend himself. The acts of Qebba were childish yet unpleasant. It rained black frogs upon Kaschak's garden, or red mud; tornadoes smashed against the cliffs, the sky grew dark from swams of insects, flocks of ravenous predatory birds. But all these things Kaschak turned aside and made harmless, and nothing he sent back against his tormentor. Then there came a plague in the garden, an invisible worm that ate the pink willow trees from within, blighted the exquisite roses, clotted the wine pools with disgusting scum. Kaschak restored his garden and drove out the invisible worm. He put seals and safeguards next over every inch of ground. Not a mote of dust could enter now. Kaschak sat before the magic window in his workroom, and he found in it the island where Qebba lay brooding. The face of Qebba had become greenish with hate, and his eyes had sunk back in hollows like two malevolent animals into their caves. His teeth were yellow and sharp from gnawing sea-

weed and the bones of fish, yellow and sharp as when he had
had the head of a wolf. One of his legs too had become
paralyzed, from lack of exercise on the narrow isle and the
dank weather. And he dragged the leg while he moved, as
once he had dragged the lizard's tail. But his heart, like the
heart of the boar, was tough and lasting.

Kaschak tried many ways to be rid of his enemy. He sent
storms to overwhelm the rock, but Qebba thrust them back.
Kaschak sent a phantom woman who bared her loins and
shook out her ruddy hair, but all lusts but one were dead
in Qebba; he flung stones till she vanished. Kaschak sent
a levin-bolt of enormous magnitude, which split the toy
island in two. But Qebba reappeared on the larger part of it,
grinning.

The two magicians had reached an impasse. Kaschak spoke
to Qebba through the magic window: "Let us cease this
wrangling. What do you want from me?"

"Your life," said Qebba. His sunken eyes gleamed with
his hate. "Your life and the life of the world. My powers are
expanding. I will see to it. None shall be happy, for I was
never happy. None shall live, for I never had a chance at life.
None shall love, save in the grave, for that is where my lover
couches."

Then Kaschak saw it was no use. Kaschak was angry, but
his anger was not like the hating grinning anger of Qebba.
Kaschak's anger was leaden, and he was also afraid.

Kaschak called four gales, and from the four hems of the
four vast garments of them, he made a supernatural net of
interwoven boiling strands. Next, Kaschak, by his arts, asked
a parley with one of the lords of the sea. How the lord came
is not recorded, but perhaps he was blue-skinned and his hair
was a stream of salt water, and his company like him, and
perhaps they rode chariots of coral drawn by teams of the
huge black and white sharks, the killers of men. Maybe their
eyes were circles of gold about a horizontal blue pupil, as
with certain creatures of the deep, and maybe they grew
impatient, finding the air of earth stifled them, and their
slender scaled fingers, bright with jewels spilled from drowned

human ships, fidgeted with the chains of little glass bowls in which gemmy fish, their pet canaries, flitted and sang in voices only the sea-folk could hear.

At any rate, a bargain was struck. A ring of oceanic magic was made to surround Qebba's minuscule rock, and no escape or sending could get by it, as it could not get by the net of gales aloft. And in return for this service, Kaschak would throw a fine jewel into the sea each year, on a certain day. And as long as Kaschak kept his part of the bargain, the sea lord would keep his.

Thus, for the second time in his wretched existence, Qebba was imprisoned. His spells were impotent, his rage turned in upon itself.

To begin with, he ranted and screamed at the insubstantial yet impervious walls of the trap, but the scream of the gales was louder. He also tried to make a bargain with the ocean's people, but in that he had no hope, having no resources, nothing to offer, and the ocean stayed dumb. At last he was weary and lay down on his face on the slimy rock among the sea wrack, and did not move again.

Only his brain worked. It gnawed inward, like a rat. His brain was all hate. Hate devoured him. It reached his heart and soul. His hate had nowhere to travel now, it could not escape. So, like any large force contained, it began to ferment, to seethe.

Time passed. Kaschak lived to a prodigious age. He performed many wonders, and was much esteemed. And every year, on a certain day, he would cast a jewel into the sea. He never forgot. Then one night, in his twentieth decade, Kaschak smiled, bored at length with living, and died. And that year no jewel was sent to the sea lord, and the sea lord accepted the pact as finished, and the magic fence about Qebba's rock dispersed.

But surely Qebba had not lived so long, devoid of nourishment, of space, of activity. The pseudo immortality, the life the monster's skin had lent him, had been amputated with the skin itself. No, Qebba could not live still, and did not. Indeed, his very flesh had vanished from the rock, his bones had even blended with it, were no more.

Yet something remained, something which would not die. The thing which had seethed, bubbled and intensified here in its prison: Qebba's unmitigated, deathless, starving hate.

Which could now get free.

Flat or round, there has always been hate in the world.

The hate of Qebba drifted from the rock and across the sea in the early darkness of night. It had as yet no form, but it had a faint smell, as of metal corroding in acid. It needed food, this entity, till now it had fed upon itself. But the earth was a granary, well stocked, the doors open.

Rough weather began. A hurricane rent the sky and spooned up the ocean. Qebba's Hate came by a foundered vessel. Her sails were torn like the sky, and her lower deck awash. In her belly her rowers shrieked and cursed in their shackles, above, a little boat was being lowered, and men were fighting for a place in it, and as soon as one had slain another, a third man came and slew him. At this spot, the Hate of Qebba supped and dined, and a new strength flooded into it.

Later, Hate drifted to shore. In a wood of pines, five robbers had caught and were knifing a traveler. Presently they cheated each other of their shares of the robbery, and fell to blows. Hate fed. In a town of many lamps, a husband mounted his wife and took his rights of her; how she loathed him and wished him in his tomb. In a yard, a woman whipped her child-slave; the slave lay huddled on the cold stone and dreamed of gouging out her eyes as the whip sliced his back with the vehemence of the woman's fury. In a cheerful tavern, two poor men plotted to murder a rich man, for they were envious of his wealth. In a tower, a girl on a velvet bed stuck pins into the heart of a wax image of her lover who had deserted her. Under a bridge, two youths fought for the favor of a third, who laughed at and despised them. On the highway, a leper was beaten to death.

Hate, fed, Hate feasted. Hate moved swiftly onward, and feasted again.

The world was wide, a great banquet-table. The dishes were various: hate which slew, hot as fire, hate which whispered and spoke lies, cold as ice, hate which merely hated, the strongest hate of all, the hate which, turned in upon itself, gained power and resonance, hate as black as a pit. All these delicacies the Hate of Qebba gorged upon. It grew vigorous, vital. It swelled and burgeoned.

Soon it could itself, by a projection of its aura, inspire hatred on the earth. Where it passed, adrift like a cloud, dislike altered to a wild gnashing thing. The girl who had tired of her sister's chat, seized a dagger and plunged it in her breast, the servant who coveted his master's goods, bought poison. All caught the sickness. Presently, the prince, enraged by petty grievances, made war upon his brother's land.

Then came a new era over the earth, the time of Hatred.

City marched against city, kingdom rose in arms against kingdom. The little individual murders by man of man were followed swiftly by greater murders, as nation tore out the throat of nation. Everywhere was blood and fire and the clashing of steel. Everywhere the air was loud with lament and maledictions.

The seed is very small; it will become a tree when nourished by good soil. Qebba's Hate had been also very small, but it had moved, a catalyst, in the soil of mankind, absorbing, growing. Now the tree covered the world with its shadow. It had taken many years, but years are of no consequence to such an entity. While it could feed, it could not die, and there were rations in plenty. Time was on its side.

And the works of Hate were not done. The earth itself, bearing these struggles on her back, began to writhe and groan with malice. Her beautiful places became battlefields, crows flapped on the corpse of her land among her burned woods and among the ruins of each vast metropolis that had been her jewel. Now the ground split with earthquake, mountains spewed up fire and the seas boiled over like cauldrons. By day the face of the sun was livid, and by night the moon was red. Plague rose from the swamps in her robes of yellow and black, Famine walked both behind and before, gnawing her own knuckles for hunger. Death was everywhere, but maybe even he, who was another of those Lords of Darkness, even Death, maybe, beheld his harvest with unease, his baskets being overloaded.

Men cried to their gods. In the morning they would slay each other; by night, fresh from the battlefield, they raved before unreplying altars. So they came to hate even the gods, and smashed their images and defiled their sanctums. "There *are* no gods!" they cried. "Then who has done this thing to us?" In the light of the riven mountains, on the shores of the wailing oceans, they did not see the shadow cast on them, the shade of the tree of Hate they had fed. "It is the worker of all evil," a woman cried in one land, a man in another, "the Master of Night, Bringer of Anguish, the Eagle-Winged, the Unspeakable. *He* has done this."

So, as towers fell, they would scream it; when the earth opened and swallowed them down, they would choke out his name. They no longer feared him. They had other things to fear.

"Azhrarn has done this to us. The Prince of Demons means to destroy the world."

He was innocent. An irony that he, creator of black deeds, had had no hand in this, save at its remotest beginning, unknowing.

He had been at some sport or game of the Underearth, had Azhrarn, something that had kept him from the world a year or two, four hundred mortal years or more. It was some beautiful boy, some fabulous woman, another Sivesh, another Zorayas, or someone he had created for himself; like Ferezhin, or one who had consented, unlike Bisuneh, and he, in his turn, had not tired of them, down below ground in the wondrous city of Druhim Vanashta, where he must have taken them. While he had lain with cool flesh, or walked beneath the black trees of his garden, or dreamed some dream exclusive to a demon's brain, a dream too strange and of too great magnitude that it be guessed at—while he had done that, Hate had chewed at the world, and the world begun to shrivel and to die.

The Demon Prince had caused illimitable pain and loss there, war and sorrow, rage and death. The Vazdru, hearing the cry of humanity ring in the bell-like psychic cavity of their inner ears—Azhrarn destroys us!—looked to see their prince smiling. But Azhrarn never smiled. He strode between the jade palaces and the iron; he mounted a horse of black oil and blue steam; he rode through the three gates. And riding away from the earth's center and its volcanos, he saw new volcanos exploding their fire across the length and breadth of earth, and where they did not burn, the cities were burning in their stead. And he saw Plague go by, and Famine, and Death walking on the horizon. The seas he saw too, in different places, drowning the land, and the broken towers poking up, and the bloated corpses floating, and where the new land had pushed from the waters he saw armies struggle ashore and begin again to fight among the sea pools and the sea wrack. And above, the bloody moon gave relentless light that he might see it all and miss nothing.

Azhrarn reined in the demon horse upon a jagged cliff top. He gazed to east and west, to north and south, and the face of Azhrarn, it is truly said, had become white. Long he looked, and long his pallor increased. A mortal man could not grow so pale and live.

A memory had found Azhrarn, of the warning of Kazir, the blind poet. How, when the Demon Lord had told him all he possessed and asked him if there were anything he yet needed that he could not do without, the poet had quietly answered him: "Mankind."

And the cold song of Kazir had come back to him, which related how all men had perished and the world was empty, and the sun rose and set on emptiness. But then Azhrarn flew in the form of an eagle over the noiseless cities, the sailless oceans, searching for men. But not one was left to fill the days of the Demon with joy and wickedness, not one was left to whisper the name of Azhrarn.

Cold fear had fallen then upon the heart of Azhrarn like winter snow. Cold fear came now. Even the dark star cannot live without the sky to hold him; there is no foothold in the bottomless abyss.

Yes, Azhrarn, Lord of Fear, was afraid. He foretold the death of humanity, he observed Hate like a black moon rising in the sky, and read human destruction in it. With such eyes as his, he could see the very shape of Hate, which had no shape, and he smelled the smell of it, of acid eating at metal, eating at the life of the world. And Azhrarn fled the earth, fled into his city underground, into a deep room of his palace, and there he shuddered, locked in and alone that none should witness his terror. Yes, terror; Azhrarn, Lord of Terrors, terrified.

Terrified.

A silent horror cloaked the demon city of Druhim Vanashta. No Vazdru mocked or sang, there came no chord of harp nor ring of dice nor baying of hounds. The Eshva wept, and did not know why they wept. By the black lake, the hammers of the Drin were still, and the red forges sank to ashes.

Then Azhrarn appeared, his face like a handsome effigy cut from stone, his eyes blazing. He summoned the Drin. He gave them a task. They were to build for him a ship with wings, a flying ship, powerful enough to pierce the highest sky and penetrate where neither mortals nor birds could go, the rare country of the Upperearth, the domain of the gods themselves.

The Drin labored with fright in their murky little hearts. They took much silver and white metal and a small portion of gold, the unloved stuff of demons and blue steel and red bronze. And as the Drin worked, the Vazdru glided in and out of Azhrarn's palace, and there they took his hands or fell on their knees before him and urged him not to leave them. But Azhrarn put them aside, and sat in stony speechlessness, tapping his ringed fingers upon an ivory book, from impatience.

Presently, the ship was ready. The sides of it glinted and gleamed from the many bands of metal there, blue and grey and yellow and red. It had a canopy of smoke, and a silver

sail woven of winds, and the tiller was the thigh bone of a
dragon. The wings of the ship were like the strong white
wings of swans, but the plumage of them was made from the
demon flax that grew on the margins of Sleep River, and
steeped in the dreams of men.

Azhrarn came to the ship, and praised it, and the ugly Drin
blushed and simpered foolishly. Azhrarn entered the ship,
and spoke to it and took the tiller, and the ship rose through
the three gates, through the vent of the one quiet volcano left
in the world, and the Vazdru shivered.

Up through the black and vulpine air of earth the ship
thrust its way, upward, till the land lay far below like seeth-
ing pitch picked out by burning lights of fire and wreck. The
wind sail blew and turned. The ship passed the congested
moon that glared huge and awful in the dark. Through the
roots of the starry gardens the ship passed, through the world's
roof. Its wings made great semi-circular beats. It flew where
no ship of man had ever sailed or wayward bird had ever
flown, in at the wide, invisible, half-nonexistent gate of
Upperearth.

There was always light in Upperearth, undying light of
enormous clarity, like and unlike the constant illumination of
the demon place. For the light of Upperearth resembled that
of a clear and icy winter dawn, though no sun shone, and sky
and land were all one.

A cold blue country was Upperearth, a cold blue which
symbolized the passionless celestial things that dwelt there.

There was no geography as such, simply this razor-edged
blueness everywhere, and in the far distance, a dim sugges-
tion of knife-edged blue mountains, capped with adamantine
snow, though these mountains seemed to have no bases, and
indeed, remained eternally distant and unreachable, even should
you walk towards them for seven years. Occasionally there
might come in view the isolated mansions of the gods themselves, each far removed from each. Such structures bore no
relation to the buildings of earth or to the palaces of Druhim
Vanashta. Rather they were like immense harps, or the strings
of harps, slender shafts of pure gold radiance that vibrated
slightly in a soundless music.

Near the invisible, half-nonexistent gateway, where the ship had come to rest, stood the Sacred Well, from which might be drawn up draughts of Immortality. But the Well was a paradox, no doubt pleasing to the gods, for they themselves did not need to drink these waters, being already immortal, while men, who craved such a drink, could never hope to reach the spot. (Once, possibly, there had formed a tiny crack in this Well—which was made of glass—through which a drop or two of the precious elixir might have spilled. Or, time being as it was in Upperearth, possibly the tiny crack had yet to come about.) Since the Well was made of glass, the water of Immortality was freely to be seen in it. It was of a leaden grey, this water, perhaps a warning. Close by, on a bench of thinnest platinum, sat two bowed, grey-cloaked figures, the Well's Guardians.

Azhrarn stepped from the winged ship, and the Guardians raised their heads at once. Neither had a face, only one huge swivelling and ever-attentive eye, and they spoke from an unlikely area in their breasts.

"You may not drink," said the first Guardian to Azhrarn, regarding him with this pitiless fearsome eye.

"Indeed you may not," said the other, regarding him also.

"I am not here to drink," said Azhrarn. "Do you not know me?"

"It is futile to know anything," said the first Guardian, "since all things below pass, alter, decline and perish, and all things here above are unchanging."

"Humankind know me," said Azhrarn.

"Humankind," said the second Guardian. "What are they that we should be interested in their knowledge?"

Azhrarn folded his cloak about him, and went by them. They, seeing he did not mean to attempt drinking, bowed their heads again and appeared to sleep beside the leaden water of Eternal Life.

Azhrarn, the Prince of Demons, one of the Lords of Darkness, went through that delicate chill region like a black reality. He walked towards those mountains that might never be reached, and, after many mortal days, he came to a huge floor of chequers that stretched from horizon to horizon. And the chequers were of two colors that were never seen on earth or under it, one the color of profound solitude and the other the color of complete indifference, and here some of the gods were to be found. A few were walking slowly about, but most stood motionless. Not an eyelid flickered, not a limb twitched, they neither spoke nor breathed.

They had the appearance of humanity, or rather, the appearance that humanity had had in the beginning, for these gods had made men. In those days, when the earth was flat, gods were permitted such eccentricities. But how fragile the gods were, how ethereal. Their hair was so pallid a gold it was almost silver, their flesh was transparent, showing that they had no bones, only the faintest of faint violet ichors that swam in the transparency without the need of arteries or veins. Their eyes were polished mirrors that reflected nothing. When they grew excited (which was rarely), at some astonishing metaphysical revelation within themselves, tissue-fine butterflies would flutter from their crystalline robes, and dissolve like bubbles in the blue, blue air.

When Azhrarn came among them, the gods stirred vaguely, like grasses in a light breeze.

Azhrarn said: "The earth is dying. Man, your creation, is dying. Did you not hear of this?"

But the gods did not answer, or look at him, or seem to see him.

Then Azhrarn told them how the earth split and burned, and men slew each other under the goad of a sorcerous enduring hatred that fed and grew more vital on destruction. He told them everything and spared no word.

And the gods did not answer, or look at him, or seem to see him.

Then Azhrarn went to a single god, or, as it might be, a goddess, for it was difficult to ascertain if the gods had two sexes or one or several or none at all. And Azhrarn kissed the god on the lips, and the eyelids of the god flickered, and butterflies rose from his garments.

"Men you made," Azhrarn said, "but me you did not make, and I will have an answer."

So the god spoke to Azhrarn at last, though not by means

of voice or tongue or language, in fact it is not known how he spoke, but speak he did. And he said this: "Mankind is nothing to us, and the earth is nothing to us. Man is a mistake we made. Even gods are entitled to one mistake. But we will not perpetrate another by saving him. Let him vanish from the earth, and earth vanish from the state of Being. You are the Demon, and humanity is your beloved toy, but we have graduated from such trivia. If you wish man to be saved, then you must save him, for we shall not."

Azhrarn did not reply, or demand another syllable from the gods. He only gazed at them, and where his gaze lingered, the edges of their crystalline garments shrivelled like paper in a fire. But no more could Azhrarn do, for gods are gods.

Thus Azhrarn returned over the blue cold Upperearth, his back to the unreachable mountains now, and he came to the Well of Immortality, and he spat in it. And such was the nature of Azhrarn, that the leaden water roiled, and for a moment grew clear and bright, before the greyness overcame it once again. But the Guardians merely snored on their bench, and Azhrarn entered into the winged ship, and left the Upperearth behind him.

6   The Sun and the Wind

The Demon stood on the flax grown banks of Sleep River; before him flowed its heavy iron waters with a dismal sound, behind him lay the winged ship, like a dead swan. The heart of a darkness can become no darker. Yet, in the person of Azhrarn had always flamed an occult brilliancy which now was gone. And his face was bitter and terrible as he stood shrouded in hollow fear upon the river bank. Here, where he had so often pitilessly hunted the souls of men asleep, strange fancies hunted the inner creature of Azhrarn.

And as he brooded there, a translucent image, like wafer-thin ivory, rose from the waters. Not the soul of a sleeping man this, few enough slept deeply in those terrifying cata-clysmic days of earth to let their souls go wandering so far. This was the soul of one dead.

Azhrarn gazed at the soul, and the soul at him. The eyes of the soul were two blue fragments of an evening, the hair amber, and about its wrist and on its shoulder lay tendrils of deep ocean weed.

"Do you know me, my Lord of all Lords," asked the soul, "or do you forget me as easily as you slew me? I am Sivesh who drowned in the green seas of morning because you hated me, who gave you only love. My bones are rotted away on the floor of that sea, but I have lingered in this parody of my human shape, for even at the amorphous gate beyond life, I loved you still, who disowned and destroyed me, and my love has bound me to the world."

Azhrarn looked at the soul of his dead lover, and what he thought no man knows, but he said: "Many thousand mortal years have passed since I parted from you. Why do you seek me now?"

"The world is ending," said the soul. "But of all things, the world you love. I have come to see if you will save the world or let her die. For in the world's death is the death of Azhrarn. Though you should live two million times a million years, without the earth yet are you dead, and you will wander as I do, and you will be as dead as I, and as purposeless."

Then the soul drew close, and through its body you could see the far shore, and the dark river going by. And it kissed the hand of Azhrarn, but the touch of it was like the touch of cool smoke only. It faded like ice in the sun.

Hate lay upon the earth, penetrated her to her deepest caves, her most secluded valleys. Hate raped the earth, and the children of Hate burst forth. And Hate, ultimate victory, had taken at last a form, a form like a huge head, or rather, a mouth. No man could perceive this apparition, which devoured him. But no man, if he had deciphered the calamity, and seen Hate as its root, could have come up against it, as a hero would go to confront a dragon, for no man could have endured this presence. For all the little wickednesses in men, in the vicinity of such concentrated malignancy the bravest or the worst of them would falter, scorch, crumble.

Only one could meet that entity which had been Qebba's Hate, only one could see, smell, find or match it. For hate, to Azhrarn, had been a familiar, a beautiful harp which might be played, a skill, a jest.

Where the location was of Hate's core, this form it had assumed, is not remembered, nor might it be written down, much as water cannot be chewed. It was supposedly some part-abstract place, neither in the world nor out of it. At any rate, the landscape was somewhat like the earth's, a range of bleak crags, their lower terraces black with burned trees, and burnished thick cloud ringing the upper pinnacles, shining with a curious brownish leaden light. When dawn broke on the tortured world, the sun would also rise upon this scene, but now it was night on earth, and night here also, and here and there a red star glittered like a drop of blood through the unwholesome haze.

Somewhere in the cloud and the haze, the head and the mouth and the core of Hate was writhing its brown bulbous lips. It could see, too, through its mouth, kept open at all times, though its sight was in no way like a mortal's. And now it "saw" a darkness on the slopes below, and the darkness took on the shape of a tall and handsome man, black of hair and eyes, and swathed in a black cloak that made him seem winged, like an eagle.

Never before had anything found Hate out, reached its citadel and stood looking at it. And Hate sensed in the figure below a powerful maleficence comparable to its own, yet imperceptibly different, a feast of evil. Hate could neither feed on nor influence.

Then Hate spoke. That is to say, it communicated. Its voice was a kind of odor, like cinders from a volcano, and the language it used was like an impulse, a twitching in the joints, nerves rasped unpleasantly, an ache that did not quite ache.

"I came from a man's brain," said Hate. "That began me. Though I have forgotten him, his human vindictiveness was my father. But you are not a man. Why are you here? What do you want?"

The figure on the slope, Azhrarn, did not answer, but instead began to climb towards the pinnacle above which the bulbous brown lips might be distinguished. He passed through one ring of dully shining cloud, then through a second. The pinnacle itself was a spike of raw grey rock. Here Azhrarn presently halted.

"There is much wickedness in you," said the lips of Hate, and they silkily slavered. "I would devour you if I could. Trade with me. Give me your wickedness, and you shall be a Lord of the world through all her final and tumultuous days."

But Azhrarn seated himself on the pinnacle and said nothing.

"You have slain many," whispered the mouth of Hate greedily. "Slay others. I will give you a whole army to slay—they will rush at you screaming and their teeth will flash in the red moonlight, and you will stretch forth your arms and they will expire, and I shall be fed. Come, I will find you beautiful women and you shall cut their pearl flesh with a jeweled knife and find rubies under the skin. I know a vault where men have buried a beautiful boy alive; I will let you see him. His flesh is like alabaster and his hair like spilled white wine. To the north of the world a great many mountains have exploded in fire. The magma runs down like golden snakes upon the cities below. To the south, the seas are running over the land like silver dogs. Come, I will give you a sea and a mountain. Come.''

Azhrarn said nothing, but he took a pipe of fine bronze from his sleeve, and he began to make music with it. When the music played, the clouds ringed about the mountains started to break up, and soon they changed to cloudy shapes that danced and embraced to the rhythm of the pipe. And the bare rock of the mountains hummed and trembled gently as if the bones of them were dancing too.

The brown mouth of Hate was dry.

''Do not treat me so,'' said Hate. ''There is no profit in this.''

Then Azhrarn took a small silver box from his cloak, and out of it he sprinkled a spangled powder, and this gave a wonderfully sweet perfume.

The brown mouth of Hate twisted.

''Ah, do not do this,'' it said, ''these things are offensive to me. You are not tender by nature, for I believe you are a demon. Yes, I am assured you are a demon. Come, be a demon, be extravagantly cruel, and please me. I cannot hurt you. We should be comrades, you and I. For, in a far past, you planted the seed which began me.''

But Azhrarn took from his belt a single flower he had found still growing on the earth. It was blue-purple, the shade the sages classified as the color of love, and when Azhrarn set it on the naked pinnacle of the mountain, the flower sank its roots in the unpromising rock, and in a minute it had sprung up into a beautiful tree, whose flowery branches brushed the low sky.

"Now," said the brown mouth of Hate, withdrawing slightly, for the color and the scent of flowers inclined it to nausea, "you are unmannerly, my demon visitor. But I shall not have to suffer you much longer. Look in the east, and you will notice you must soon be leaving."

Azhrarn turned, and looked as the mouth of Hate suggested.

There, through the turgid haze, one dim yellow sword had struck—the first omen of the dawn.

No demon could remain above ground once the sun came there, this was well known, and even Hate knew it.

Azhrarn had put aside the bronze pipe and the silver box, and leaned his back on the flowering tree.

"You have said much," Azhrarn murmured, "now it is my turn. None could meet you save I, for who does not recall the cunning the wisdom of demons? None but I, my vile companion, could destroy you."

Then Hate opened wide its brown lips, and showed the cavern that yawned behind them, a gigantic maw, without teeth or tongue or throat, a pit that could never be filled.

"Destruction is my prerogative," Hate said. Then its lips drew in again, and it said. "The light is stronger. You had better be gone."

But Azhrarn took his ease, leaning against the tree as if on cushions of silk. And he watched the glow in the east, where two rose swords were lifted now on either side the yellow. And Azhrarn's eyes were half lidded over as he gazed, and he smiled, though his lips were white.

The mouth in the sky grew abruptly pale also, ugly pale as something diseased.

"Come," it said, "you should be going. A demon may not face the sun."

But Azhrarn made no move, and now there were ten swords in the east, seven of silver and three of gold.

"Ah, but this is foolish," said Hate, quivering, "you are acting out a symbol of self-sacrifice—but what is the world to you? Let the world go. There shall be others. See. How bright the sun is growing. You have only an instant or so more. Once the sun rises—only think of it. The agony of that light, the light that fades the things of the demon country and turns its folk to dust. Oh, Azhrarn, Azhrarn!'' howled the mouth of Hate, recognising him suddenly, shuddering and contorting, causing the clouds to swirl and the cages to rumble, ''nothing is worth such hurting. Run, Azhrarn, fly, Azhrarn. The Underearth is cool and shadowy. You cannot love the earth so much that you will sacrifice eternal life for her.''

There were twenty swords now in the east; five were silver, twelve were gold, three were of white steel. Azhrarn rose, and stood beneath the tree. All about the sky and the land were rocked by the convulsions of Hate as it strove to move him. But Azhrarn was motionless as the rock and the sky had been. He stared straight in the direction of the sun, as does the eagle still, in memory of that stare of his.

Every sword was white now, and beneath, the rim of a whiteness that was not of white but of blindness—black. The sun rose.

Two slender nails pierced the eyes of Azhrarn, two more his breast and three his loins. Dark glowing blood ran from the corners of his mouth and from his nostrils and his finger tips. He did not, the Prince of Demons, cry aloud at the agony that blasted him, though it seemed to linger many centuries, and every moment it grew harder to suffer, and sweet, needle-threaded singing pain, the roaring oxen of pain that trampled beneath. And then at length came a golden pain, worse than all the rest, and at that he must have cried out, even Azhrarn, the Prince of Demons, but in that second he was turned to smoke and to dust and to silence.

These, the ashes of Azhrarn, were blown across the face of Hate.

Hate could not bear it. Hate fed on hate, and now perforce it fed on love, and love choked it. Even the love of Azhrarn, the wickedest of all the wicked, the love of the Demon for earth that no god, gods being above such things, any longer cared for. There was an explosion of many lights and thunderings as the love of the Demon for the earth destroyed the earth's Hate, as the sun had destroyed Azhrarn.

*   *   *

Hate was dead, and the Demon was dead. Nothing could follow but an age of absolute Innocence.

The face of earth was much altered, seas now where continents had been, mountains fallen or upraised, forests withered, new forest springing from rank, haphazard seed. The race of mankind had survived, due to the intervention of Azhrarn. Now, puzzled, it gazed about. Without a ruling Hate, the small hate that remained in men had shrunk, and not for several ages would it grow again to its old, honest, filthy and natural proportions. This day, all men were brothers. They fell on each other's necks and sobbed, and led each other from the fallen ruins into the bright new day. And there they built altars, and blessed the aloof gods, who never noticed, and in three centuries, or less, the name of Azhrarn was forgotten, as they forgot the night at the coming of the day.

It was a unique time in the world, then, and no mistaking it. Kings who were just, few thieves and fewer murderers. The scars healed, and the soil of the lands was bathed in flowers and grain, and tall trees mantled the shoulders of the hills, and the fires of mountains slept in their high blue towers. It is said that tigers would follow a young girl like dogs and never harm her, and unicorns would act out mock battle with their golden horns in broad daylight, and that every fortieth fruit of the orange tree contained a wish, and the cats learned how to sing and did it most charmingly.

That was the earth. But below the earth there was no singing. Three centuries had passed, but little had passed with them. What the earth forgot, the Underearth had cause to remember.

Druhim Vanashta mourned. The Drin by their cold furnaces, among their neglected rusting heaps of metal, cried and snivelled, and their tears raised the level of the black lake on whose shores their forges stood. The Eshva wept, and the snakes that coiled in their long tresses wept too, tears of polished serpentine. But it was the Vazdru who railed and cursed mankind for its forgetfulness. The Vazdru did not weep easily, yet the water ran from their eyes. They put on mourning robes—yellow, for the sun which had slain their beloved Lord—and they tore their hair and bared their breasts, both male and female, and scourged themselves with whips of jade.

"The world dishonors Azhrarn," the Vazdru princesses cried.

"Let us go above ground," the princes of the Vazdru shouted, "and make the accursed ones burn with shame."

Then, by night, the Vazdru visited the innocent new earth. They passed like phantoms along the sea shores and through the tall standing corn, they crossed the highways of men, and in the cities the lamps glittered on their ochre garments and their beautiful distraught faces. And they smote stringed instruments as they passed, and shook the sistrum, and called loudly: "Azhrarn is dead! Azhrarn is dead!" And they cast black blossoms before them, and scratched with briars of black iron on the doors.

The dogs began howling and the nightingale was quiet.

The people said: "Who is it they speak of? Azhrarn is a name we do not know. But surely he must be some great lord or king to be so mourned." And they bowed respectfully to the Vazdru, and offered them wine or money, not knowing they were demons. And the Vazdru had no heart for wickedness with their Prince dead, and they went off crying into the darkness.

There was also an Eshva woman who came to the earth by night, but she came more quietly. It was none other than Jaseve, the demoness Azhrarn had poured from a ewer to be the solace of Drezaem. Primroses no longer grew in her hair, the silver snakes were back in it. Her eyes were dry, for she had thought unaccountably of a curious place, half in the world, half out, where a tree of blue-purple flowers sprang from a barren mountain top.

A long while Jaseve searched, several years. She went to the world's four corners and returned from them. At length she found the curious place, and the way into it. She walked where Hate had died, no longer over mountains, for they had been shaken down, no longer through a blackened wood, for it had put forth leaves, copying the fertile world. The moon had risen. It showed a terrible scar in the very sky itself,

puckered and luminous—the wound where Hate's mouth had
been torn out of it. Beneath that scar stood a tree, as in the
dream of Jaseve, though its flowers were not the shade of
loving now, but grey as ashes.

Jaseve ran to the tree. She kissed its narrow stem and dug
in the rubble of the mountain to free it. Her hands bled, and
her blood fell on the roots of the tree and they seemed to
struggle up towards her. Then it was loosened, and Jaseve
drew it from the stones and put it on her back, for it weighed
very little. She carried the tree from that ground on to the
earth, but there she must set it down, for she was weary. At
once the tree thrust its roots into the fruitful soil. Jaseve
became aware they were in a forest, the tree and herself, a
forest thick and close and ancient, one spot which had escaped upheaval. Here, with the boughs knotted so intense and
dark above, and the trunks massed round about like sentinels,
no speck of sunlight could get in, even at high noon. Jaseve
observed this and smiled dreamily. She lay down beneath the
tree, caressing its grey bark with her hand.

At the edge of the ancient forest was a highway, and by the
highway a farm of many fields, orchards and vineyards.

Now the farmer had seven daughters, the youngest being
fourteen and the eldest twenty, for each had been born within
a year of the other, and though all seven were lovely, all
seven were virgins, for this was an age of innocence. However, they lacked a mother's guidance, she being dead, and
small wonder. From the eldest down, the meanings of their
names were as follows: Fleet, Flame, Foam, Fan, Fountain,
Favour and Fair.

Now it happened that these seven sisters were not as
modest, lacking a mother's guidance, as they might have
been. Their father, a bluff insensitive man, had not seen his
girls tricked out as they should have liked, while in the town
nearby was a sly silk merchant, who had said to each of
them, at one time or another: "Your magnolia flesh would
look far better in a gown of silk than in that homespun. Come
and visit me one night, and I will see what can be done."
None of the seven maidens had gone to him as yet. They did

not like to, for they had noted, ignorant though they were, that his fat yellow fingers had a tendency to roam over them as much as over the bolts of silk, while the youngest had declared he housed an animal in his britches that pushed them out in a most peculiar way whenever she bent over him to admire the new silk samples, as he constantly invited her to do.

Still, the old villain kept on at them, and they kept on thinking of the silk, and one night the seven agreed upon a plan.

The silk merchant was in the back room of his shop, doctoring his books to deceive the king's tax collectors, when a delicate scratching came upon the door.

"Who is there?" demanded the merchant nervously. Though there were few robbers in those days, he—being one himself—was ever conscious of their existence, and invested the night with them. "Beware my sixteen servants and my mad dog."

But a sweet voice called through the keyhole: "It is I, dear merchant, Fair, the farmer's seventh daughter. But if there is a mad dog—"

However, the merchant had leapt up, overjoyed at his luck, and flung open the door.

"Enter my unworthy shop," he cried, leading Fair inside. "There are none here but I," he added, "you misheard me. Mad dog! What nonsense! Do not be so timorous but come closer, and then I will see about the silk for a dress. Of course," he assured her winningly, "I cannot fit you when you are clothed; you must remove your garments."

Fair promptly did as he suggested. The merchant licked his lips and rolled his eyes, and Fair noted that the strange animal was about him again.

"And now," said the merchant, "just stand by the wall there, and I will measure you."

Fair demurely obeyed, and the merchant, unable to restrain himself further, flung himself at her.

"But is this quite necessary?" inquired Fair, as he covered her with repulsive slobberings and kisses.

"Indeed, yes," avowed the merchant, undoing his britches and preparing once more to advance.

"No, but I do not think so," said Fair, and, raising her voice, screamed for her sisters. At once all six, who had been attentively waiting outside, rushed in, brandishing various household items, with which they set about the merchant.

"This is I, Fleet, the farmer's first daughter," yelled Fleet, cracking him on the left shin with a huge meat-hook.

"And this is Flame," yelled Flame, cracking the other shin with a small griddle.

"And this Foam," a blow on the buttocks.

"And this Fan," a blow on the back.

"While I am Fountain," announced Fountain, appropriately pouring a jar of cold oil over him.

"And I, Favour," added Favour, hitting him about the head with some tongs.

The merchant roared and skipped and soon slipped over in the oil and fell on the ground. Here the seven daughters beat him unmercifully till he entreated them to take all the silk they could carry, and let him alone. This turned out more generous then he had intended, for the seven had prudently brought their father's oxen and cart with them, and loaded it high. The merchant wailed and wrung his hands.

"And now," said Fleet, "you will tell no one we have been here."

"You must say robbers attacked you," advised Flame.

"If you do not," said Foam.

"And if you accuse us," said Fan.

"Of *anything*," said Fountain.

"We will also tell how you made our little sister stand naked against the wall of your shop," went on Favour.

"And meant to take a vicious wild animal, probably your mad dog, out of your trousers and set it on me," finished Fair indignantly.

The merchant accordingly roused the town with cries of twenty gigantic black-bearded robbers toting clubs of iron, while the sisters rode home along the highway with a cart full of silk.

But, as the laden vehicle came up to the farm where it

stood against the black curtain of the ancient forest, the sisters beheld, in the moonlight, a most beautiful lady waiting in the road.

"Why," said Fleet, "she must be very rich. See, she was silver snakes in her hair, so cunningly wrought they seem alive."

"But look," said Fair, "her hands have been bleeding."

"What can she want with us?" said Fan.

When the woman came nearer, the oxen sighed and halted, and shut their large eyes. She walked three times about the cart, studying every sister in turn, and then she walked away up the road and aside from it into the dark forest.

"She must be a sprite," said Foam.

"Or a deranged princess," said Flame.

Fountain and Favour sniffed haughtily.

Jaseve meantime, who had been attracted, as were the demons ever, by the scent of this little wickedness of theirs returned to the grey-flowered tree, and embraced it. Next, on the flat mossy lawn between the close knit trunks, Jaseve began to dance.

A wild dance it was, a dance to wake the night and the air, to call creatures and things. A black hare came first, and sat to gape at her with round pale eyes, then foxes who did not even seem to notice the hare, and after them two stags with daggered horns, and owls on wings like banners, and a lion, pale as smoke with age. Even water beasts stole up, drawn from the deep pools of the forest and the swamps there by the silent irresistible dancing of the Eshva woman. At last even the wind came from the east to the forest, pulled by her magic.

When Jaseve heard it shaking the leaves on the trees, she loosed her sash and the wind swirled into it, billowing there as if in a sail. And Jaseve swiftly knotted the sash together so the wind could not get free, for such things demons had power to do. Then she stopped dancing. The animals ran away. The wind struggled and complained in the sash as Jaseve tied it securely among the boughs of the grey-flowered tree.

*   *   *

The seven daughters of the farmer made for themselves dresses of silk, but did not dare wear them by day for fear of discovery. Then somehow they got the notion to dress up at night, and steal out to the edge of the ancient forest. Here they would flounce up and down, pretending they were princesses, and discussing the weather, as they had heard princesses exclusively did, since everything else was within their jurisdiction, and therefore, bored them.

"How strange it is," said Fleet, "that there is no east wind tonight."

"There has been none for days," said Flame.

"The ships are becalmed at sea," said Foam.

"And the windmills must be turned by teams of men," said Fan.

"As for the buzzards and other floating birds," said Fountain, "they sit on the fences and grumble, unable to sail the air currents."

"And the scarecrow stays still, and does not scare off the pigeons," said Favour.

"Yet," added Fair, "the foul smell from the midden no longer blows into the vineyard at dawn."

Just then, the seven sisters glimpsed a figure standing before them among the trees. It was none other than the beautiful lady they had come across on the night of the robbery.

"What does she want?" the sisters asked each other. "Now she is beckoning us to go with her. But we must not follow," they said, finding they already were. The forest was ebon and mysterious, yet they were not afraid. The woman led them deeper and deeper into the gloom, and somehow they did not wish to turn back. Finally they came to a tree unlike the other trees, a tree of flowers, but they were grey, and in its branches was a sash that blew about by itself.

As they were looking at it, Jaseve began a second time to dance. But on this occasion none came near, for the dance was for the tree and for the wind bound in the branches and for the seven virgin sisters. And suddenly the sisters began dancing also, unafraid and unwondering, as if they were only natural that they, clad in silk, hand in hand and led by a woman with snakes in her hair, should circle round and round a grey-flowered tree in an archaic forest at midnight.

They danced till a marvelous sensuous weariness overcame them, and then the seven virgin sisters sank down in a ring about the trunk, and their heads fell back on the springy moss, and their eyes were glazed by dreams. Jaseve stole by them and, reaching up, she swiftly loosed the knot in the sash and shook forth the wild east wind. Furious to be free, the wind was. It lashed the tree so all the grey flowers were violently tossed in it, and from their petals the greyness flew off in a thick cloud. It was actually ash that had turned them ash-grey, and now the ash was sucked up into the wind as it flew about the tree, and next, as the wind raced in a circle, the ash scattered from it. It settled upon the seven maidens beneath the tree and, as it did so, each one moaned and twisted as if some invisible force of pleasure had seized her. And then each cried out aloud several times, and lay quiet. The ash had vanished and the wind had fled. Jaseve sighed, and she too went away, patiently to wait.

Seven girls woke in the morning, woke in the ancient forest dressed in silk. Seven girls remembered an unusual experience, and seven girls blushed. Over their heads a tree of blue-purple flowers was not as they recalled.

Bemused, whispering, giggling, they crept home and took off their silk, and hid themselves virtuously in their beds.

Some months later, there was no hiding anything.

"Oh, my daughters!" bellowed the farmer. "All seven deflowered. All seven with child."

It was true enough, no mistaking the signs. Seven lovely girls with high round bellies, lowering their demure eyes.

"Who is the wretch—the wretches?" bawled the farmer.

"A dream," murmured Fleet.

"A dream of a tree," murmured Flame.

"A flower from a tree," murmured Foam.

"No, the wind," murmured Fan.

"A fiery wind," murmured Fountain.

"Ash on the wind," murmured Favour.

"No," said Fair the youngest, "it was a beautiful man with black hair and eyes like the burning coals."

"The shame!" howled the farmer. But he told the neighbors his seven daughters had a strange malady, highly infectious. And he secluded them in the house and allowed no visitors. It was an age of Innocence, he was believed, though for seven months the "malady" persisted.

On the last day of the seventh month the sun went down, and seven sisters each gave a scream and fell on their beds. For seven hours there was screaming. In the last minute of the seventh hour, seven sisters each gave a triumphant shriek.

The old servant woman of the house, who had been assisting the labor, began to scream instead. The father ran in and shook her, "Well, are they sons or daughters?"

The servant woman, regaining her natural fortitude, remarked: "I declare that never in my long life, which now has doubtless been shortened by this shock, have I witnessed such a thing. Fleet has given birth to a little baby's arm, and Flame to another little arm, and I will be struck dead if Foam has not give birth to a leg and Fan to another leg, while poor Fountain brought forth a whole torso, and Favour a head."

"And Fair?" whimpered the farmer.

"Well," said the servant woman wisely, "I am sure I cannot say what Fair has given birth to, but rest assured, it is a fine specimen."

The farmer wept, and when he had ceased weeping, he commanded all these pieces of a child's body, so unnaturally accrued, to be bundled in a sheet and buried. But no sooner were the portions of anatomy in the sheet together than the sheet began to writhe.

The farmer fled, but the wise servant woman peeped in, and she saw a wonderous joining had taken place, and a whole healthy child, of striking beauty, lay there sleeping.

"Now," said the servant woman, "which of you girls has milk to give this infant?" She had got herself in a mundane mood, but she was to be tested still further. None of the seven daughters were found to have any milk upon them and, in any case, it was not needed. For, turning to the child again with clucks of commiseration, the servant woman saw he was prodigiously grown. Indeed, the child in the sheet was now a handsome boy of perhaps eleven years. "Steady, my chick," cried the servant woman disparagingly, "you will overtax yourself." But to no avail. In another minute the child had grown further, and further yet. Now a toothsome, adolescent youth lay there, jet black hair, thrilling to look on, so the old servant trembled all over. Then, even the youth was gone. A man was stretched upon the sheet. He seemed made of dark light, he glowed with beauty, and his naked body was like a god's, or as they thought a god's should be, the eight who shivered awestruck above him. His sleeping face deprived them of speech.

But abruptly Fair, the youngest of the seven sisters, crept to the window, and there in the east she saw a single yellow sword uplifted, the token that the sun was coming. What made her do it she never knew, but she hurried to the incredible man, and, kneeling by him, she kissed his mouth, and whispered: "Azhrarn, awake, for the sun returns to earth and you must return to your own kingdom."

And the man's eyelids flickered up, and two dark fires blazed suddenly between the bladed lashes, and he smiled, and touched the lips of Fair with his cool fingers. And then he was gone.

The room was filled with screaming yet again, while a black eagle rose unseen into the sky of earth, turned on its broad wings, and vanished without trace.

Moments after, the bright sun rose. But be sure, the age of Innocence was ended.

DAW

TANITH LEE

"Princess Royal of Heroic Fantasy"—*The Village Voice*

The Birthgrave Trilogy
- [ ] THE BIRTHGRAVE   (UE1776—$3.50)
- [ ] VAZKOR, SON OF VAZKOR   (UE1972—$2.95)
- [ ] QUEST FOR THE WHITE WITCH   (UE1996—$2.95)

THE FLAT EARTH SERIES
- [ ] NIGHT'S MASTER   (UE1657—$2.25)
- [ ] DEATH'S MASTER   (UE1741—$2.95)
- [ ] DELUSION'S MASTER   (UE1932—$2.50)
- [ ] DELIRIUM'S MISTRESS   (to come)

OTHER TITLES
- [ ] THE STORM LORD   (UE1867—$2.95)
- [ ] DAYS OF GRASS   (UE2094—$3.50)

ANTHOLOGIES
- [ ] RED AS BLOOD   (UE1790—$2.50)
- [ ] THE GORGON   (UE2003—$2.95)

DAW

DAW Books now in select format

Hardcover:

☐ **ANGEL WITH THE SWORD**
by C.J. Cherryh
0-8099-0001-7 $15.50/$20.50 in Canada

A swashbuckling adventure tale filled with breathtaking action, romance, and mystery, by the winner of two Hugo awards.

☐ **TAILCHASER'S SONG**
by Tad Williams
0-8099-0002-5 $15.50/$20.50 in Canada

A charming feline epic, this is a magical picaresque story sure to appeal to devotees of quality fantasy.

Trade Paperback

☐ **THE SILVER METAL LOVER**
by Tanith Lee
0-8099-5000-6 $6.95/$9.25 in Canada

THE SILVER METAL LOVER is a captivating science fiction story— a uniquely poignant rite of passage. "This is quite simply the best sci-fi romance I've read in ages."—*New York Daily News.*

NEW AMERICAN LIBRARY
P.O. Box 999, Bergenfield, New Jersey 07621

Please send me the DAW BOOKS I have checked above. I am enclosing $_____ (check or money order—no currency or C.O.D.'s). Please include the list price plus $1.50 per order to cover handling costs.

Name _____

Addres _____

City _____ State _____ Zip Code _____
Please allow at least 4 weeks for delivery

DAW

DAW PRESENTS THESE BESTSELLERS BY
MARION ZIMMER BRADLEY

DARKOVER NOVELS

☐ DARKOVER LANDFALL	UE1906—$2.50
☐ THE SPELL SWORD	UE1891—$2.25
☐ THE HERITAGE OF HASTUR	UE1967—$3.50
☐ THE SHATTERED CHAIN	UE1961—$3.50
☐ THE FORBIDDEN TOWER	UE2029—$3.95
☐ STORMQUEEN!	UE1951—$3.50
☐ TWO TO CONQUER	UE1876—$2.95
☐ SHARRA'S EXILE	UE1988—$3.95
☐ HAWKMISTRESS!	UE1958—$3.50
☐ THENDARA HOUSE	UE2119—$3.95
☐ CITY OF SORCERY	UE1962—$3.50

DARKOVER ANTHOLOGIES

☐ THE KEEPER'S PRICE	UE1931—$2.50
☐ SWORD OF CHAOS	UE1722—$2.95
☐ FREE AMAZONS OF DARKOVER	UE2096—$3.50

NEW AMERICAN LIBRARY
P.O. Box 999, Bergenfield, New Jersey 07621

Please send me the DAW BOOKS I have checked above. I am enclosing
$_____ (check or money order—no currency or C.O.D.'s).
Please include the list price plus $1.00 per order to cover handling costs.

Name _____

Addres _____

City _____ State _____ Zip Code _____
Please allow at least 4 weeks for delivery.

AN OPEN LETTER
TO THE AMERICAN PEOPLE

Astronauts Francis (Dick) Scobee, Michael Smith, Judy Resnik, Ellison Onizuka, Ronald McNair, Gregory Jarvis, and Christa McAuliffe understood the risk, undertook the challenge, and in so doing embodied the dreams of us all.

Unlike so many of us, they did not take for granted the safety of riding a torch of fire to the stars.

For them the risk was real from the beginning. But some are already seizing upon their deaths as proof that America is unready for the challenge of manned space flight. *This is the last thing the seven would have wanted.*

Originally five orbiters were proposed; only four were built. This tragic reduction of the fleet places an added burden on the remaining three.

But the production facilities still exist. The assembly line can be reactivated. The experiments designed for the orbiter bay are waiting. We can recover a program which is one of our nation's greatest resources and mankind's proudest achievements.

Soon Congress will determine the immediate direction the space program must take. We must place at highest priority the restoration and enhancement of the shuttle fleet and resumption of a full launch schedule.

For the seven.

In keeping with their spirit of dedication to the future of space exploration and with the deepest respect for their memory, we are asking you to join us in urging the President and the Congress to build a new shuttle orbiter to carry on the work of these seven courageous men and women.

As long as their dream lives on, the seven live on in the dream.

SUPPORT SPACE EXPLORATION!

Write to the President at
1600 Pennsylvania Avenue,
Washington, D.C. 20500.